6001

THE SLEEPERS

Published in Australia by
South Head Press
ABN 75823432905
P.O. Box 7135
Bondi Beach
N.S.W. Australia 2026

The National Library of Australia Cataloguing-in-Publication entry:

Author: Widerberg, W.R.
Title: 6001 the sleepers/W.R.Widerberg.
Edition: 1st ed.
ISBN: 978-0-9808096-1-9 (pbk.)

Cover design by Alli Spoor

Text typeset and designed by Mercier Typesetters Pty Ltd, Granville NSW

6001

THE SLEEPERS

Book 2 of The Camarilla Chronicle

W. R. Widerberg

To my granddaughters

Natasha

and

Charlotte

The Author

Bill Widerberg grew up in Clovelly in Sydney's Eastern Suburbs. His first novel, *The Big End of Town,* an adult thriller, was published in 2005 to great reviews in all media Australia wide. His second, *6001 ICEWORLD,* which also received good reviews, is the first of the trilogy, *The Camarilla Chronicle.*

6001 THE SLEEPERS is the second book of the series which is written for young adults.

Widerberg's short story, *Sunday Morning at the Bay,* won first prize at the Stroud Writers Festival in 2009. The following year, his story, *The Target,* won the Dymocks Award for the best short story at the Bundaberg Arts Festival.

During his business career, which spanned the production and marketing of soft drink, canned fruit and beer, Bill Widerberg was named by *Business Review Weekly* as the top marketing man in Australia.

Acknowledgements

I thank Lauren Nitschke and Alli Spoor for allowing me to use Lauren's beautiful face on the front cover and Rod Mercier for his advice and assistance in the presentation of this book.

Chapter 1

Biscetti held Dumperty's hand, in her anxiety squeezing it until the pressure was too much for him and he pulled free. Like all those waiting below the summit of the mountain the Camarilla had named the sleeping hare, they stared up at the rock face that now hid Tasha, Dram, Snotty and Mangrove from view. The roaring in their ears persisted, rising and falling, never stopping, drowning all other sounds.

"Where are they? What's happened to them?" The tiny Dumperty looked up at Biscetti, seeing the concern on her face, wondering as Biscetti did whether the four who had gone ahead were now victims of whatever was making the noise that shook the air with its intensity.

"I wish I knew," Biscetti said and saw that she had failed to hide her despair from him.

In the months since they had been driven from their homeland by the Torterats and forced to travel south, Dumperty had shared the hardship and disappointments of the Camarilla. Small as he was, he was aware that that the suffering may have been for nothing.

Biscetti looked at Dumperty and could have wept. It was too much. *We're just children. Why did it come to this?* But she knew well enough. The Camarilla, the small trusted band, was the last remnant of humankind on earth and their time could be running out.

From the day of her birth she had been told the stories of the Good Times, that long and happy period that went into decline when greed warmed the planet and drought ravaged the land until food crops would no longer grow. Biscetti, like every Camarilla child, had grown up with the legends of the Good Times and how they had ended, but Biscetti had seen more. She had been in the belly of the mountain carved by ghosts.

As she waited, dreading what might have befallen the advance party, she recalled that night in the hollow mountain when Dram had by accident activated the film left by the ancients; an archive to tell the story of the end of civilisation.

Biscetti tilted her head again to search the summit – nothing. Dumperty pulled at her tunic. "What if..."

She put her finger on his lips. "Shh. They'll come for us soon."

"But the noise?" He held his hands to his ears, imagining that no one could survive, that his idols, the Foragers he cherished most, the boy hunters Mangrove and Snotty, might have gone already to Endless Night.

"Shh." Biscetti was thinking of Tasha, two years older than herself, Queen of the Camarilla and bearing responsibility for the safety and welfare of the band. If Tasha was gone, the clan would be leaderless. If the boys, if Dram...

Her eyes roamed the ridge above; still no sign. She smiled at Dumperty, trying to raise his spirits and her own. Behind the smile her thoughts centred on Dram, and even though Tasha had ruled that Dram was forgiven, Biscetti had too many memories of the tall and beautiful girl. Pictures of past events were vivid in her mind: Dram's willingness to desert Biscetti and leave her to freeze in the ice; Dram abandoning Tasha at the makeshift bridge across the crevasse; later in the forest of Kaldor leading the revolt to depose Tasha. There were many things Biscetti held against Dram, no matter how she had redeemed herself.

Again Biscetti craned her neck and in frustration screamed into the wind and the raging turmoil of sound. "Where are you?"

On the crown of the sleeping hare, the four who had gone ahead had no chance of hearing her. There the wind blew even more fiercely, screaming in from way beyond the ocean's horizon with nothing to slow its progress. Borne upon the wind was the endless crashing of waves that far below foamed and tumbled to the shore.

Tasha, Mangrove, Dram and Snotty gazed in wonder at the ocean, turning to look at the land which they had travelled so far to find and for so long. No one spoke, each reflecting on the green expanse of rolling hills and dales that lay before them, turning again to look in awe at the wild beauty of the ocean. This place to which they had come could not have been more different from their homeland, the land of ice, the land from which they had been driven by the Torterats.

Facing the ocean, leaning into the wind, the hair of the Foragers streamed behind them and their tunics of soft animal skin pressed so hard against their bodies that ribs were outlined.

Snotty grinned with pleasure and shouted his joy to the others. "I love all this."

Forcing his way against the wind he walked to where the sleeping hare fell away in a vertical drop to the sea, the only flaw in the smooth rock-face the minor protrusion of a single ledge.

He looked down to where hundreds of metres below, waves pounded at the foot of the cliff. The grandeur of all that lay before him was overwhelming.

"This is where the land ends and the rest of the world begins." He whooped his delight to the sky, to the rushing air and to himself because he thought that this wonderful day would be forever etched in his memory.

Snotty spread his arms wide, marvelling that wind which was only air, which was really nothing, could blow so hard that he could lie against it without falling. He tilted his head for the pleasure of wind on his face and as he did so it snatched away the feather in his hair.

Dram saw him try to grasp it, but the feather spiralled up and away, out of reach, out of sight, gone. With foreboding she watched it go. The feather had come from the raptor that Snotty had killed in saving Mangrove. It was a trophy Manny had taken from the bird, a badge of honour for Snotty to wear. For a moment Dram feared that its loss could be a bad omen and she looked again at Snotty. Carefree, he had no thought for the feather.

"Come here. Come and see this." The words were plucked from his mouth and flew unintelligible to Mangrove and the girls.

They laughed at the sight of Snotty with arms wide, standing angled toward the sea. Dram and Mangrove pushed their way to him, leaning forward as he did. With one hand, Snotty took one of Dram's and raised it. With the other he held Manny's so that the three of them stood with arms spread wide against the wind. A stronger gust caused them to stumble backwards. Laughing they recovered.

Tasha watched the enjoyment before turning her attention to the valleys that promised so much. Her people would love this land. She sat and hugged her knees and gave thanks to the stars. Behind her the others played with the wind.

"Come on." Snotty pulled Dram and Manny toward the edge, pulling them further until below them there was only the sea and they were looking straight down at it.

This is madness, Mangrove thought. He glanced at Snotty and saw him held by the wind, heedless of any possible risk. Dram too was rapt, weightless from the pressure of the rushing air. Their euphoria was contagious. Manny followed suit, resting feather-light on the wind, his caution overcome by sheer joy.

Never could the Foragers have imagined such an experience. Their feet were on solid ground, but they were floating on air, as close as they ever would be to flying. Within each was the sensation that this was how a bird would see the world.

They squeezed hands, thrilled to feel so free. The way they stood, on the edge of the cliff, leaning beyond it, they looked like skydivers from the twentieth century, daredevils with hands linked, bonding together in the sky.

A stronger gust lifted them, as though they were hinged, blowing tears to streak from their eyes, making them laugh. But the gust was followed by quieter air. Off balance, briefly unsupported, still joined by their hands, the three fell into space.

"Ahh." Dram's scream was caught by the next blast of wind and blown across the plateau of the sleeping hare.

Dram's cry hit Tasha so that she jumped in fright. She looked to see why a scream would come from the three who were having so much fun.

Tasha saw nothing. Dram, Manny and Snotty were gone. "Where..."

She got to her feet and ran to the cliff's edge, knelt and with her heart thumping in her chest saw the three lying on a ledge four metres down. Far, far below them, the turmoil of the sea vented its fury on the foot of the cliff.

Tasha opened her mouth and cried out in horror. The wind blew between her lips and through her teeth, strangling her cry, putting her in her place; an insignificant mortal in the vast universe of ocean and sky and rushing air.

She tried again, "Manny, Manny." Screaming his name, then calling to Snotty and Dram, wanting to hear one of them say that they were all okay. The three lay limp, not answering. Tasha looked at arms and legs for some slight movement. She sought eyes that might be open and could see hers. There was no movement. Eyes were closed.

Her thoughts in turmoil, Tasha rose to go for help. The clan was waiting, the rope would be needed. Willing hands would bring the three to safety. She knelt again. There was no way that she could leave. *If one of them rolls or ...* Tasha imagined Dram or one of the boys falling from the ledge, falling to hit the rocks or to drop into the sea and, if not already dead, to drown. She would have to stay, try to rouse them and make sure that they didn't move while she went for help.

"Snotty, Dram, wake up, tell me you're okay." Tasha shouted again and again, looking all the time for some sign that she had been heard.

The only sound was the wind tearing at her ears.

She stared down at the crumpled bodies lying on the ledge and saw Dram lift a hand to rub her head. Snotty grimaced and raised his knees. Manny moved his shoulders, testing for injury.

Tasha felt relief flood through her. A faint smile touched her face. "You're alive." Yelling at them, the smile widening to a grin, as Dram nodded and waved. When Snotty and Manny did the same, Tasha laughed aloud. "I'm going for help. We'll get you up." Tasha gave a final smile of encouragement and was gone.

Mangrove carefully shifted position and looked down. It was a long, long way to the sea. "Just watch how you move. If we fall..."

Snotty took a look. "Hmm."

Dram sat up and huddled at the back of the ledge, quivering with fright. The joy of seeming to fly was gone. In its place was the terrible fear that she would fall, fall into the darkness of Endless Night.

"Don't worry, Dram," Snotty said. "Tasha and the others will get us off here."

Dram shuddered and pressed hard against the rock wall. Not only was there the danger of toppling from the ledge, if she was to be rescued it would mean clutching a rope and being hauled up the face of the cliff. She would be battered by the wind. She knew that she would lose her grip and fall. No matter how hard she tried to keep her eyes fixed on the sky, they kept returning to look down at the sea. Each time her stomach shrank a little more, tightening into a ball.

"Dram, it'll be all right." Manny could see how scared she was. He was not too relaxed himself, regretting that he had been so caught up in the exhilarating moments of riding the air that he had not heeded his first reaction to Snotty's wild idea. *It was madness. We should never have done it.* But it was too late for regrets. The three of them were stuck on the cliff-face. Getting off safely was all that mattered.

Waiting for the call to recommence the climb, not knowing what was going on, Biscetti was filled with misgiving. She looked up at the trees as if they might have the answer. "Where can they be?"

Even as she asked the question, Tasha re-appeared on the rocky outcrop that was the shoulder of the sleeping hare. A surge of emotion gripped Biscetti so that her voice cracked as she called out to those behind her that she could see Tasha and from the line of those waiting a happy shout rose loud enough to pierce the never-ending roar assailing their ears.

Biscetti's relief was short lived. Tasha was beckoning them to climb, to come on up to the mountain top, but her action was hurried and she was not smiling. Something was wrong.

In one quick glance, Dumperty saw the doubt on Biscetti's face. "What's the matter?"

"I don't know, but it doesn't look good."

"Let's go." And then he was off, Biscetti by his side, scrambling up the slope to join Tasha and with the wish to know what lay beyond.

More slowly others followed. Belle took old Ingamo's arm to assist him and motioned to Vellum to do the same for Jemma, Ingamo's wife, but if their progress could not match the speed of Dumperty, they shared the same concerns. Not one of the clan could resist interrupting the grasping of tufts of gorse that would make the climb easier, to look up to where Tasha stood urging them on. Occasionally, while raising a head to check that she was still there, someone slipped from what had seemed a firm foothold, or dropped the load that had been humped month after month across snow and desert. But it didn't matter. A new foothold was found and the pack retrieved. The goal was to get to the top to find out what had gone wrong.

Like ants the line ascended the rock face to where their Queen stood. As calmly as possible, she told them of the fall.

"Are they hurt? Can we get to them?" Dumperty spoke quickly, worried that he might never be again with his heroes.

"The rope's in Snotty's pack. We'll use it to haul them up the cliff."

With Tasha leading, the line passed between the ears of the sleeping hare and across its flat summit. However they came, singly, in pairs, or in small groups, the moment they saw the view spread before them, people gathered to stare and to gasp. Tasha hurried them on. The rescue could not be delayed.

Biscetti got the rope. Tasha with Dumperty at her side went straight to the cliff top. The wind blasted in from the ocean, tearing at their clothing. Tasha motioned him to the ground. Together they crawled the last few metres.

"Oh." Dumperty took in the immense height, his friends trapped with scarcely room to hold them on the narrow ledge, the possibility that one or all would slip from it, or that the wind would tear them from the rock so that he would see them falling, falling, to finally hit the sea.

Snotty saw him peering over the edge, saw the apprehension and waved. "Hi, little guy. Don't worry. We're okay."

Dumperty swallowed. The situation looked horrible.

Tasha mouthed that she would lower the rope and got the answering wave. She fed it over the edge. The rope dropped less than half a metre before the wind took hold and flung it back in Tasha's face. She tried again and again. The rope was too flimsy in the teeth of the wind. At a distance the clan watched with mounting concern.

"Tie the rope to me," Dumperty said. "I'll take it down."

Tasha touched his wind swept hair. "Little one..."

"I can do it, Tasha."

She looked at him. He was so small.

"Let me do it?" He took the end of the rope and knotted it around his waist.

Biscetti saw what was happening and crawled closer, arguing that she should take the risk, not Dumperty, that she was bigger and stronger.

"Yeah, you are bigger. That's why I'm the best to do it. It won't be so hard when you have to pull me up."

"But..."

Dumperty ignored her and looked to Tasha. "There's no room on that ledge for Biscetti, but I'm small enough to fit."

Tasha knew that he was right. Another Forager on the ledge would be impossible. Dumperty might just find space. Even then the danger would be increased, but what other way was there.

"Okay." She tightened the bowline he had knotted and

touched his hair again. "Take care, little one."

He waited while Tasha called Sola, Situ, Kalich and Belle to join her and Biscetti in holding the rope. There was to be no mistake, no further mishap. Six would let Dumperty down and six should easily haul up each of those on the ledge.

Dumperty stood at the brink of the cliff, facing the six Foragers who had his life in their hands. "I'm ready."

The crew on the line let it slip slowly through their hands and Dumperty was lowered to disappear from the view of those behind Tasha. Only she, standing at the very edge, could follow his progress.

Dangling in mid-air, buffeted by wind so that he had to use his feet to avoid being bounced against the rock-face, Dumperty descended until Snotty could reach him and guide him to stand on the crowded ledge.

Snotty tapped Dram's shoulder. "You first, Dram."

She did not answer him, did not move, simply stared at the ocean below.

"Dram, you can go up now. Come on."

She shook her head. "I'll fall."

Snotty encouraged her, talking her round, telling her that she would die if she stayed, that he and Manny and Dumperty would be lifted to safety, leaving her if they had to.

Dram closed her eyes. "I won't make it."

Manny grasped her arm. "Yes you will. Now stand up so that Snotty can tie the rope around you." He spoke harshly, treating Dram like a naughty child.

She drew up her legs and pushed herself upright, staying flat against the rock wall, glued to it.

Snotty turned her round to face the cliff, broke the bowline to free the rope from Dumperty and remade it around Dram, leaving a long tail. This he tied around Dumperty. The little fellow would be needed to bring the rope down twice more, once for Manny and then for Snotty.

Snotty signalled to Tasha that she could commence the lift.

The two hung at the end of the rope. Unrelenting, the gale

blasted at them, banging them at the cliff- face, twirling them to spin like tops, but gradually they were raised until Dram touched the top of the cliff and rolled to safety at Tasha's feet. Tasha flicked the bowline loose for Dram to scramble out of the way.

Those on the line began to let it out. Dumperty was on his way back to the ledge.

Tasha watched the rope as it inched over the lip of the cliff. The rock was sawing at it. She could see the rope fraying.

Again Snotty guided Dumperty to stand while the knot was released. Manny was secured and in turn the process repeated for Dumperty. Snotty waved and the two commenced their ascent.

At the cliff-top the rope dragged across rock. The fraying worsened. Tasha could see that whole strands were splitting. There was nothing she could do about it, except hope that it would be strong enough to get Manny and Dumperty to the top.

Mangrove kept his head up, checking the distance yet to go. He could see the rope wearing as pieces parted. He placed his feet against the cliff, trying to bear some of the weight and so ease the burden on the line. Under him, Dumperty saw what he was doing and followed suit.

Below them, waiting for his turn, Snotty also saw the rope thinning, conscious that before it was lowered again, more would wear away. On his reckoning Dumperty would be able to make another trip to the ledge, but they would be lucky if they made it up. The rope would more than likely snap with their combined weight. He watched Manny reach the top and release the knot. Before Dumperty could be lowered again, Snotty waved to Tasha, both hands crossing and recrossing above his face, the signal to stop the operation.

"The rope's going to part. Don't send Dumperty down. Leave me." Yelling to be heard above the roar of the wind.

"No, Tasha." Dumperty jerked at the line in her hands. "We can't leave him."

Tasha looked at the worn rope, at strands that were no longer part of the weave, but loose ends of no use. It's always the same, she thought, whatever I decide will be wrong. I can't leave Snotty marooned on the ledge, yet if we try to raise him the rope will probably break and he and Dumperty will be lost. She struggled with the problem.

"It's okay, Tasha." Dumperty looked into her eyes, pleading to be let down. "It's the last time and we can't leave Snotty."

That was the unknown; whether the line would continue to hold. Snotty had his head tilted so that she could see his face, the face she knew so well, the face that so often wore the cheeky grin. She couldn't abandon Snotty. Dumperty could be right, the line might hold.

"No, we can't leave Snotty." Tasha fed out the line and Dumperty stood again on the ledge.

Snotty loosened the rope, took a long tail and knotted it about Dumperty again. "You're leading this time, little guy. I'll be under you." He tied another bowline about his own waist and signalled Tasha to haul them up.

The final ascent began. In one hand Snotty held the Swiss knife, a sharp blade bared.

The rope crept over the lip of the cliff. Tasha, Dumperty and Snotty all watching strands parting until the diameter of the rope was a fraction of what it had been. The boys were a metre and a half from the top. Snotty put the knife to the line. He would cut it between him and Dumperty. With most of the weight gone, the little fellow would make it to the top.

"No, Snotty, no," Tasha screamed at him.

Dumperty glanced down and saw the blade. He kicked out at Snotty's arm, shouting at him not to slice the rope.

Above them the strands continued to part.

Snotty shook his head. "Don't worry about me. Look after yourself."

Tasha dropped to the ground, lying on her stomach leaned over the edge and reached for Dumperty. "Grab my hand."

He stretched his arm toward her, fingers touching. Biscetti and the others stopped hauling. Tasha moved her body further over the edge, one hand moving into Dumperty's until their grip tightened.

She looked down at Snotty and yelled at him. "Don't cut,

Snotty."

Biscetti ran to Tasha and held her legs. The others recommended pulling with Tasha using all her strength to lift Dumperty and spare the rope from his weight. Snotty held the knife against the line, his eyes on it as it inched over the angle where cliff-face became the firm ground of the sleeping hare. If he had to, he'd cut himself free.

Tasha reached with her other hand, held both of Dumperty's and raised him to crawl to safety. The rope was parting. Lying close she could hear it scraping on rock and the ping of strands as they snapped.

"Hold me, Biscetti." And Tasha moved almost her whole body over the cliff and stretched to reach Snotty. He pulled himself higher and heard the crack of the rope as it parted for good. One hand reached for Tasha's. The loose end of the rope fell by Snotty and still tied to him whipped about in the frenzy of the wind.

Tasha held him and he hung in space, only she preventing him from dropping to his death.

He put the knife between his teeth and grasped her other hand. Kalich ran to lie beside Tasha and he too stretched down to take an arm and together they raised Snotty until they could pull him on to the flat summit of the sleeping hare.

Exhausted, he lay on his back drawing air into his lungs, staring at the sky. Tasha lay beside him, all her strength gone. He reached out to touch her arm. "Thanks, Tasha."

"You're welcome."

Mangrove stood looking down at them, holding the Camarilla's precious possession, the now shortened rope. "You know you're crazy, Snotty."

"Sorry, Manny. I'll fix it as soon as I can."

"I'm not talking about this." Mangrove glanced at the rope. "I mean making out as if we were birds."

Snotty grinned. "It was fun though, wasn't it? Admit you loved it."

"Yeah, for a while it was." He reached for Snotty's hand and helped him to his feet then did the same for Tasha.

Snotty looked for Dumperty, found him, winked and raised a thumb. "You did well, little guy."

Dumperty grinned with pleasure.

Dram had joined the onlookers. As it turned out, events had ended happily, but the vivid memories of falling, of being on the ledge high above the sea, of dangling in mid-air would not leave her. There had been no fun in that, whatever Snotty might say.

Chapter 2

Tasha called everyone together. The near disaster was behind them. It was time to enjoy the spectacle of the new land.

From the height of sleeping hare they could see a series of valleys that ran in parallel from the ocean to finally be closed off by a cliff rising to a plateau. Running from east to west, each was separated from the next by a rolling hill, as though the earth had been folded to provide the succession of secluded valleys. They could see that some were separated from the sea by sand dunes. Others lacked the dunes, but – apart from the land directly below, through which a river ran – what lay within the more distant valleys was hidden by the intervening hills. Far to the south, a wisp of smoke or steam curled from the cone of a snow capped mountain.

Whatever those further valleys might hold, whatever caused the wispy vapour to float from the distant peak would be discovered in due course. For the moment, attention was focused on the breaking surf and the ocean stretching to a distant horizon.

Of all those looking down from the mountain, Tasha was conscious that only five had any conception of the sea. When Dram had activated the screen in the belly of the mountain carved by ghosts, Tasha had watched with her, Biscetti and Manny and Snotty, scenes of polar icecaps breaking up to float away as huge icebergs. They had been shown the sea invading low lying coasts, and islands disappearing below its surface.

The scenes, they knew, were meant to inform them of how the Good Times had come to an end, how mankind had ignored the warnings of global warming and how that warming had caused sea levels to rise. Although unintended, the moving pictures provided an additional lesson for the Foragers. They saw planet Earth as a sphere and that most of its surface was covered by water.

On return to Homecave, everything that they had seen was recounted to all the members of the clan, every one of whom had listened avidly. Seeing these events on a screen, hearing the story told and re-told by the Foragers had made their impression, but to see the real thing in all its enormity was overwhelming.

Blue, bluer than the sky, the ocean appeared to be rolling toward the beach and from the tops of the swells white caps were hurried by the wind, white horses to prance wildly for a few metres before laying down to become blue once more. The overwhelming noise that shook the air came from waves that approaching the shore towered and crashed in a wild tumble of foam.

Tasha stood by Mangrove and Snotty. "Isn't it magical?"

"It is. Let's stop looking and get down there." Snotty lifted his pack.

"You're right." Tasha hefted her own load to her back. "Do you think we could find shelter for tonight? We're all sick of sleeping in the open."

Snotty glanced at the sun. "If we hurry."

Their actions began a general movement among the crowd. To one side, Cloud remained sitting, looking into the distance: Cloud, the short sighted girl, who, with the spectacles Dumperty had found in the ancient military bunker, had gained vision that was superior to all; Cloud, who at times fell into a trance and with eyes wide foretold the future from her dreams. Something had caught her attention.

Snotty called to Dram to give Cloud a shake. They were going down.

Cloud heard and turned toward him. "There are animals down there amongst the trees."

"Where?"

She pointed. "And I saw some running on one of the distant hills." Her voice had the tone of concern.

Snotty laughed. "Don't worry about it, Cloud. That's just what we need. Tomorrow Manny and I will go hunting."

Cloud looked at Snotty through the round lenses of the spectacles. "Some were very big."

But Snotty did not hear her. He had already begun the descent.

The cavalier attitude, the dismissal of her concern did not surprise Cloud – it was typical of Snotty – but across the hills and valleys spread below, eyes were attracted to the movement on the sleeping hare, eyes that saw strange beings and the minds behind the eyes registered intrusion. The imprint of strangers was made without emotion; a cold appraisal of beings now entering territory that did not belong to them.

The going was relatively easy; steep, but not dangerous and with boulders that provided resting places where loads could be put down while strength was regained. Manny and Tasha went down together, assisting each other in the more difficult sections, listening to the light-hearted chatter going on around them.

"Manny, I'm so happy."

"Everyone is, Tasha. Look at this country."

He stopped to take in the valley below. It appeared to be wider than those more distant, with a river that cut its way through hills and wound a few kilometres to empty into the sea. Along its length, the river banks on either side varied from grassed meadows to groves of trees and in parts reeds grew from the water.

"There'll be fish in the river. We'll never go hungry again."

"No." And Tasha thought of the years of famine they had suffered and the perils encountered in the journey from Homecave.

In her mind flashed pictures of Torterats and Dandle and the others who had succumbed to become wraiths in the forest of Kaldor. She felt again the crushing power of quicksand and heard the roar of the monster among the rock towers. The memory caused her to touch her leg where it had been injured and a shudder ran through her body. Momentarily she closed her eyes, inhaled deeply and opened them again to gaze on the valley and the ocean. The past was behind them. A new life in a new land was about to begin.

"We must find a cave to make our home."

"I've been looking, "Mangrove said, "but..."

"Then let's go to where the water breaks upon the sand." Tasha laughed and called aloud for all to hear. "C'mon. We'll go to the big water."

Her gaiety was infectious, the whole clan caught up in the spirit of good humour as they hurried along through lengthening shadows. Above them birds were flying, calling as they went. To the clan the birdsong was a welcome. Pleasant melodies had been rare in the extreme cold of the north. Those they now heard added another wonderful dimension to the land in which they planned to settle.

The air began to cool. The ball of the sun was dipping and would soon slip behind the plateau.

Tasha picked up her pace. Life had found new meaning, but to spend the night unprotected in a strange place would be unwise.

"Manny, could you go ahead? Find us somewhere to rest."

"Sure, I'll take Snotty. There could be caves in the cliffs beyond the beach."

Mangrove indicated the sleeping hare. Coming down into the valley they had had the benefit of a steepish slope, but on the ocean side was the sheer rock wall that rose all the way to the peak. He knew that cliff-face well, too well.

"We'll see what we can find."

A sliver of sun was all that showed above the plateau. In seconds it was gone. Mangrove and Snotty began to run, heading across the grassed floor of the valley toward the perpendicular cliff that faced the sea. They crossed a dune, slid down its wall of sand to the beach and hurried on. In the east, above a sea that tossed before the wind, the sky was already darkening.

"Hey, what do you reckon?" Snotty was looking at the base of the cliff where at some time in the past a geological fault or erosion by the sea had created an overhang.

"Maybe." Mangrove walked into the open space that was not really a cave, but a broad bite out of the cliff. Nevertheless it extended well into the base of the towering rock face.

Initially well above his head, the rock roof in its interior sloped down to meet the sand. Not ideal, the place was unenclosed and would never have the warmth or the feeling of Homecave, but it did provide shelter.

"Well?"

"Yeah, it'll do until we can find something better."

"Okay, let's tell Tasha." Snotty had seen enough.

The chamber created below the overhang was, as Mangrove had judged, not ideal, but the clan saw it as a reasonable place to stay in the circumstance. The ocean, the valley, all that they had seen from the summit of the sleeping hare, had been a break point in their lives. As refugees they had fled before the onslaught of the Torterats. They had suffered unthinkable privation in the long desperate journey, but the journey was over. They had found a new land which had all the appearances of being a wonderful place to settle. The general opinion was that until more suitable accommodation could be found, the roomy cavity under the cliff would provide somewhere to sleep and to stow belongings.

In a bustle of activity, sleeping places were selected and the communal cooking pot set up. It was filled with water from some of the gourds that had been carried since Kaldor. Those still holding water were set down in depressions made in the sand floor. With driftwood lying about on the beach, there was little more to do than gather sufficient for the fire.

The last of the day gave way to night and with the ocean as backdrop, the clan ate game caught when crossing the mountains. Lips were licked in satisfaction; the doubled pleasure of eating the first meal in a land of promise.

Tasha's sister, the blonde Biscetti, took the wooden flute from Tasha's pack. "Play for us, Tasha."

The newfound home filled with music and the dancing began. Old as they were, Ingamo and Jemma swayed to the rhythm.

Biscetti took Hock's hand and led him. Snotty and Dram, Belle and Vellum, Cloud and Kalich, the whole clan joined in the dance, totally happy that at last they had found peace.

For hours the music and the singing continued, but one by one people tired and found their sleeping places. The fire died so that the only light came from the glowing coals and the clan slept.

The scream was magnified by the low hanging roof. It echoed and re-echoed as Dram leapt from her sleeping place still shrieking, running about wildly, totally disoriented, unsure of where she was.

"Tasha, we're drowning." Scenes from the screen in the hollow mountain re-played in her mind. She remembered pictures of islands being submerged and coastlines disappearing. "The sea is taking us."

And now, before her eyes, the past was being relived. Wave after wave was washing through the opening, coming with force to hit the back of the cave and rebound. With each new wave the water rose higher. Furs and packs were swept this way and that, tumbling about, banging into legs and knocking people over.

The fire had been extinguished by the first flush of water. In the darkness, Dram's initial scream was joined by cries of despair from all around. The pandemonium of panic exaggerated the fear of those stumbling about. Unable to see what was happening, feeling trapped by rock walls on three sides and the overhang of the roof, drowning seemed inevitable. The next wave, or the one after that, would flood the cave and take them all into Endless Night.

The weak reflection of moonlight from the ocean did little to help, but it was a beacon to which they could flee. Stumbling, most crying in terror, the clan fled from the overhang and still splashing through water made for the dune and climbed to stand trembling; the first to arrive assisting others to the higher ground. All the while, the water rose.

Ingamo, his clothes wet and spattered with sand, wrapped his arms around himself, moaning. "I knew it was too good to be true. We're doomed."

"Be quiet," Jemma snapped. "You're only making things worse. Here, get that before it floats away." A back pack was coming by, lifting on waves, bumping along the beach.

Snotty stayed Ingamo with his hand and jumped down from the dune. He grabbed the pack and two more that had washed from the cave and flung them to the top of the wall of sand. He turned to look for more.

"Snotty, leave it." Mangrove was shouting in anxiety. "We'll be carried away if we stay here. We have to get to higher ground."

"But we'll have nothing."

"We'll be alive."

"Do as Manny says, Snotty." Dram's voice was breaking with fright. "We have to run before it's too late." She could see the water rising just as it had done on the screen.

Snotty began to argue. Tasha called to him over the rush of waves. "Look at the river. It's running backwards."

He stared at the river-mouth in disbelief. What had been, and seemed eternal when they first entered the valley, no longer existed. Water was no longer flowing into the sea. The bar was deep under water, the ocean racing in, a great upwelling of current, swelling the river to rise at its banks.

"We have to leave, Manny." Despite her concern, Tasha spoke calmly. Even stronger than her distress at the oncoming flood was the ache within her ribs, the intense disappointment that her hopes of a new life had been dashed. The world was once again to suffer inundation and in doing so take from her and her people the happiness they thought they had found.

She began to count. Who was present? Who might be missing? Fear exploded in her chest. "Dram," Tasha shouted. "Is Dumperty with you?"

"No."

Heads turned, searching the dune and the beach where belongings tumbled in surf that was now sweeping up to the dune and crashing over it.

"There," someone cried.

Dumperty appeared, was knocked from his feet to disappear under the foam. His head rose above the turmoil. "Snotty." His scream for help piercing the night.

Still rescuing property, Snotty stood with water swirling around his chest and let a returning wave take him toward the little boy. Dumperty raised an arm, Snotty reached for it, touched with outstretched fingers, but a wave hit Dumperty and he was gone.

A cry of intense dismay rose from those on the dune. Water was rising around their legs, but they didn't move, staring at the surging surf, wishing that Dumperty would survive.

Mangrove called to Tasha that it would be best if the band left the valley. "They can do nothing here. Take them up the slope to the sleeping hare. Hurry, we may not have much time."

"What about Snotty and Dumperty?"

"Get going," he said. "I'm staying to help."

Mangrove slid into the surf. Barely able to keep his feet he forced his way to Snotty. "Where is he?"

Snotty shook his head, eyes searching. Hair broke through white water. Snotty grasped, held a handful and pulled, raising Dumperty's head above water.

"Hey, little guy, are you still with us?"

The boy nodded, coughing and spitting.

"Good." And with Dumperty clinging to his back, fought his way through deep water where the beach had been. A wave lifted them. They were on the dune.

Mangrove followed on the next wave. "Come on, let's go while there's still time."

Dumperty ran with one hand held by Snotty, the other by Mangrove. At times his legs left the ground. He didn't care. His throat still burned from the salt water he had swallowed. All he wanted was to be away from the rising ocean, far from the possibility of drowning. He glanced back and saw a great plume of white water rise high as a wave crashed at the dune.

"The water's coming to get us."

"Just run," Mangrove said. "Catch up to the others."

The fretful group they chased was four hundred metres ahead at the foot of the slope that led to the sleeping hare. The full moon, white, serene and distant, shone pale upon their scrambling ascent.

The figures, washed out of home, climbed in desperation, seeking the elevation that would put them above the sea flooding the land. In every mind was the fear that no matter how high they went, it would not be high enough.

As he ran, Mangrove looked at those ahead, pallid in the moonlight. He saw Tasha turn and wait. *Go, go on. Don't stop.* Not shouting, there was no point. With the distance separating them he wouldn't be heard.

Behind Tasha and those with her, behind the three racing to catch them, the ocean roared, never ceasing, spurring them on.

The slope slowed progress and at times hands were needed to claw a way over an obstacle. No longer dragged along by Snotty and Manny, but by their side, Dumperty kept pace as they made their way up the mountainside. The ragged line of climbers above, tired by the effort, was faltering. The three finally joined them, shouting to Tasha that they had arrived.

Half way to the summit, Ingamo was forced to sit. "I can't go on."

Jemma, his wife, looked at him and knew that he had reached the limit of his endurance. She sat beside him and stroked his forehead. "I'll stay with you."

Calling to Tasha, Jemma motioned to her to continue climbing. "Take the others higher, Tasha. Ingamo and I can go no further. We'll take our chances here."

Tasha looked toward the ocean. Waves were surging where she had recently stood. Once again she was faced with dilemma. Argument and counter argument played in her head. She had responsibility for the lives of the whole clan, how could she leave Ingamo and Jemma? Yet to carry them up would delay the progress of all and that could be fatal. *Why must it always be like this? Why is there never a clear cut answer?*

But in the past the crucial events requiring Tasha's decision had been decided by her compassion and again her nature resolved the issue. "No, Jemma, you can't stay here." And, her eyes darting to people above and below where she stood, Tasha quickly rounded up Belle, Zita, Vellum and Hock.

"Help Ingamo and Jemma, please. If necessary, carry them."

Jemma stood. "Thanks Tasha. I can manage. It's Ingamo who needs the help."

"Okay, let's get on with it."

The gang of four knew what to do. Hock and Vellum each took Ingamo by an arm. To be sure that Jemma could manage the steep slope, Zita and Belle accompanied her. Confident that the old couple wouldn't falter again, Tasha gave the signal to recommence the ascent.

Leaning forward, bent over as they struggled up the incline, Biscetti and Cloud had been overtaken by Mangrove, Snotty and Dumperty. They climbed like that with the sound of surf driving them on, in their anxiety occasionally glancing back.

Biscetti looked at Snotty's hair where the raptor feather should have been, the feather that had blown away with the wind. That portent of bad things to come was now reality. Biscetti feared that worse was in store for them all.

Exhausted bodies clambered up the slope, but short of the summit began to fall. Scattered about they lay slumped on the rough ground. Once more the clan was suffering. The hope they had shared was now shattered. In its place was an emptiness; the loss of everything.

Snotty rolled over to stare down at the beach. He squinted. In the pale moonlight, the ocean, the sand of the dune, the valley, the river, were almost colourless. He concentrated, trying to make out how quickly the water was rising, but the distance and the monochrome sameness of the landscape gave him difficulty.

"Cloud, it's hard to separate outlines. What's happening down there?"

Breathing heavily, Mangrove also looked down at the scene and was taken back to nights when he had sat on Home Mountain and gazed out at snow that stretched to the horizon.

It was an illusion of the light, he knew that, but the moon gave pallor to the ocean, to the river, to the whole countryside, so that it could have been snow he was looking at. Homesickness welled within his chest. If only they could return.

"Look, Tasha," he swept an arm toward it all. "We could be on Home Mountain."

Her lips formed a sad, half smile. It could be true. If she let her imagination take hold, the dull sheen of moonlight that had bled all colour from every object could be a blanket of snow.

Tasha shook her head to reinstate reality. This was no time for nostalgia. The land was disappearing, the ocean eating at solid earth like a grub chewing a leaf. They had to keep climbing. She shouted to all to continue upwards, setting the example, moving quickly with Mangrove at her side.

"Wait, Tasha. We must know how fast the sea is rising," Snotty pleaded. They were threatened, but if Endless Night was about to take them, he wanted to know when that might be.

Determined to take the clan higher, Tasha urged people on.

"Tasha, please." Snotty shouted to make sure he was heard.

She stopped. "Okay, but be quick."

He repeated his request to Cloud. Could she tell him how far the ocean had progressed? What more had happened?

With the exertion Cloud's glasses had slipped a little. She pushed them to sit more firmly on her nose. "Nothing!"

"But the water, how far has it come into the valley?"

Cloud shook her head. "It hasn't. The waves are not coming as far any more."

"What do you mean?"

"The water has receded from the dune. The waves are only washing halfway up the beach."

"What?" Biscetti said. "That's not how it happens. The water keeps on coming. In the pictures we saw in the hollow mountain, the land is submerged and disappears."

Cloud was still looking down. From what she could see there was no doubt. The sea was retreating. Waves were petering out metres from the back of the beach. On the higher level of the dune, the sand remained dry.

"Whatever we saw, it's not like that now."

"I don't understand," Biscetti said.

Snotty glanced at her. "Nor do I."

He yelled to Tasha that he was returning to the beach.

"Snotty you mustn't. It's too dangerous. You'll drown. We have to go higher."

He reasoned with her that Cloud reckoned the water had stopped rising. "She says it's going backwards."

The startling news and the counter warnings not to return were shouted across the hillside. Everyone heard, stopped climbing and stared down at the beach, but in the moonlight, the ocean, the whole countryside was drained of colour. As Snotty and Biscetti had found, it was difficult to distinguish the detail Cloud had described.

"Tasha, I'm going back. I have to know, we all have to know what's going on and anyway everything we own is down there."

"All our stuff is lost, Snotty." It was Dram's voice. "The water has taken it. Don't go back."

"I'll be all right."

Mangrove, who was with Tasha, put his hand on her arm and quietly told her that Snotty would go, no matter what anyone said. "It's his nature. You know what he's like." He paused for a moment. "I'll go with him."

"Manny?"

"I owe it to him." And Mangrove shouted to Snotty to wait. "I'm coming with you."

High on the mountainside, wherever they were standing, people watched the two descend. Tears filled Dumperty's eyes and rolled silently down his cheeks. Dram knelt by him and held him tight, both believing that this was the last they would ever see of Manny and Snotty. Water would overwhelm them and send them into Endless Night.

Chapter 3

The boys slipped and slid, searching for footing as they moved down to the valley. Looking at the ground, watching disturbed stones tumble by them, both suddenly checked and froze unmoving.

"Wolf?" Manny whispered.

The sound that had come through the night came again, a howl from far away, faint but unmistakable, a noise that they had not heard for a long time.

"Sounds like it."

The howl was repeated and taken up in a chorus of baying.

Manny pointed to the full moon.

"Yeah," Snotty said. "But they're a long way off. Come on." He continued downward.

Manny followed, wishing that they had not lost their bows. The knives they carried would be of little use against wolves.

In the valley the going was easy. They took the same path over which they had recently hurried. Manny looked at the river, its surface smoothly reflecting the moonlight. The river appeared no different from the day before. Again its current was running east, running to the sea. But there is a difference, he thought. There was just a murmur coming from that direction.

"Snotty, a short time ago the air was full of the sound of breaking waves. Now it's quiet."

"Yeah, otherwise we wouldn't have heard the wolves."

"True, but I wonder why the waves are quiet."

Snotty shrugged. They were getting close to the beach. He turned from the river to head directly for the dune. Mangrove cautioned him, suggesting that if the sea suddenly rose they would be washed away and would certainly drown. He reminded Snotty that in all their years of fishing through holes in the ice, they had been careful never to fall into those freezing waters. An innate fear, that in the river below the ice death waited to smother them, had given them great respect for water.

"I know, but the waves *are* quiet and Cloud said the water was falling not rising." He turned to grin at his friend. "And when has luck ever let us down?"

"Yes, but..." Oh, Mangrove thought, what's the use? "Snotty, I just hope that one day we don't regret your willingness to take risks."

Mangrove was remembering their time as slaves of the Torterats. If it had not been for Dram's hysteric grabbing of the lever that turned night into day, he was sure that he and Snotty would have met their end. *Still, I have to admit, life's never dull with you.*

They crossed grass and moved between trees to come to the dune, the buttress of sand where the green of the valley ended and the beach began. They stood looking down at the beach just three metres below. Randomly scattered about, left where they had floated when the water had receded, were the packs, the utensils, the weapons; all the goods and chattels that had been abandoned by them all when they had fled.

"Hey," Snotty said. "There's the cooking pot."

The big, hard-baked clay pot lay on its side, part filled with sand.

"Yes."

Mangrove looked at it and at the other items that lay among bits of driftwood and the kelp that littered the beach. Apart from the newly arrived flotsam of the clan, the beach looked as it had when they had first seen it. If there was a difference, it was that the ocean had lost its wildness. The waves were no longer crashing and tumbling. Instead, much smaller in height, they were breaking gently, easing their way to shore in a leisurely way. *This is weird.*

"Snotty, I can't work it out. This is how the beach was when we arrived. A few hours later, when we were all asleep, the water rose. We thought the land was about to drown, just as it had in the time of the ancients. Now the water has gone down to where it was."

"Yeah, well…" Snotty slid down the wall of sand to the beach. "Be happy that we've got our stuff back."

As they collected the scattered belongings, the white disc of the moon continued its passage across the sky. Mangrove looked up to gauge how much longer they would benefit from its light. A few hours remained.

The clan owned very little, but being few, these possessions were invaluable. Nothing should be overlooked.

The howling of the wolves that had caused Snotty and Mangrove to stop in their tracks came clearly to those waiting further up the mountainside. Concerned that the boys and possibly all those around her could be attacked, Tasha had gone to where Cloud was sitting and called every one to gather round. Wolves tended to stay clear of a crowd.

"Were they wolves, that you saw yesterday, Cloud?" Tasha asked.

"No. The animals I saw were much bigger."

Faces in the group close to Cloud sought other faces. Eyes met eyes and while no words were spoken, Tasha could see that many were unsettled. The weapons needed for hunting and defence had swirled away in the water, water that might rise again to claim their lives if by then they had not already been eaten by wild animals.

Tasha raised a calming hand and swung attention to Snotty and Mangrove. "Can you see them, Cloud?"

"Yes."

She gave running commentary, following their progress by the river. What was clear to all, even in the ghostly light, was that the water was no longer an immediate threat.

"They're at the dune," Cloud said. "Now they're on the beach, moving about. They seem to be collecting things. I can't make out what."

Biscetti stepped to stand by her sister. "Shouldn't we join them, Tasha?"

Tasha hesitated. Who knew what the water would do. Had it retreated to gather strength for another, stronger, assault? Yet the valley lay quiet below. Cloud could see the boys on the beach and Tasha herself could tell that the ocean was calm. Was she worrying over nothing and yet was it right for Snotty and Mangrove to be alone at night in this unknown land?

"Let's go back," Jemma said. "We'll all live, or we'll die together."

Dram said nothing, but the thought passed through her mind that it was all right for Jemma to say such a thing. Jemma was old.

Tasha looked into the faces pale in the moonlight, saw the nods and heard voices give support for the idea.

"Very well, we'll go back to the beach."

The crowd began to descend. Tasha had gone a few steps when she heard her name called. She looked back to see Cloud still sitting, her eyes staring at nothing, Dram and Dumperty kneeling at her side.

"Tasha, come quickly." Dram was supporting Cloud who, deep in trance, would otherwise have collapsed to lie on the earth. "She's dreaming again."

Tasha ran to the girl whose mind was no longer on the mountainside, but in some strange place. She sat and taking Cloud's hand held it gently. "Wake up, Cloud. We're going back to the beach. Everything's all right now. Wake up."

Tasha leaned forward so that her eyes peered directly into Cloud's, but Cloud looked through her, seeing only the faraway images in her mind. Held by those imagined pictures, oblivious to all around her, Cloud's lips began to twitch, her mouth to move, until eventually she spoke. The voice was not her voice and yet it was.

Those making their way down the mountain had heard Dram's anxious cry. Some looked back and drew attention to what was going on and soon all returned to gather around, to look and to listen.

Shaking, as though what she witnessed was cause for alarm, Cloud uttered words that made no sense. "Milk from cow to calf is given, dogs of yellow snarl and bite, flying manes of horses ridden, evil dragons out of sight."

"What's she saying?" Belle looked at Jemma, but spoke loudly. The question was really addressed to anyone who might be able to give an answer.

Jemma shrugged. Much was unintelligible to her. Words that had no meaning were mixed in with those she knew. *And dragons?* They were creatures of myth that appeared in the frightening tales told in Homecave late at night as the clan huddled around the embers of the fire; scary stories, but just stories.

Tasha watched the reactions in the faces of the assembly. No one could understand what Cloud had said. For Tasha too, so many of the words were foreign that nothing could be made of them.

"Don't worry." She waved a calming hand. "You go on. We'll wake Cloud and soon follow."

The bystanders recommenced the downhill journey. They had all listened to Cloud's premonitions in the past. Understandable or not, words of her dreaming seldom augured well for the clan.

In the east the sky began to pale and before the moon had slipped below the horizon the first light of the new day made progress easier.

Tasha paused to look up. The Southern Cross was low in the sky, Venus, the morning star, almost extinguished by the light. Many of the stars had already faded from view. But, she thought, they will return. Tonight those old friends will shine on us again. Hope rose in Tasha. Not everything was new and unknown. Some things remained steadfast. She gazed at the lightening sky and hoped that good would come to the clan in the new land.

Working in the green-gold light of dawn, everyone scouring the beach, the search for lost articles became a treasure hunt. The joy at finding things that had been believed lost forever brought laughter and cries of excitement. Almost everything was lying somewhere on the sand.

The rising sun made the search easier. Items that had floated to sea and been carried back by the waves further down the beach were also recovered.

As the sun rose higher, belongings were re-united with rightful owners and common property set to one side. Either laid out on the dune, or hung in the nearby trees, by noon everything was dry and with a fire going, the idea of eating took hold.

Tasha looked at the gourds that had held the supply of fresh water. Empty, some holding sea water which they knew was salty, her first thought was that a source of drinking water had to be found. She wondered if the river might provide fresh water, doubting it since she had seen the sea rush in. Nevertheless it was imperative to find drinking water.

Mangrove, Biscetti and Belle volunteered that they would make the search.

The river was the first to be investigated. Belle scooped up water to her mouth and immediately spat. "Forget it. The river's salty too."

She had found that estuarine rivers are dominated by the sea; fresh water coming down from up country overpowered by the ocean.

The three walked along the bank, looking about, intrigued by so much that was novel. Alongside them, a point of reference for direction, the river ran swiftly to the sea, returning water that had swept inland during the night as they had fled.

A small hillock, the only unusual feature on the otherwise flat field of grass with its few trees, rose a short distance away. Biscetti ran to it, wanting to stand at its crest like some queen on the battlements of her castle from where she could look down upon her minions. She climbed the slope and as she did saw white amongst the green of the grass. Curious, she scraped a little earth and grass away until she could see that there were shells beneath. She knelt and dug a little more and still on her knees called to Mangrove and Belle to come and see what she had found.

Together they cleared a larger area and the few shells uncovered became many. It was soon obvious that the whole hillock was composed of the bleached remains of shells.

"How did they get here, Manny?"

"I don't know, but someone must have put them here."

He examined one and saw that the shell was made of two parts. Joined at a hinge, the shell had the appearance of a pale butterfly. Mangrove put the shell in his pocket. He would show it to Snotty when they were back to the beach.

The three returned to the search for water and a few hundred metres further on a shallow creek interrupted their way. Biscetti bent to taste the water and found it sweet. Relieved, the three filled the gourds that hung at their belts and around their necks. The potentially serious problem had been resolved.

Over time, the creek had carved its way through the river bank before dropping into the water below. Perhaps it always ran with fresh water.

Mangrove wanted to be certain. "Let's see where this water comes from."

The group left the river and followed the course of the creek for four or five hundred metres across grassed areas and through trees. In a rocky grotto at the base of the mountain they found its source. Vines, that had taken root in the crevices and ledges of the rock face above, hung in a thick curtain, hiding what was behind, but, like a spring, water bubbled from between rocks, splashing in a tiny waterfall that fed the creek.

Belle and Manny knelt to drink directly from the fountainhead. Cold from its long, dark passage through the mountain, water had never tasted so fresh and pure.

"We have water." Mangrove looked to the girls and smiled. "The best we could possibly have."

The new land had begun to live up to its promise.

At the beach, hunger rumbled in the bellies of those waiting. Trying to occupy their minds with thoughts other than eating, they sought diversion in what was going on around them.

Four small birds were at the water's edge, running whenever a wave slid up the sand, pecking with long red beaks in a search for food. The birds ran with quick, short steps, stopping, eating, hurrying on to repeat sharp jabs at a new patch of sand.

Snotty was intrigued and leaving the others went to see what the birds were eating. They chirruped and flew twenty metres down the beach to begin again their search. He laughed and walked into the surf to splash about. He called to those watching from a distance to join him. They held back, their respect for what they had experienced the night before keeping them well away.

The waves were surging around Snotty's legs, rising to his knees, falling back to just cover his ankles. Something pressed hard under his foot. He felt it move a little and bent to pluck a shell from the sand. As he did so he saw the lips of the bivalve closing and, disappearing between them, a strip of white flesh. He took the Swiss knife from his pocket, levered a blade between the lips and winkled them open. Fresh meat pulsed on the plate of the shell. With a twist of the blade he severed flesh from shell and tipped it into his mouth to chew and swallow. Those watching saw the look of pleasure on his face.

Snotty waved, beckoning them to the water. "You have to try this. It's so good."

For a moment he looked at the opened shell in his hand. As with Mangrove, the shell reminded him of a white butterfly. Pretty as it was, the shell was no longer of use. He dropped it, his feet searching for another.

Dumperty slid down the wall of sand. Zita and Hock followed. Entering the water, keeping close to the shore they prodded the sand with their feet. Zita faced the ocean, not trusting it, walking backwards wriggling her heels. She felt the hard lump, bent and plucked the shell and then another from their hiding place. A shell in each hand, she looked at them and then not wanting to delay the pleasure, smashed them together. The shells split. Zita broke pieces away to fall into the water and scooped flesh into her mouth. Juice ran down her chin. She smiled, relishing the taste.

It was enough. In a rush everyone found a place along the water's edge, working feet into sand, finding shells, breaking them open to gorge on the flesh. The clan had discovered pipis.

Dumperty spat sand from his mouth. The shellfish were nice, but they did have sand in them.

Jemma watched and felt sympathy for him. "We should cook the shells," she shouted to Tasha. "They may be better that way."

It was agreed. Easily found, the shells filled pockets until they would hold no more. One by one people re-crossed the beach and climbed the dune to drop pipis into the pot now boiling with sea water.

As Jemma had thought, cooking opened the shells. With a wooden spoon she lifted one from the pot, blew on it to cool it and with her flint knife scrapped the meat from the shell and offered it to Tasha.

She chewed the warm flesh as everyone watched. Swallowing, she grinned. "They're even better when they're cooked and the sand has almost gone."

The pipi feast began. Shell after shell was taken from the pot and as bellies filled, a pile of butterfly shells grew on the sand. Snotty watched the heap grow. Had he known, members of the clan were not the first to cast their shells upon the dune. In the distant past, long before the civilization of the ancients, long before the period the Camarilla referred to as the Good Times, primitive people had gathered there to eat; tribes who had lived in much the same way as the clan. These Stone Age tribes had roamed the valley, eaten together and left the shells to mount in middens. The shells being thrown to the new heap were symbols of human existence that had gone full circle.

Interesting as it might have been to know such history, Snotty was totally unaware and like the others he ate with enjoyment until his belly stretched to bursting. Only when Mangrove returned, would they realise that the hillock in the valley was a mound of pipi shells, a place where tribal dinners had been held long, long ago.

Sitting above the beach on the dune, chewing the succulent flesh, Dumperty was suddenly alert. He stared at waves that progressively seemed to wash a little further up the beach.

He stood in alarm and ready to flee, shouted a warning. "The water's coming up again."

The whole crowd rose, eyes fixed on water creeping up the beach.

"We have to go," Ingamo cried. "This time it may not go back."

People ran to grab whatever they felt could be carried. Ingamo was right. A second time they might not survive.

"Wait," Snotty shouted. "Wait."

Fearing the worst, ready to run, some were stepping away from the dune, already on their way to higher ground.

Tasha called to them, calming the rising panic. "Do as Snotty says. We know we can run faster than the rising water."

Some were reluctant, but gradually the band gathered above the beach and watched.

Without the wind to drive them, the waves advanced gently up the beach, reached their high point and commenced to recede.

The clan could not know that the ocean rose and fell at the command of the moon, that the inundation they had all feared was merely the rising tide. Nor could they know that on the previous night with the moon's face fully lit – because of its alignment with the sun – the power of gravity of those heavenly bodies was strengthened. What had seemed a catastrophe was simply the ocean being lifted, as if the moon was a magnet that would attract everything it could from planet Earth.

As time went by, Tasha and her people would learn that the ocean rose and fell in regular sequence. They would come to know that twice each day the water would creep up the beach and dutifully return and that every twenty-eight days the full moon would pull the tide higher than normal. Similarly, they would learn that when the tide was low, things usually hidden from view could be seen and touched and new-found foods eaten. They would come to understand that the ocean on a rising tide entered the river so that it flowed west and that when the tide changed to run out, the river flowed east. It was this regular, unstoppable force of the tide that meant the river was salty. The ocean was the master.

But gaining this knowledge would take time and Tasha was fully aware that until immediate needs were met, the survival of the clan was in jeopardy. When everyone had finished eating, she put forward her plan; the ways and means by which they might settle comfortably into the new land.

Dram, Biscetti and Cloud would explore the extent of the valley, the valley in which the clan had spent their time so far. The three were to note anything of interest, but their main task was to find a suitable cave in which they all could live. If game or anything edible could be found, it was to be brought back for the cooking pot.

As is common with estuarine rivers, sandbanks had formed where river and ocean met. Snotty and Mangrove were to cross to the other side at low water. A headland further along the coast prevented them from gaining access to the next valley from the beach. Therefore they would climb the rise on the far side of the river and make their way from there, the intention being to see how hospitable the next valley might be. Was it different from the one they were in? What animals if any lived there? Would any provide a source of food? Naturally if the boys came across a cave that met the clan's requirements, they should mark its location.

The main body of people would remain in the vicinity of the dune. Since the exploration parties were expected to be away for two or three days, those who stayed behind would set up the sorts of shelters they had used during the exodus from Homecave. The abundance of pipis that could be caught fresh daily would feed them until alternatives were found. To bring variety to the menu as soon as possible, Belle and Hock were to use their lines in the river while Zita and Vellum fished off the beach.

Falling into their former roles at Homecave, the twins Sola and Situ would fetch water from the spring and gather plenty of firewood. They would carry hunting weapons at all times; meat would be a welcome addition to the diet. As a precaution against possible attacks from the wolves – that had been heard if not seen – fires would be set up at intervals around the boundary of the camp and lit at nightfall.

When she had finished outlining responsibilities, Tasha asked if all was understood and was answered with general murmurs of assent.

"What about me?" Dumperty came to stand before Tasha. "I should go with Snotty and Manny."

She smiled and tried to reason with him that the mission could face unknown dangers.

"It's because I'm small isn't it? You don't think I'll ever be a Forager."

"You will be one day. It's just..."

"How will I ever learn if you never let me go with them?"

Tasha looked to Snotty for support. Dumperty's logic was faultless, but she was sending Snotty and Mangrove into territory totally unknown. It was a risky undertaking.

"He's right, Tasha." Snotty said. "And remember that without Dumperty, Dram and Manny and I might never have got off the ledge. Let him come." Then turning to Mangrove. "How about it?"

Mangrove was thinking that Dumperty had proved his courage already and that he had to learn the ways of a Forager sometime. A few days away from the clan would be a good introduction. If on the other hand he and Snotty ran into trouble, Dumperty would be an unnecessary responsibility. Or, there was the possibility he would add to their firepower; an extra man against whatever they were up against. Mangrove considered the pros and cons.

"Yeah, why not?"

"Are you sure?" Tasha asked. "I don't want Dumperty to come to any harm."

"With us?" Snotty grinned. "No chance. Anyway who says *he* won't be protecting Manny and me?"

Dumperty listened to the conversation, his eyes bright with anticipation flitting from one to the other as his fate was decided.

"Hey," he shouted and laughing flung himself at Snotty. "I'm coming. I'm a Forager."

Snotty hugged him. "You'll be the best Forager there ever was."

Chapter 4

Dram licked her finger and ran it along the string of her bow, testing its readiness. She applied pressure and watching the bow flex, smiled with satisfaction. Once again she was back in her element.

Biscetti examined the heads of her arrows, feeling them with a thumb, honing the flints with a sharpening stone where necessary. As she moved the stone back and forth the thoughts in her mind were that she wanted no surprises, but if danger threatened she would be ready. *Well, as ready as I can be. Who knows what's out there?*

Cloud, the third member of the cave locating party, watched the preparation. She had never fired an arrow. Until Dumperty gave her the spectacles he had found in the bunker, her vision had been restricted to objects held a few centimetres from her nose. She hoped that in time one of the Foragers would teach her how to use a bow. Until then her eyes, aided by the lenses from the twenty-first century, were her greatest asset. Her only weapon was the knife in the scabbard worn at the belt in Camarilla fashion.

Belle and her team checked lines and hooks. Pipis would serve as bait for both beach and river fishing. They sat in the sun, legs crossed, talking, discarding hooks blunted from use and replacing them with fresh, sharp barbs of bone. Stones were attached as sinkers, selected for shape and weight so that when the baited lines were hurled, they would fly well out from the beach or river bank. As they prepared the lines they chatted cheerfully, exchanging exaggerated forecasts of who would catch the most fish.

Snotty and Mangrove wasted no time. For them it was just another foray into the unknown. Their prime concern was that Dumperty came prepared. They checked him out, nodding approval and praising him as he laid out his gear.

Watching each group prepare, Tasha prayed to the stars that those who would probe the surrounding countryside would return safely. "So much depends on you," she whispered. "May no harm befall you."

"Okay, all set?" Snotty confirmed with Mangrove that he and Dumperty were ready to go.

He got their nods and signalled Tasha. Dram and Belle gave her the same thumbs up. They too were on their way.

With all the characteristics of a carefully planned military operation, the groups set out on their assigned tasks. In knee deep water, Mangrove, Snotty and Dumperty crossed the bar at the mouth of the river, their bare feet disturbing sand that eddied away with the current. Two hundred metres upstream, Belle and Hock were saying goodbye to Dram, Biscetti and Cloud.

"Good luck," Hock said. "Find us somewhere nice to live."

Dram smiled. "We'll be trying. And good luck to you."

At the dune – the base camp until all returned – those who remained watched the explorers depart, gave their final waves and commenced erecting shelters.

Leaving the fishers, Dram headed west along the river bank, Cloud following, Biscetti in the rear. Each carried backpack with provisions and weapons. With a broad field of grass and a few trees contained between the river and the steep rise to the top of the range, there was nothing to interrupt their view but the small hillock that Biscetti had earlier found to be composed of shells. It was of no consequence. For two kilometres ahead all appeared normal, but appearances could be deceptive. They were Foragers and their eyes continually searched ahead and to either side.

Dram raised a hand to halt. She knelt examining the droppings of some animal. Biscetti and Cloud watched.

The girls recognised dung that must have lain on the grass for many days. The manure was dried and weathered, but rather than being confined to a single pile, it had fallen separated over quite a distance. They stood over it, trying to determine from what animal it had come. The droppings were larger than any they had previously seen. Dram drew her knife and poked at a lump the size of an apple, cutting into it, endeavouring to identify what the animal had been feeding on.

"Hmm," Dram said. "Cloud, you saw big animals from the top of the sleeping hare."

"Yes."

It was obvious. Big droppings could only have been left by a big animal and, strung out as they were, the beast was probably running in fright when he had emptied his bowels.

Dram sliced the 'apple', shaving sections from it, trying to reveal from what it was made. She bent low and sniffed the dried dung. "This animal ate grass. Look you can see it."

"That dung's pretty old, Dram. Whoever dropped it is long gone."

"Yeah."

They moved on, keeping to the riverbank but with a clear view of the mountainside. Any openings that might house the clan would be easily seen. Where the open field gave way to scrub and trees, the slope of the mountain changed rapidly to become an escarpment. Before reaching that point, it was Dram's intention to veer to the right until close to the slope and then proceed to explore the foot of the cliff until the light failed. In the meantime, sticking by the bank gave Dram the opportunity to examine what might exist in the clear waters of the river.

The girls enjoyed the heat of the sun. It warmed their clothing and pressed on bare arms and bare legs with caressing energy. Biscetti looked up at the sky, cloudless and so brightly blue that she thought it could have been newly scrubbed.

"Isn't this a great place to be?"

"I love it here," Cloud replied.

That was Dram's feeling too.

Biscetti began to whistle. Life was as sweet as she could imagine. She raised her face to the sun and with eyes closed relished the warming of her skin.

"Uh, what's that?" The rapture on her face had changed to disgust. The smell thickening the air was revolting.

Dram grimaced. "We'd better find out."

The stench was wind borne, so strong that its source could not be far away. She held her nose, eyes partly closed. "That's bad, really bad." She came to an abrupt halt. "Oh, look at that."

In a dip in the ground was something they had never seen before and from which the terrible smell was coming. A dripping mass of hair and ragged strips of hide lay in the sand, all entwined, rolled into a ball that was held together by thick red mucus. Within the slimy wad they could see individual teeth, big teeth, long and yellow, across which were streaked threads and gobbets of red and there were hooves at odd angles, no longer attached to the legs to which they had once belonged. It was as though the whole congealed mess had been vomited as an unwanted part of some terrible meal. Around it, crawling all over it were flies, constantly buzzing.

"What a stink!" Biscetti had half turned her face away, grimacing at the assault on her nose and eyes.

"Hmm," Dram grunted, but she continued to examine the ugly mass, finding it hard to believe that there existed an animal so large, or so fierce, that it could consume another that from the size of the teeth was itself big. Hooves she recognised. They were different from those of a goat, but they were the feet of some animal and, like the teeth, had once belonged to something very big. A quiver of fear rippled through her.

"What did this come from, Dram?" Cloud was peering at the mess.

Dram had moved upwind to escape the stench. From there she could look without the full force of the smell assailing her.

"The dung we saw came from a big animal. Perhaps it was also responsible for this, but..." She hesitated.

"But what?"

"The dung was spread, remember. It lay in clumps that were in line, as though it had fallen from a running animal. You know what I mean. We've seen that sort of trail when we were hunting in the snow."

"Yeah," Biscetti said.

The girls knew from experience that it was the hunted animal whose bowels failed when the realisation came that escape was impossible and death was but seconds away. The possibility remained that the dung and the red mess in front of them came from the same creature. It didn't really matter. Either way, hunter and hunted must be huge, much bigger than anything they had ever previously encountered.

"I hope our bows are strong enough and our arrows sharp enough." Doubt was in Biscetti's tone.

Fear fluttered again through Dram. She trembled a little. "I hope we don't have to find out. Let's go."

"What about this?" Biscetti kicked sand at the ball of regurgitated body parts.

Dram shuddered. "Leave it."

"We should warn the others we've seen this." Cloud said.

"Yes."

Eager to get away, Dram returned to the river. "Look at that." She pointed to the water close to the bank. "Belle and the others should have no trouble."

A school of fish was lazily nosing at the sandy bottom, searching for prawns, worms or tiny shellfish, anything on which they could feed.

Biscetti looked back to where they had left the fishers. "Manny and Snotty reckon if you hope to catch anything, you have to fish where the fish are. Maybe Belle and the others should come here."

But as they continued along the bank more fish could be seen. Dram made the comment that the clan was very lucky to have found a river so full of fish.

The offshore breeze – light air that blew from above the heights at the end of the valley and out to sea – puffed gently at their faces, ruffling hair and providing a cooling counterpoint to the warmth of the sun. The girls were about half way to where the bush began and had left the river to cross to the escarpment. They were walking through long grass when Cloud called softly to Dram. "There are animals near the trees."

Immediately the three stopped, eyes focused on the dozen or so four legged creatures seven hundred metres ahead. All had long necks stretched to the ground, grazing peacefully.

"What are they?" Biscetti lifted her hand to guard her eyes from the sun. "What are…"

"Shh." Cloud touched her, cautioning her. "There's something else in the grass."

The others strained to see what had attracted Cloud's attention. Not far from the feeding animals long stems of grass momentarily shivered.

Dram concentrated. "Yes."

She had caught a brief glimpse of a dark, heavyset body, a thick clawed leg, before the parted grass sprang back to hide the figure.

With the animals upwind, human scent could not be detected, but the girls remained still, not wishing to betray their presence with movement. Unused to foraging, Cloud asked Dram what was happening.

"The animal in the grass is stalking the ones eating. The stalker looks very powerful. I don't want him coming at us."

Like sculpted figures the girls held still, unwilling to even sink to the cover of the grass, but the creature had but one interest; the grazing herd.

Every little while the screen of tall grass was brushed aside and in those moments the motionless girls were able to see the hunter; never a whole picture but a collage of partial views of his body that with mounting apprehension they put together.

"Oh." Dram's voice cracked and she swallowed. "He's huge, so thick and so ugly."

Biscetti stood mute, unable to get out of her mind the size of the claws that protruded from legs that had the girth of tree trunks. She imagined the legs stomping on her, crushing her and the billhooks of claws raking her flesh.

Cloud was trembling. The yellow tongue, deeply forked, kept darting to feel the air, as if it were a third eye to feed more information to the animal's brain. She saw teeth, long and sharp and what might have been blood oozing from its mouth. Speaking as if to herself she said, "It's a dragon."

"Dragons aren't real." Biscetti spoke hurriedly, her tone rising, but as she denied their existence there was a lack of conviction in her voice.

"They are real. I saw them in my dream."

Biscetti looked at Dram and for a moment they stared at each other. Neither spoke.

Unaware, the long necked animals continued feeding. Minutes passed and from where they stood the girls watched the gap closing. Stealthy, taking great care, the dragon scarcely disturbed the curtain of green.

"He's so close to them," Dram said.

They watched. All was still.

In one explosive leap the dragon shot from cover, trampling the grass, rushing at speed toward his prey.

"He's so fast. I can't believe..."

The dragon was hurtling over the ground. Startled, those grazing looked up to see death racing at them. In a wild flurry of movement they began to run. From the distance the girls could see individual muscles bunch and flex under the skin. Highlighted by the sun, the satiny haunches drove hooves at the turf, legs gathered and stretched, but for the short, sharp burst the dragon was too fast. He hit his target at the neck, dragging him down, tearing out the doomed animal's throat. Before his lungs and heart had ceased to function, the prey was being eaten.

Those lucky enough to escape were running in terror, long hair on their necks streaming in the wind.

In shock, Dram saw herself supporting Cloud in the moonlight and in her mind heard again the words coming from the depth of Cloud's trance. *Flying manes of horses ridden. Evil dragons out of sight.*

"Are they horses, Cloud?"

"They must be."

The thunder of galloping hooves filled the air; a relentless drumming that faded as the horses wheeled into the trees and flying manes were lost from view.

At the kill, the Komodo Dragon, an animal that over millennia had evolved to become the largest, deadliest lizard on earth, was tearing the fallen horse apart.

At more than one hundred and fifty kilograms, three metres in length, the Komodo could hardly be called a lizard. He was a true dragon. A wily killer that hunted by using cover to close unnoticed on his quarry and then with a great burst of speed catch and overwhelm it. In more than forty million years the Komodo's serrated teeth had developed to cut chunks from bigger animals with ease. The bones of his skull had evolved to become flexible, enabling him to swallow the enormous sections of meat and bone he ripped from a carcase. Worse still, the dragon's mouth was full of virulent bacteria that dripped blood- red from his gums. Once bitten no prey could escape. The wounded animal might get away, but poisoned, die within days. The smell of the rotting corpse would be picked up by the dragon as far off as ten kilometres. Uncaring whether the meat he ate was fresh, the Komodo would then gorge on the carrion.

In the new land to which the Camarilla had come, the Komodo was king, feared by all.

The Foragers watched in amazement the consumption of the horse. Chunk by chunk its body was disappearing. In ten minutes half the horse was gone. In twenty-five nothing was left of it. The dragon had eaten it all.

"How can it be?" Biscetti asked. "And look at him now!"

The Komodo was rubbing his face on the earth, tearing up grass with the swiping of his head.

"He's wiping his face."

It was true. The dragon was ridding himself of the evil smelling bacteria that had flecked his face as he ate.

Cloud's hand moved slowly to touch Dram. "There are more of them."

Dram heard the warning with dismay. Bubbles seemed to suddenly invade her veins. Her heart began to race and her scalp shrank. Tasha had given her responsibility, put the safety of Biscetti and Cloud in her hands and on this bright shiny day, monsters far worse than those she had fought at the lake and among the pillars of rock, had appeared from nowhere. Dragons that were invisible until they charged and from whom there was no escape.

"Where?"

"In the shadow of the trees." Cloud moved a finger.

Dram saw them, not together but separated. Whereas the Komodo that had killed the horse was black, one of the new arrivals was grey, the other the colour of red clay.

"Just two, are there just two?"

"That's all I can see."

"What about those we can't see?" Biscetti's eyes were searching the grass. "They could be stalking us right now."

Dram drew air deep into her lungs a number of times. She had to be calm. She had to think. "Don't say that. We've seen three, that's all and we are downwind. If there are any more they won't know we're here."

"So what do we do?"

Dram had the picture of the Komodo standing high on hind legs, the claws of his forelegs ripping into the horse. The size, the weight of the dragon was enough to terrify, but Dram could not forget the sight of his jaws loosed so wide in unnatural separation.

"We could go back." She shuddered as she spoke.

"How can we do that? On the beach, on the dune, we would all be so exposed. The dragons would find us. We'd be easy meat."

"Don't talk like that, Biscetti." But Dram knew that it was true. "Okay, we have to avoid the dragons and we have to find a place to live; somewhere where they can't get at us."

"Huh?" Biscetti was remembering Dram at the ice crevasse, thinking that if they ran into trouble Dram might crack.

"You said yourself we can't go back until we find a safe place for the clan to live."

Biscetti nodded. The facts were plain enough. She and Dram as Foragers were duty bound to carry out the assigned task, regardless of the risk. Good sense and good planning should minimise danger, but the code of the Camarilla was cast in stone. Foragers had a selfless duty.

"Okay," Dram said. "Here's what I think."

She outlined her plan. They would discreetly backtrack to approach the escarpment less directly. In that way she hoped the dragons would remain unaware of their presence. They would make their way along the base of the cliff. A cave if it could be found would have to be elevated, high enough to be out of reach of the Komodos.

Biscetti was thinking that a search from the ground did not sound good. With scrub and trees growing close to the cliff they would never see danger until it was upon them. From what she had seen the dragons were smart. They thought ahead. She had seen how they gained surprise and how well judged was the final charge. If any good had come from the scene they had witnessed, it was that they now knew how ferocious and how clever the dragon was. Putting that knowledge to use would be the trick; making use of it to stay alive.

"If we can find a ledge and climb to that..."

"If there is a ledge!" Dram looked at the wall of rock. "What can you see, Cloud?"

"I'm looking. The cliff isn't sheer. There are ledges, but I'm not sure whether they are continuous." Cloud traced the rock face from where the mountainside altered to form the escarpment. "If we climb there." She pointed. "There seems to be a way along, but I can't be sure."

"There's only one way to find out," Dram said.

She looked again toward the Komodos. The big black one was moving slowly toward the river, dragging his distended stomach along the ground. The grey and the red appeared to be snapping up scraps, the remnants of the kill. She could see only the three.

They cut back toward the north-east, moving away from the Komodos and toward the mountain. The breeze had picked up a little, swaying the grass. Here and there wildflowers showed in pink and yellow. Above, the ball of the sun radiated from the peerless blue of the sky. The only intrusion into the idyllic scene was the odour carried on the wind; the stink issuing from the mouths of Komodos.

The girls began to sweat with the effort of climbing the slope. Biscetti pulled at the strings of her tunic to open it wide. The others did likewise. Judging themselves to be high enough, they began the traverse toward the escarpment. Fallen rocks provided some cover, but often the girls were scrambling across open terrain.

"If those things are looking this way," Dram said. "They must see us."

Cloud reassured her. The red Komodo and the grey were still roaming the area where the horse had been butchered, their tongues flicking at the ground in the search for left over flesh or bone. The black dragon was lying in a scrape in the sand.

"He's digesting his meal," Biscetti said.

Dram nodded.

The slope steepened, changed from the earth of hillside to rock cliff.

"Here," Cloud said and stepped onto a narrow ledge, a mere fault in the rock before it continued the drop to the valley floor. "We're above the treetops."

"Hmm." Biscetti followed. The shelf running along the cliff face was not as wide as she would have liked. Remembering Manny's advice at the crevasse, she did not look down.

Dram followed her. "You okay, Biscetti?"

Biscetti stared ahead. "Yeah."

Cloud turned around to smile at Biscetti. "This is fun. It's like walking in the air."

"Not for me."

Cloud led. The ledge narrowing until it ran to nothing. "We have to step down here. The path continues, but it's lower."

Some geological idiosyncrasy had brought an abrupt end to the layer of rock, shearing it to recommence half a metre lower down.

Biscetti grimaced. *Why did I ever suggest this?* She watched where Cloud placed her feet and the handholds she used. *Okay.* She did the same.

The shelf had become wider and the geological shift a million or more years earlier had caused the rock layer to angle downward. The girls were moving across the cliff face, but gradually descending. They were down to the canopy of the trees, pushing foliage aside when they came to a fissure in the cliff, a split that ran upward from where they stood for three or four metres. Cloud held a branch and stepped by.

"Wait," Biscetti said. "There's cool air coming from there." She put her face to the opening feeling the air dry her sweat.

Dram nudged her. "Keep moving."

The ledge widened. They walked normally, no longer needing to hug the cliff face.

"This is better. We can..."

She broke off. Cloud was stumbling backward, holding part of the tree away from her body, using it as a shield. Biscetti grabbed her, fearing that she would lose her footing and tumble off, questioning why Cloud had without warning acted in this way. Cloud was whimpering, still retreating so that Biscetti was pushed into Dram. The three were jammed on the stratum of rock, the cliff rearing above, a drop of thirty metres below.

"Cloud what are you doing?" Biscetti's voice was high and sharp. "We'll fall."

It was then the wave of fear passed through her and she heard Dram catch her breath and felt Dram's fingers clutch at the back of her tunic. The red Komodo, a female, was in a fork of the tree. She had seen them, climbed to lay in wait and was about to devour them. The split ends of her yellow tongue were repeatedly flicking toward them.

"Dram, what do we do?" Cloud was shaking. She was closest to the animal. She would be the first to be eaten, imagining an arm become a stump, a leg being crushed between Komodo jaws.

Dram tried to speak but no words came.

All senses of the three girls were reeling. Up close they could see every detail: the eyes moving in their sockets, the swollen and bleeding gums from which some bloody substance oozed across the saw-edged teeth, the huge size of the clawed legs, the individual bony scales of the Komodo's armoured skin. From her opening, closing, mouth the stink of bacteria blew at them, the girls wishing that their nostrils would close, that they could stop breathing. Hammering their ears was the full throated hiss of the hunter who had cornered his prey.

The Komodo shifted her huge muscular tail and with claws gripping the thick branch began to cross the last few metres separating them.

"Dram, Dram." Biscetti was pleading, her voice raised. "Move. Move now."

Dram was fixated on the progress of the Komodo. Massive bowed legs enabled it to hold the limb of the tree, ten centimetre claws cutting through bark and into the wood beneath. There was no hope of the animal falling. It would continue along the branch until it could step on to the ledge and then...

Cloud was arching backwards, crowding Biscetti.

Biscetti drove an elbow into Dram. "Get going or we'll die!"

Dram took a step backward. The others had freedom to move. Half turned they began retracing their steps, walking sideways like crabs, backs to the wall of rock, unwilling to take their eyes off the dragon. They saw the Komodo heave its body on to the ledge.

Dram moved faster, feeling her way, one hand brushing along the cliff, thinking that the rock strata would soon come to the shear, that they would have to climb to the higher level and in that time Endless Night would take them all.

Her hand touched the edge of the fissure and felt cool air. She glanced at it, stepped past and stopped. "Biscetti, see if you can squeeze in."

Saying nothing, Biscetti threw her pack into the darkness, wriggled sideways, twisting her head and was gone.

"It's okay," she called from within the cliff.

Cloud made to follow. Dram nodded and Cloud too was gone.

"Come on, Dram, hurry." Biscetti's voice echoed as though she called from some vast, empty space.

"I'm not coming. I have to tell Tasha what's happened. You'll be safe in there."

"Dram, you'll be killed."

"I have to get help and..."

The Komodo was lumbering toward Dram, not running, coming at her with a rolling gait, knowing that for this kill there was no need for speed.

Dram slipped her bow from her shoulder, fitted an arrow and fired. The arrow glanced off the armour. The Komodo reared its head and hissed.

"I'm going, Biscetti. Good luck, stay safe." Dram turned and was off.

The Komodo stopped. Her tongue speared into the crack through which Biscetti and Cloud had disappeared. The forked tongue licked the air, tasting the scent of the girls. The Komodo pressed her head against the rock. Sensory organs in the scales of her chin picked up the movement of their feet as they recoiled from the whispering tongue. With one foreleg the dragon struck blindly into the crevasse, claws ripping at the rock, scarring it with deep, parallel lines. It struck again in fury, opened its jaws and roared.

A little more than three metres away, the girls cringed. The sound was unlike anything they had ever heard; loud, harsh, low pitched, a sudden exploding volume of compressed air that narrowed to a long, terrifying hiss. In dim light they clung to one another, watching claws scrape against the walls of the narrow passage.

"Where's Dram?"

"She's gone, Cloud."

"To Endless Night?"

"I hope not." With eyes tight shut, Biscetti quickly prayed to the stars that Dram had got away. "No, she knew the dragon would never be able to enter this passage. She must have hoped that it would waste some time trying to get at us, time for her to escape."

Biscetti's voice was strangely loud. The hissing, the smashing of claws against rock had ceased. More light was coming through the thin passage. The Komodo had left.

"It's gone after Dram," Cloud said. "She should have come with us."

"No, Cloud." Guilt weighed on Biscetti that she had screamed at Dram. "We would have been trapped. Tasha and the others would never know where we are. They would learn of the dragons too late to save themselves. Dram risked her life for us and the clan. I just hope…"

"You're not sure are you?" Cloud's eyes filled with tears. "The dragon will kill her."

Biscetti bowed her head. She could *not* be sure.

Chapter 5

The three who crossed the river as Dram's party bid goodbye to Belle, were well armed and carried food for two days. Coiled in Mangrove's pack was the communal rope. Corded from animal tendons, kept supple from regular greasing, the rope was a precaution. In the past it had saved Biscetti's life, it had saved them all from the Torterats at the crevasse. More recently it had played the key role after the flying incident. The damage it had suffered had been repaired by Snotty, who had collected tendons from whoever was using them as binding for one thing or another. All agreed that the common good had precedence.

Maybe, Mangrove thought, the rope won't be needed. *The thing is, you never know.* Pushing against the current, he mentally ticked off the array of items they carried. Drinking water might present a problem, but otherwise they were as well prepared as they could be.

"Hey, Manny, look at all the stuff lying about."

The bar crossed, Snotty left the water and ran across soft, dry sand to pick up what had once been the trunk of a sapling. Lying among the driftwood, aged and weathered, abraded by sand and time to a uniform smoothness, the grey stick was perfectly straight. He ran his hand down the clean roundness and stood it upright in the sand like a pole, half as tall again as himself. He pulled it from the sand and with his arm bent thrust it back and forth, feeling its weight.

"Watch this, Manny." And taking aim at a clump of kelp sweeping up the sand in the wash of a wave, he threw hard. The pole flew fast and true to stick quivering in the kelp.

Dumperty ran to retrieve it.

"Good shot," Manny said.

They looked at each other, each understanding that hitting the kelp had been a game, but with the immediate knowledge that Snotty now had a spear. A new weapon had been added to their armoury.

They left the water and with foot coverings on again – the same scuffed animal skin shoes they had been wearing since the days of Homecave – set off for the ridge that hemmed the southern extremity of the valley. It lay about a kilometre distant.

Snotty scanned the ground they were about to cross. "What can you see, little guy?"

"Open ground, trees dotted about except for over there." He pointed to where the trees grew thicker, as though this was the main wood from which the others had wandered to take root.

"Anything else?"

Dumperty searched the whole area before them, even glancing back to the river. "I don't think so."

Mangrove listened with amusement to the exchange between teacher and pupil.

"There's a small animal, could be a hare, by the trunk of that tree with the broken branch. He's in shadow and hard to see, but he's there."

Dumperty narrowed his eyes and found the outline of the animal. "Sorry, Snotty."

"That's okay. He'd be nice to eat. Do you think you could get him?"

Dumperty nodded eagerly.

"Go on then. Make yourself small and..."

"I am small!"

It was Snotty's turn to apologise. He went on to explain that Dumperty should take a roundabout route as though not interested in the animal and then close in at an angle from behind the tree. For the last fifty metres he should crawl and finally edge forward on his elbows until he felt sure that, if he fired, his arrow would hit the mark.

Mangrove and Snotty sat down to watch their apprentice. He followed his instructions until judging that he was within range, slowly rose to kneel and take aim. The movement was enough to startle the hare. His big ears twitched and with eyes bulging he bounded away.

Dumperty let the taut bowstring relax and walked back. "What did I do wrong?"

"When you rose to your knees, he took fright. If you'd rolled on to one shoulder, you could have made a shot with the bow parallel to the ground. No guarantees, but less chance the animal would see you."

Dumperty nodded. "Are you angry?"

"No, and you know something. That wasn't a hare."

"But it looked like one."

"Not quite." Mangrove had also noticed the difference. "The hind legs and the ears, the whole body, all were too small for a hare."

"Anyway it doesn't really matter," Dumperty said. "I missed him."

Snotty and Mangrove consoled him. He had to learn and more opportunities would come his way.

Approaching the slope of the hill that was their objective, Mangrove bent to examine paw prints in earth that had been excavated from a series of holes. "Look, whatever that animal was, he lives in these burrows."

"We'll set a snare on the way back," Snotty said.

They moved up the hill.

Mangrove stopped, his arm raised. "Listen." His heartbeat had risen at the sound. In alarm he glanced at Snotty and saw fear flit in the eyes of his friend.

In the mind of each, memory was playing the yipping of Torterats. But fear subsided. Just as the rabbit had at first sight appeared to be a hare, the sounds coming from the far side of the hill took on their own shape of length and pitch and timbre.

Snotty shook his head. "Not Torterats."

"No."

Even as they dismissed the possibility of the old enemy, other sounds intruded to intermittently blanket the high pitched yaps.

Snotty cocked his head, trying to identify the deeper notes, to put form to whatever was making the noise. "What *is* that, Manny?"

"No idea."

"Okay, Dumperty, you find out. Go ahead, keep low and check what's over the ridge."

Again alarmed that Dumperty, the novice, should investigate, Mangrove's doubt showed on his face.

"He has to learn, Manny."

Determined that this time he would do it right, Dumperty moved in a crouch until close to the brow of the hill. The last few metres he covered wriggling on his belly. Slowly raising his head he looked into the next valley and his eyes widened. Still as stone, he gazed on the drama being enacted.

Behind and below, Snotty and Mangrove waited for the signal that all was clear or for Dumperty to return. Nothing came from him. Totally engrossed in the scene, the real purpose of his observation was forgotten.

Impatient, Snotty and Mangrove remained where they were. Good sense and years of experience demanded that they take no action until the forward scout gave some indication of what lay ahead.

"What's he doing, Manny?"

"I warned you. We shouldn't have sent him in this situation."

Snotty slipped his bow from his shoulder and loosely fitted an arrow. "I'm going up."

"Not alone you won't. We'll go together."

The ridge provided the perfect vantage point. Sight and sound let the three boys witness the life and death struggle that had virtually hypnotised Dumperty.

Snotty nudged him. "You should have come back."

"But what are these creatures?"

"The ones attacking aren't Torterats and they're definitely not wolves."

"What about the two big ones being attacked?"

"We've never seen anything like them," Snotty whispered, although it was unlikely the animals below would be aware of the humans because of distance and the favourable wind.

Like citizens of ancient Rome at the Circus Maximus, the boys watched the battle unfolding, the age old battle of hunger versus self-preservation, of those who would eat versus those who had no wish to be eaten.

One of the attackers darted from the pack.

"Look at the colour of his coat. It's yellow, like the sand when we were crossing the desert."

Mangrove studied the animal and turned his attention to the six milling about, each looking for an opportunity to snap at the two larger creatures. All the attackers were of similar appearance with broad heads and erect ears, but it was their coats of sandy yellow, which around their chests and bellies was a lighter, creamy shade, that attracted his attention. Mangrove concentrated, trying to recall things Tasha had said to him, the words she had used when recounting Cloud's dream on the mountainside, when he and Snotty had been on their way to the beach. He tried to bring them to mind, but the words had made no sense and were forgotten.

"Snotty, what was it Cloud said?"

"When?"

"The night we had to run from the rising water. We had gone back to the beach, but Tasha told us what Cloud had said in her dream."

"I don't know. Anyway, Cloud's so difficult to understand."

"Manny, I remember what she said." Keen to make up for the mistakes he had made, Dumperty smiled. "I was there. I remember exactly."

In the way of a children's nursery rhyme, Cloud's words had stuck in his little boy's head. Whispering, he repeated the lines he had heard as he knelt by Cloud in the moonlight.

Milk from cow to calf is given,
Dogs of yellow snarl and bite,
Flying manes of horses ridden,
Evil dragons out of sight.

"Yes, *dogs of yellow.* She must have meant them." With his eyes he indicated the pack in the valley. "Yellow dogs snarling and biting, they're not wolves, they're *dogs.*"

He focused on the distended udder of the bigger animal, on the teats hanging from it. Mangrove, as were all the clan, was familiar with mothers suckling their young. Milk was the food of babies. "And that is the *cow* with her *calf.*"

The strange words that Cloud had uttered in her trance had once been in common use, but had disappeared with the coming of the ice. For uncountable generations these expressions must have remained in the unconscious of Cloud's ancestors, unspoken but inherited. From the depths of her trance this innate connection with her past had surfaced. The words had re-entered the language, reborn and alive with meaning.

Mangrove touched Dumperty's head. "You did well, little guy. Now we know what Cloud was saying, well, some of it anyway."

Dumperty beamed.

Snotty pulled them back to the present. "But just look at those dogs, they're after the little one."

The dogs were chivvying the cattle, surrounding them, constantly looking for an opening to attack the calf. Each time one came close the cow would lower her head and swipe with her horns at the dog, at times tossing one high. All the while the calf and cow were bellowing, the attackers yapping and those that had been gored whimpering in pain, but the cow was tiring, the dogs wearing her down. When she fell, the life of the calf would be over.

"Can't we save him?" Dumperty pleaded.

"Hmm," Snotty said. "We'll try. He'd look good in the cooking pot."

"I meant..."

"I know what you meant."

Mangrove looked at Snotty. "It's not a bad idea."

"What! The calf is good meat."

"Milk from the cow may give us many meals."

"How?"

"Every day we can take some of her milk. We'll share it with the calf."

Snotty spent a moment in thought. "Yeah, I guess so."

"Come on then." Dumperty's face lit with joy. "Let's do it. Let's save her."

"First things first." Mangrove scanned the area of the valley that was in view.

In the open grassland he could see nothing that might threaten them but the dogs. Nothing else appeared significant. What might lurk within the plentiful groves of trees was unknown, but he figured that the racket made by the dogs and the bellowing of the cattle would have attracted other meat eaters if any were nearby.

"Okay, let's go."

The dogs had the cow and calf encircled, harrying the desperate mother. Blood was running from her flanks, where sharp teeth had sunk into her hide. The Foragers began to run toward the pack, fanning out as they ran.

Snotty carried his spear like a javelin, raising it and shouting. "Yah, get out of there. Leave her alone. Get away. Get away."

Mangrove and Dumperty took up the cry, yelling at the dogs, holding their arms wide as they ran. Yellow heads, ears pricked, turned to the new commotion running towards them. It was the first time that the dogs had seen humans, but the intent of the two legged animals was clear. Some went onto their haunches before leaping away, others simply ran. The pack – no longer working in concert – scattered.

The exhausted cow sank to her knees. The calf nuzzled her face, at times mooing, begging her mother to rise.

"Keep watch on the dogs, Dumperty."

Mangrove dropped his pack to the ground and taking the rope prepared a noose. With Snotty's help he slipped it over the head of the calf.

The cow, her sides heaving, her nostrils running with mucus from the trauma of the attack, lifted her head and bellowed.

Mangrove took one of the gourds and laid it before her. The dark tongue of the cow, long and rough, lapped the water. Cautiously, with a slow deliberate movement, Mangrove placed his hand on her neck and stroked her; a gentle action to assure the cow that she would not be harmed.

With every movement conducted in slow motion, Mangrove pulled some grass from the ground and using it as a cloth wiped at the blood oozing from the gashes in the cow's hide. She bellowed again, turning her head to see what he was doing. He took another gourd and poured water over the wounds, wiping them again with clean grass. The cow seemed to know that Mangrove was helping her, that without the intervention of the humans, she and her calf would have been eaten by the dogs. She mooed and drank again.

Snotty held the calf, keeping an eye on Dumperty and the dogs that now sat a hundred metres distant. "Manny, you've just about run us out of water."

"I was thinking we can lead the calf back to the base on the dune. After she's rested a bit, the cow will follow. We can get more water and head out here again."

"Great idea, Manny," Snotty said. "We'll do that. I don't think the dogs will worry us again."

They let the animals rest until the cow, in the clumsy, rocking way of cattle, regained her feet. The calf immediately nudged the udder and with legs splayed sucked at a teat.

"Time to go, Snotty," Mangrove said and called to Dumperty that they would return to the beach.

Eager to remain involved, Dumperty asked if he could lead the calf. The cow followed close behind, mooing occasionally. Snotty and Mangrove were the rearguard, just in case the dogs had a mind to attack again.

The journey to home base was slow. It was not in the nature of a cow to move quickly and with her injuries her pace was even more leisurely. The calf, as Manny expected, was the lure to attract and keep her going.

Dumperty looked back at Snotty. "Are you going to set the snare where we saw the hare?"

"Yes. I'll use fishing line. See if you can find me a stout stick to anchor the line."

In the age-old role of the apprentice, Dumperty was learning: observing the example set by Manny and Snotty, listening to their instructions, doing his best to put them into practice, determined not to repeat his mistakes. He was also learning that his masters delegated to the apprentice the menial tasks of fetch and carry.

Dumperty didn't mind. Just to be with the Foragers he idolised, to be with them on the expedition, to be able to look forward to being with them every day made him happier than he'd ever been. He could have sung with the birds whose calls rang out over the valley. Running to the nearest stand of trees, he selected a branch from among those lying about. Long fallen, the dried and leafless wood would suit the purpose. With two hard blows of his stone axe he cut the branch to size.

On return he held the half metre long stick out for inspection. "How's this, Snotty?"

"That's just what we need."

The patch of disturbed earth that they had seen was dotted with holes. Tracks, the paw prints of animals, led to them and all around droppings littered the sand. Snotty examined both carefully and concluded that, while similar, they could not have been made by hares.

"Maybe a cousin of the hare, but smaller," he concluded and gave Dumperty his instruction. "Dig a hole about here." He indicated a spot central to the many burrows of what in fact was a rabbit warren. "And hammer the stick in hard. We want a solid anchor for the line. When you're satisfied it's set firm, fill the sand back in."

Using the back of his axe, Dumperty did as he had been told, smoothing the ground to the way it had been.

"Now watch carefully."

Snotty cut a length of line with the steel knife that had come from the bunker in the forest of Kaldor. With one end he looped repeated hitches around the stick, jerking each loop tight. Making a circle with the line to gauge the size he needed, Snotty tied the loose end in a slipknot.

"There! Sooner or later one of these hare-cousins will put a foot into the circle and jag the line. The knot will slide and we have him caught by the leg."

"Do you think we'll have one by the time we're back here again?"

Mangrove handed the rope to Dumperty, and laughed at his eagerness. "Here take your calf. The quicker we get her and her mother to the beach, the quicker we can return. Then we'll see how successful the snare has been."

From where they stood, they could see the distant camp on the dune.

"They won't be expecting us," Snotty said.

At the dune behind the beach, shelters had been erected. Some of the fish caught in the surf by Vellum and Zita were already bubbling in the cooking pot. Others had been scaled and cleaned and were suspended over smoking fires to be preserved. The scene was one of people going about their chores, happy with what they were doing, enjoying the warmth of the sun.

Tasha was content. All was going to plan. Yet again, she surveyed the camp. Although intended as a temporary place to stay, it had a tidy, appealing appearance. Smoke drifted her way, bringing the smell of curing fish.

"Hmm." She sniffed and her mouth began to water, grateful that Vellum and Zita had been successful on the incoming tide, wondering if Belle and Hock were having the same luck. Then there were other matters; what would the outcome be from the two parties exploring the valleys. Prompted by the thought, she looked across the river toward the southern ridge and was immediately alert. In the distance a group of figures was gradually growing larger.

Tasha squinted, trying to make out who and what was approaching. She called to those working near her and soon the whole camp was looking.

Kalich identified Snotty and Mangrove. "And Dumperty's leading some animal tied to the rope. There's a bigger one as well."

The strange cavalcade came on, everyone watching. Tasha raised her arm and waved, heard Manny's distant whistle and saw him wave in return.

"Tasha." There was urgency in Kalich's voice. "Look!"

She turned her head to see him pointing and farther up the valley saw Sola and Situ running. Dram was between them. Tasha saw Sola take Dram's pack from her and then each of the twins took one of Dram's hands, still running, dragging her along. Much further back, Belle and Zita, their packs loaded with fish, were struggling to hurry.

"Something's wrong." Tasha walked quickly between the shelters. *Where are Biscetti and Cloud?* Asking herself why Dram was running, why those she could see coming down the valley were desperate to get back to camp. *What's happened? What has gone wrong?*

The twins assisted Dram into the camp, supporting her as she sank to the ground.

"Dram." Tasha knelt by her. "Why are you alone? Where are Biscetti and Cloud?"

Her chest heaving, unable to speak, Dram looked at Tasha and at the crowd gathered around her.

"They were attacked," Situ said, explaining that he and Sola had seen Dram running down the mountainside, gone to meet her and learned of what had happened. "She made sure Biscetti and Cloud were safe and then headed back to warn us of the dragons."

"Safe where? What dragons?"

But already Cloud's words were playing again in Tasha's mind. "Dram, is it true?"

Dram nodded, breathing heavily. "Yes. Tasha they are evil. We can never beat the dragons."

"Tell me about them."

In front of the assembled crowd, Dram described seeing the black Komodo stalk and kill. "It tore great chunks from the horse, swallowing them so fast. It ate everything: meat, hair, hide, hooves. Then when we were on the ledge of the escarpment another one, a red one this time, climbed a tree and attacked us. Oh, Tasha, I thought we were going to Endless Night."

Tasha stroked Dram's hair. "You're safe now, but where is my sister and Cloud."

Dram described the split in the cliff face. "They squeezed through. They must be still inside."

Tasha continued to calm Dram. "You did well."

Already crossing the bar, helping Dumperty drag the unwilling calf through the water, Manny could not understand why no one had come to greet them.

"What's going on, Snotty?"

"I don't know. They all seem to be standing around Dram."

Dumperty, Snotty and Mangrove and their newly acquired livestock made their way from the water and entered the camp. The cow mooed long and loud.

Heads suddenly turned.

"Just look at them." Kalich said. "What are those creatures?"

The big eyes of calf and cow, wide and anxious, pools of brown surrounded by white, stared at the crowd staring at them.

"This is a calf. That's her mother. She's a cow." Dumperty said, proud of his knowledge.

For Tasha, for everyone listening, the lines from Cloud's dream had become reality. Dragons had attacked the girls. The boys had found the cow and her calf. As they examined the strange creatures, the calf nudged her mother's udder and began to drink.

Jemma stooped to confirm what was happening.

"Milk from cow to calf is given." She spoke loudly for all to hear, watching creamy milk dribbling from the calf's mouth as he sucked, drawing the same conclusion as Mangrove. "The cow has so much milk. The calf will share it with us."

A murmur of approval went up from the crowd.

Chapter 6

Snotty's attention was not on the cattle. He was looking at Dram, seeing the exhaustion, seeing the lines of worry on her face. For a few moments he searched for Biscetti and Cloud.

"Tasha, what..."

"Oh, Snotty, I'm so glad you're back. There are dragons in the valley. Biscetti and Cloud are holed up in the escarpment."

"I don't understand."

Belle and Hock struggled into the camp, their return unremarked. They put down packs heavy with fish and listened.

Tasha knelt again beside Dram, encouraging her to retell the story of the Komodos.

Snotty and Mangrove stood by, often interrupting, asking Dram to repeat some detail or to define more clearly how the dragons used teeth and claws; information they felt was necessary if they were to estimate the dragons' size and speed in attack.

"Well," Snotty said. "We can't delay. Manny and I'll go for Biscetti and Cloud."

"Hang on." Mangrove raised a hand. "Did you hear what Dram was saying? Arrows bounce off the dragons and they may run faster than we can." He looked directly at Snotty. "And they're big and you don't see them coming until maybe it's too late."

"We can do it, Manny."

Mangrove shook his head. *Sometimes I wonder...* "We've never come across anything like this."

"True, but we can't leave Biscetti and Cloud."

Always the dilemma, thought Tasha, always the same answer. None of the clan would ever be left to an unknown fate. Whatever the risk, rescue had to be attempted.

"Won't you go, Manny?"

"Of course I will. I'm saying that we can't just race off. We have to come up with a winning strategy. We have to think and plan, otherwise..."

Tasha agreed. "And I'm coming with you two."

With the whole clan listening, ideas were put forward, considered, discarded. Nothing in their experience had prepared them for defence against Komodos.

Thinking of the Torterats, who had forced them to come south, Mangrove was philosophical. "Sometimes there are enemies who are stronger or too numerous."

Snotty argued that in the new land they had everything: food, sunshine, warm days. At Homecave, living in the snow and ice, the clan had starved.

"Snotty, I know what you're saying. It's great here, except that killers are out there." He waved his arm toward the upper valley and reminded Snotty of the ugly ball of hair, teeth and blood. "What Dram saw must have once been a horse. The dragon vomited up the bits he couldn't digest."

Tasha intervened. The fact remained. Biscetti and Cloud had to be rescued.

"Yes, I know that," Mangrove said. "So let's make sure we succeed."

In case they had forgotten, Dram spoke of the monster she and Tasha had faced at the lagoon. "He backed away from fire."

Standing behind her, old Ingamo moaned. "In the tales we tell of dragons, they breathe fire. Dragons aren't afraid of fire."

"Be quiet, Ingamo," Jemma scolded him. "You know nothing. Those stories we tell in the dark of night are just stories, nothing more."

Tasha was considering the idea of fire. The flames Dram had thrust at the crocodile had proved their worth.

"Dram's right. I was there. I saw it happen."

"Then that's the way to go," Snotty said. "Okay, Manny?"

Mangrove nodded. He had other ideas mulling in his head, but he needed more time to round them into a workable plan.

It was decided. Tasha would accompany Snotty and Mangrove. They would carry the usual weapons and take with them torches prepared for burning when needed. These they made by splitting the ends of sticks and jamming into them, and wrapping around them, strips of old leather from unwanted clothing. The leather, soaked in the oil of fish would burn for a long time.

Dumperty pressed Tasha for permission to take part in the rescue.

"No. You must stay here with Dram. Your job is to mind the cow and her calf."

He protested.

"No."

"Then can I go back to the snare Snotty set? We might have caught something."

Tasha reasoned with him that it was more important for the clan to stay put and set up stacks of firewood and grass around the camp; a ring of bonfires ready to be lit if danger threatened.

"Okay."

Finally, Dram again briefed Tasha and the boys on the perils of the ledge and where to find the split into which Biscetti and Cloud had fled.

A bright column of light shafted through the cliff face, but the narrow fault continued for only three or four metres before it broadened. Its size, its location – running off the escarpment ledge – was comparable to a crack in a wall through which a mouse might run.

Now crouched in semi-darkness, the mice were Cloud and Biscetti. Here the light from the valley diffused, becoming weaker with distance from its source. The girls tried to make out what sort of place they were in. It took some time to begin to see outlines, but gradually they realised that the crack through which they had squeezed had led them into a cavern of great size.

"Can you hear water falling, Cloud?"

"Yes and look." Way above, another geological fault or the flow of water for millennia had formed a hole in the roof of the cathedral-like cavern. Whatever the cause, a thin stream of water was falling from the hole to drop into a pool on the cavern floor.

As their eyes became accustomed to the gloom, strange shapes gained substance; some small, some majestically massive, rose from the floor. Others held like tapered candles to the uneven sides of the cave or hung like chandeliers. Strangest were those that resembled drapes, rippling from where a sloping rock jutted from the cavern wall. The shapes were mainly white, but here and there mineral salts had given colouration in red and green.

The girls had entered a cavern, which itself had been eroded by water over countless centuries, water that in soaking its way through rotting vegetable matter had absorbed carbon dioxide to become slightly acidic. Over endless time the acid in the water dissolved the limestone of the mountain, ever so slowly eating into it. Water continuously seeped from the mountain top, finding its way through crevices and hairline cracks in the limestone, tirelessly enlarging the cavern.

The chemistry of nature had further wonders to work. As acid in the water leached the limestone away, some calcium carbonate from the limestone entered the water. The water took and also gave, continuing to drip only occasionally, but with never ending persistence, building always building. Biscetti and Cloud were seeing stalagmites rising from the floor, stalactites hanging from above. Other oddities grew like crystal mushrooms or toadstools at the damp edges of thin fissures in the walls of the cave.

"Cloud, this really is a magic place. How beautiful it is."

Biscetti began to walk among the columns, at times tipping back her head to admire the forms high above. She touched the smooth surface of a stalagmite, crystals twinkling like stars. For a moment it seemed to her that she was again out in the snow, looking at the ice of Home Mountain. *No, I will never be there again.* Sadness flitted on her face. The sadness came and went. The enchantment of the cavern was too strong for memories.

Cloud stood by the pool, listening to the tinkling sound of falling water. She saw movement and stooped for closer inspection. Fish were swimming, tiny fish without eyes and yet they didn't bump into each other, nor crash into the side of the pool.

Water overflowed from the rock basin that held the fish and made its way along a shallow channel. Curious, Cloud bent low to see whether fish were there too. In the poor light and with her spectacles stained with dried sweat and dust she could not tell. Cloud removed the glasses and dipped them in the channel to clean them, but the water was cold, tingling her fingers, the wet frames suddenly slippery. She lost her grasp and they were gone, tumbling along in the flow.

Myopic, fumbling in the dimness, on her hands and knees in the water of the channel, Cloud chased the spectacles.

"Biscetti, Biscetti, I've lost my eyes." The pitiable cry of a girl who knew that unless she found them, near blindness would again be her lot.

Startled, Biscetti looked for Cloud. She could hear her splashing, could hear the pathetic sounds of moaning from someone deeply in trouble. "Where are you?"

But Cloud was intent, no other thought in her mind but to find her artificial eyes that were flipping end over end in the water.

The channel had begun to slope. Cloud hurried, her hands feeling ahead. The downward angle of the slope increased. The channel became a chute, a water slide dropping down a wide hole in the floor of the cave. Cloud could see nothing, scrabbling toward it, her knees slipping on the limestone running with water.

The whimpering, the splashing directed Biscetti. She hurried, stepping around the beautiful shapes until she could see Cloud and the gaping hole a metre ahead of the crawling girl.

"Stop, Cloud, stop."

Cloud was still moving forward, realising that despite Biscetti's warning she could not stop.

Biscetti ran, seeing the danger, screaming for Cloud to get out before it was too late.

Cloud had her hands forced against the bottom of the channel. She was still sliding forward, unable to stop, unable to stand. The limestone was too smooth and slick, polished by aeons of running water. She could get no grip. She was sliding down the chute and then it became almost vertical and Cloud was gone.

Biscetti screamed in horror, knelt by the hole and called Cloud's name. The only sound to reach Biscetti was the fall of water.

Snotty chose to cross the mountainside high up. Although boulders sat here and there, he reasoned that a dragon would not find the cover needed for an attack. Should one approach them from the valley floor, they would have ample warning.

The slope steepened as Dram had advised. Snotty examined the wall of rock, seeking the ledge. They would need to descend a little to reach it. He jabbed the air with a finger. Tasha nodded that she understood. Third in line, Mangrove followed.

Moving along the face of the cliff all three scanned the area near the trees for Komodos. None was obvious.

"One could be waiting for us." Mangrove kept his voice low. "Like Dram said, up a tree."

There wasn't much they could do about it.

The ledge sheared. Like flies on the cliff face they crossed the gap, feeling with feet for where the fault recommenced at the new level. A shadow darkened the escarpment, shielding them for a moment from the heat of the sun before the quick moving shadow sped up and over the wall of rock above them.

Mangrove looked at the sky. Scud was rolling in from the south and as he remarked on the coming change, the first flurry of cooler air gusted around them. He paused to gaze southward, recognising the place on the far side of the river where Dumperty in his role as apprentice had stalked the hare-cousin. In the distance, smoke from the snow capped cone was bent before the wind, streaming toward them, a dark stain high in the sky. As

Mangrove watched, grey clouds enveloped the cone, took it from view and soon the smoke was lost. A rumble of thunder came faintly on the wind and the first fat drops of rain began to fall.

"Let's get off this ledge." Mangrove steadied himself against the cliff. He looked toward the river and watched its surface change, progressively darkening with the sudden eruption of waves. The wind hit the near bank and swathes of grass lay over. "Tasha, Snotty be careful. The wind..."

The words were blown from his mouth. The front hit them, pinning them to the cliff face. "We've gotta get off here."

Rain was falling, running down the rock, sloshing on to the ledge, bouncing off to cascade into the valley. Tasha shouted to Snotty that they would have to get off the ledge or they would be washed off. She looked down. From that height no one would survive a fall.

Tentatively, Snotty inched forward, feeling for sure foothold before putting his weight on it, wishing that the ledge would widen, looking for the gap through which Biscetti and Cloud had found escape. Rain was getting into his eyes. He found it difficult to see.

In the rear, Mangrove was worried. The rain was intensifying. Tasha was right. They had to get off the cliff face and soon, otherwise either wind or rain, probably both, would send them crashing off the ledge.

"Snotty, haven't you found the split?" yelling with all his might, wind distorting his lips, rain running down his cheeks into his mouth.

Snotty heard only the drumming of rain and the howl of the wind. He was making slow progress, bending his head to protect his eyes, still unable to keep them clear of belting rain. He wiped at them and returned his hand to the rock, feeling his way, feeling the pressure of the sheet of water running down the cliff.

"Where are you?" Talking to the opening as if it might hear and reveal itself.

His hand moved into open space. Air blowing through the passage chilled his fingers. Snotty thanked the stars. He stepped by and with a flick of his head motioned Tasha to enter. She turned sideways, attempted to squeeze into the gap and stopped. Her pack stuck in the confines of rock walls.

"Take it off. Give it to me."

Tasha understood, handed the pack to Snotty and moved in a metre, reaching back for the pack. Mangrove followed, adopting the same procedure, passing on his pack to Tasha, reaching for Snotty's.

They were inside, shaking themselves like wet wolves, brushing water from clothing, wiping it from faces, arms and legs.

"Biscetti, Cloud," Tasha called, barely able to see. The low hanging mass of nimbus, the thickly falling rain had reduced the light entering the cavern.

From somewhere in the darkness, Biscetti answered. "Tasha, come here."

"I can't see you. Where are you?"

"We should shut our eyes for a time." Mangrove said.

The three rescuers stood with heads bowed, eyes closed, waiting for pupils to dilate, for their eyes to become accustomed to the dim surroundings. Biscetti was calling to them and unseeing they called to her; shouts that carried the grim news that Cloud had disappeared.

"Tasha, I'm scared for her."

"Stay where you are. We're coming to you."

Opening her eyes, Tasha saw the glistening formations and called again, trying to identify the blonde Biscetti among the columns.

Snotty took a torch from his pack. "We need light."

On the floor of the cavern, Mangrove oscillated the fire stick between his palms, its blunt point in the groove of wood. He smelt smoke as friction generated heat and placed a handful of grass around the groove. Heat gave off its glow and the grass flamed. He added more grass. Light flickered on stalagmites and stalactites, crystals seemed to move with dancing light and in the strange subterranean place Snotty held a torch over the flames, saw it catch alight and then lit another and another until four torches were throwing their light wide into the cavern. The weapons intended as defence against Komodos had taken on a different role.

Still at the hole, down which Cloud had disappeared, Biscetti watched the torches flare and their light brought relief. She was no longer alone. Together they must be able to find Cloud.

"Tasha, I'm here."

"There she is." Snotty held his torch in Biscetti's direction.

Tasha, Snotty and Mangrove walked toward the kneeling girl, keeping to the side of the channel now running fast.

Mangrove peered into the hole. "Cloud went down there?"

"Yes. I yelled at her to get out of the water, but it was too slippery and see, the channel has worn its way deeper." Biscetti pointed to the where water was racing. "She tried, but she kept sliding along and the channel dipped steeply and she was whisked down this hole."

Snotty lay on the limestone and lowered his arm into the hole. Light from the burning torch revealed the chute as a millrace, water rushing down it.

"I can't see Cloud."

Mangrove looked to the hole in the roof high above. What had been a succession of drops plinking into the rock basin when Biscetti and Cloud had entered the cavern was now a column of water, falling to thrash the surface of the pond that boiled white, spilling over the rim to run deep in the channel before falling through the gap in the floor.

"We've got to find her, Snotty."

Biscetti put her head into the hole and called again and again for Cloud. No answer came.

"She's been carried along with the water somewhere, or she's unconscious. Either way she could drown," Mangrove said.

"Yeah, and Manny, we don't have the rope."

They could see Dumperty leading the calf and wished that there had been another way to control the animal or that one of them had had the foresight to slip the halter from the calf and place the rope in a backpack.

Mangrove ground his teeth in frustration, trying to think what could be done. Every moment of delay diminished the chance of saving Cloud. He looked at the water pouring down the chute. Rain from the storm was adding its volume. Perhaps unable to escape, the water level could be rising somewhere in the darkness below, rising over Cloud's head. Maybe that had already happened. *Think*. The word silently screamed in his head. *Think*.

Under pressure, seconds ticking by Mangrove berated himself for not bringing the rope, pushed the thought from his mind and concentrated. He stared into the darkness. *To save Cloud we've got to know what's down there.*

"Snotty, do you still have a fishing line in your pack?"

"Yeah, why?"

"We'll tie it to a torch and lower it into the hole. We've got to know what's at the bottom."

Tasha ran to Snotty's pack and around her torch quickly looped hitches in the line – once known as *gut* – made from the split tendons and intestines of game caught long ago. She drew the hitches tight and gave line and torch to Mangrove. Lying beside him, leaning over the hole with him, she watched Manny pay out the line, the torch descending. Initially they heard the hiss as a drop splashed on the flaming torch, but the oily rag-ends of leather burnt bright, too hot to be extinguished.

Mangrove continued to let the line feed through his fingers seeing that the chute was really an eroded depression in the wall of another chamber below; a half- pipe worn into the sloping wall. Light from the torch flickered in the chamber.

"There's another cave below this one. It's quite big."

Tasha leaned further into the hole. "I can't see Cloud."

Mangrove fed out more line. "There she is."

Ten metres below, the torch dangled above the still figure of Cloud.

"Manny, she's not moving." Tasha looked at the wet, white face, at hair that spread clinging to limestone, at soaked clothing.

Cloud, eyes closed, was lying on a shelf of rock, her legs trailing in a pool that seemed to be very deep. From the height, in the flickering light, there was no obvious movement of Cloud's chest.

"Manny, we have to get to her." Tasha clutched his arm, emphasising her anxiety. "We can't wait."

"I'll go down." Snotty said.

"How?" Mangrove looked at his friend, smoke from the torch drifting up to pass between them.

The scene was one from a hellish wonderland; torchlight casting shadows that danced capriciously, tendrils of oily smoke curling amid the glitter of crystals imbedded in stalactites and stalagmites.

"I'll use the line."

Mangrove grimaced.

Snotty saw the disbelief. "I'll double it and double it again. It should take my weight."

Mangrove nodded. Maybe the fishing line would be strong enough. "But how do we get you and Cloud up again? You may have to carry her and the line won't bear the weight of two."

"I'll work out something."

"What will you work out?"

Snotty took the line from him and hauled up the torch. Cloud was again lost in the darkness.

"Help me, Manny."

By the light of torches now stuck in cracks in the limestone, the two boys brought the ends of the line together, knotted them and roughly braided the doubled end through the twin lengths of gut to make a four stranded line.

Mangrove inspected it, worried that the original splices might come apart under the strain. No fish they'd ever caught had been as heavy as Snotty was. Snotty waved away the concern.

The girls and Mangrove became the anchormen for Snotty. Taking one torch with him he tried to abseil down the chute, but his feet found no traction. Constantly falling water had polished the stone to a glassy slipperiness. Without some friction, there was nothing to give him an orderly descent. Snotty wildly kicked his feet into the waterfall, trying to slow his progress. He failed and was free falling. The line snapped taut. Mangrove heard the ping of splices separating. The rope that he, Tasha and Biscetti were holding went slack. From below came the sound of a body plunging into water.

"Snotty." Shouting his anguish, Mangrove leaned into the hole. *I knew I shouldn't have let you do it.*

Tasha grabbed a torch, tied it to the broken line and lowered it. Cloud's body lay wet and still on the rock shelf. There was no sign of Snotty, only the blackened remains of the flame he had held floating on the pool.

Tasha let out more line. Her torch hung close to the surface of the pool. Deep down she saw a string of bubbles rising, saw a head, arms flailing, and from the depths Snotty burst into sight, gulping for air, grasping for the edge of the rock shelf. Tasha, Biscetti and Mangrove watched as Snotty dragged himself from the water and lay beside Cloud. He lifted a hand to signal that he was unhurt and turned to Cloud.

Kneeling, he bent over her, placing his cheek by her lips to check if she was breathing. A soft, regular puff of air brushed cold on his wet skin. He examined her arms and legs in case they had been fractured. All were normal. Recalling the time in the bunker when he had found Dumperty with a head-wound, Snotty lifted Cloud's head while his fingers searched: no cuts, no blood. As the others watched from above, he shook Cloud's shoulder, repeated her name and asked if she could hear him.

Slowly Cloud sat up, her lids screwed to slits. "My eyes, I've lost my eyes."

Although Snotty was close enough for her to recognise him, she cried out loudly as if he wasn't there. Her voice echoed in the chamber so that the three watching and listening from above heard Cloud's lament come doubly and triply to their ears before it echoed again in the large cavern of crystal formations, repeating and repeating her loss until her voice faded to nothing.

"Snotty, I can see them," Tasha shouted. From the bedrock of the pool, through water clean and clear, the spectacles reflected the flames hanging just above the surface. "Cloud's other eyes went into the water. They've sunk to the bottom."

Snotty shielded his eyes from the torch and peered into the pool. The glint of lenses came from way, way down.

Cloud shifted position, lying with her face almost in the water, unable to make out what others were seeing. "Are my eyes there, Snotty?"

"Yes. I can see them at the bottom of the pool."

"Can you get them for me?"

"Cloud, I'm not a fish. The water is so deep."

Snotty looked at her and in the light from the flickering flames saw the tears rolling down her cheeks. He turned away and stared at the spectacles mocking him from the depths, daring him.

The three above listened to the echoing conversation.

Without looking away from the drama below, Biscetti nudged Mangrove. "What's Snotty doing?"

"He's trying to work out how he can get the eyes."

"But, Manny, he can't swim. None of us can swim."

"I know."

Snotty continued to look into the water. He and Cloud had fallen into the pool and pulled themselves out. They had gone in by accident, but had survived. *I went down a long way. I wonder...*

He stood up, still concentrating on the spectacles, still thinking, nodding slowly. "Okay," he said quietly to Cloud. "I'll try to get your eyes." Then turning to look toward the hole above announced. "Manny, I'm going to dive for Cloud's eyes."

Before anyone could speak, Snotty plunged into the pool. Working his arms as though tearing at the water and as though gravity was hindering not helping his descent, he clawed his way downward. The blurred image of the spectacles spurred him, but the increasing pressure of the water was painful to his ears. His lungs hurt and he had to breathe. He had to have air.

Snotty turned and fought for the surface.

He dragged himself onto the rock shelf, sucking air, knowing that to drown would be a terrible way to enter Endless Night.

"Snotty, are you okay?" Mangrove's concern echoing, re-echoing.

Snotty gave a brief wave. "Yeah."

For some minutes he lay unmoving, resting, feeling his strength returning.

Cloud stroked his hair. "Don't worry, Snotty. Leave them."

He sat up and looked again into the pool. Far down, the challenge shimmered.

"No, Cloud, I'll get your eyes for you."

Standing, Snotty dragged air into his lungs, expanding his chest. Three times he did that, making oxygen enter his bloodstream until he felt that he had no need to breathe. He halted the process and held his breath, seeing himself diving down, gauging the distance to the bottom, imagining going deep and measuring his reserve of air against the depth. At last he opened his mouth and breathed again. *Yeah. I reckon I can do it.*

He sat again until his breathing returned to normal. Rested, he stood and began again to ventilate his system. With one last lungful of air, he dived.

Down, down, his eyes on the blurry image he pulled himself downward. He calculated that he had passed half way and clawed at the water. A little air escaped from his lips and rose in a pretty, wobbling trail of bubbles. Snotty went on down.

The spectacles became clearer. He reached for them, realised he had misjudged and kept on, digging at the water like a dog unearthing a bone, diving deeper. His ears began to sing with the pressure, a hum increasing in intensity, hurting.

The spectators above could see him clearly. Biscetti had held her breath as Snotty dived into the pool, wanting to share his experience and to have some idea of how difficult it would be. She had long given up and with rapid, shallow breaths watched with growing anxiety.

"Tasha, he won't make it."

Tasha had the same thought. She looked at Mangrove for reassurance and saw on his face the pain of someone who believed he was about to lose a dear friend. They watched and hoped.

In the silent depths the spectacles were clearly visible to Snotty. He let out more air. His lungs were bursting, the need to breathe becoming unbearable.

Snotty reached for the spectacles, felt the frame in his fingers and kicked off the bottom. Far above he could see red and yellow, the flame of the torch that Tasha dangled. Thoughts were running contrary in his mind. *I've got to breathe.* The instinctive urge was almost uncontrollable. Snotty's brain was at the point of losing command. Breathing was the absolute necessity for life. *Don't breathe. Not much longer. Don't breathe.*

Carbon dioxide levels in Snotty's blood had risen to dangerous levels. Receptors within his body that were meant to control the rhythmic cycle of breathing were being overridden by his determination, but the conscious part of his brain could put a stop to breathing for only so long. The command centre of his nervous system was sending its signals to inhale immediately.

He willed himself to go on. If he opened his mouth he knew that he would drown. His strength was almost gone. He clawed at the water, pulling himself upward. Unable to prevent the inevitable, Snotty opened his mouth.

His head broke through the surface, sweet air filled his lungs.

For some time he clung to the edge of the rock ledge, breathing, breathing. How good it was, he thought, to fill his lungs with air.

Cloud was laughing and crying. The spectacles were once more on her nose. Snotty had given her back her eyes. She clapped her hands in delight. "Come on. I'll help you out."

Grasping an arm she assisted the exhausted Snotty to climb from the pool. Three faces looking down shouted out their joy. Happiness bounced around the caverns in repeated echoes.

"Snotty," Mangrove called to him. "What now?"

The broken line dangled over the pool. Snotty looked at the frayed ends and shook his head. There was no way he would be able to use it.

"I'll have to explore down here. There's probably another opening to the valley."

"What makes you think that?"

Snotty replied that the well of the pool was just the dropping point for water from the cavern above and that it then flowed into the darkness. "I can't see where the stream goes, but I'll take Tasha's torch and follow it. It's gotta come out somewhere."

"Snotty," Tasha called to him. "How will we know what happens to you?"

"If there is a way out, I'll come back here and tell you. If there isn't, we'll have to come back anyway."

"Okay, good luck."

There was little more that could be said.

Tasha swung the line. Like a pendulum the torch swung to and fro until Snotty was able to reach it and untie it. He held the flame high and with Cloud close behind began to follow the flowing water.

Within minutes the figures had disappeared from view. All that the heads craning into the hole could see was the dancing of light on the cavern walls that became fainter until only blackness remained.

Tasha, Mangrove and Biscetti settled down to wait.

For a time, Snotty and Cloud were able to walk upright, but gradually the cavern narrowed and the roof lowered until they were in a tunnel that required them to stoop as they followed the stream at their feet.

"I don't like this," Cloud said.

"If it gets us out, that's all that matters."

Soon they were bending low, Snotty forced to hold the torch so close he could feel its heat.

"Stop, Snotty."

"We have to go on, Cloud."

"No wait. I can see something. Let me pass."

He edged as close as he could to the wall of the tunnel. Cloud squeezed by. "I can see light."

"Let me look."

Far ahead a pinpoint of light glowed and from what he could make out, the passage grew no smaller.

"Cloud, we've found the way to escape."

They moved on, buoyed by the natural light, its glow growing stronger as they came closer.

"Listen," Snotty said.

They paused and heard water falling.

Pale light was filling the tunnel. It seemed to be filtered and as they approached, still crouching, they saw that vines hung thickly to shroud the opening, letting in only a fraction of the outside daylight. Snotty parted the vines, pushing his way through, holding them apart for Cloud to follow.

He laughed aloud. "Look, Cloud. This must be the spring that Manny found."

The stream that had led them from the cavern bubbled between moss covered rocks to form the creek that ran to the river. Cloud and Snotty had emerged at the spring whose water tasted so good.

"Wait here. I'm going back to tell the others."

At the pool, he shouted the good news through the sinkhole. Relieved, Tasha, Biscetti and Mangrove passed again through the split to the ledge on the face of the cliff. The rain had passed over. Big patches of blue were growing, the grey of storm clouds pushed aside to allow the sun to shine through. No longer fierce, the wind had dropped to a gentle breeze. In high spirits the three hurried across the mountainside and descended to meet Snotty and Cloud at the spring. Joyously reunited, they hugged each other.

Snotty grinned. "I told you I'd work something out, Manny."

"Yeah, I know."

"Perhaps a bit of luck helped."

Curious, Snotty touched the curtain of vines, feeling the texture. Selecting a length, he held it between his hands, tried to snap it and failed. The vine was strong. He cut a piece of about three metres and coiled it easily.

Mangrove watched the manipulation of the vine, which was roughly the thickness of Snotty's thumb, guessing that he was testing its suitability as a rope. "Will it do?"

"I reckon it will." He cut more. "I'll plait these together. They should give us a good long rope. We'll have a spare."

Mangrove agreed. Snotty's ingenuity had given the clan another valuable asset.

Chapter 7

The scene on the dune was chaotic. The storm had wreaked its havoc on the camp. The timber used as rough framework over which clothing and bedding had been draped for shelter had been blown over. Wood, jackets, furs were scattered willy-nilly across the dune and soaking wet. Attempts were still being made to gather items and to restore some order. It was a slow process. Drenched and unhappy at the setback, people went about the task of recovery as though it were scarcely worthwhile.

With everyone busy, it was Dumperty who saw the party returning. "Hey. They're back. Snotty and Manny and Tasha have found Biscetti and Cloud."

He ran to them. "You did it. You found them."

"Yes." Snotty lifted Dumperty and whirled him in the air. "We did it."

"What happened? Did you see a dragon?"

"We'll tell you all about it," Tasha said and as the group entered the camp, people dropped what they were doing and gathered around.

The return of the Foragers brought some smiles and a squeezing of the hands of Biscetti and Cloud. The rescuers were congratulated, but despite the show of welcome, Tasha recognised that many appeared to have lost heart. The storm had damaged the flimsy structures. It had also affected morale.

In turn, sometimes interrupting to add a colourful detail that had been omitted, each of the five gave his or her impressions of the limestone cavern and the way Cloud had come to grief.

"She lost her eyes and then I lost her," Biscetti said. "But when Tasha and the boys came and Manny lit the torches, we saw Cloud in the chamber below."

The story unfolded and the clan was roused a little by the latest instance of Snotty's courage. People patted his shoulder. Another chapter had been added to the legend of his exploits.

"Well," Tasha said. "That's it. Now we'd better clean up."

Mangrove looked at the remains of the bonfires. Flattened by wind, lying in the sand, too wet to burn, they were useless against any marauding dragon.

"Tasha, we have to do something about this."

She nodded and wondered what. Apart from the destruction of the shelters, the clothing everyone was wearing was still damp. Body heat and the sun were having their effect, but if the sun set before clothing was dry, it would be an uncomfortable night.

Dram came to stand by her. "We can't stay here, Tasha. The dragons know we're in the valley. They'll come for us."

"I know." Tasha thought for a moment and motioned everyone to sit. Their plight needed serious consideration. Her people would need to talk in General Council.

Briefly she described the situation. The clan had nowhere under cover to stay. Until decent accommodation was found they would be forced to live in the open air. This left them exposed to attack from dragons and any other predator. "But we've survived danger and privation before today. No matter what the trials, we came through. The storm has been an annoyance, but many hands do make light work." Tasha looked into individual faces, appealing to the spirit she knew existed. "These are tough times, but we, the Camarilla, will continue to find a way."

"We will," Kalich called and other voices gave their support.

"At least we have food." Hock looked at those seated around him. Murmurs of agreement rippled through the crowd. "And we have water."

Tasha saw the mood changing. "We'll build defences against the dragons. They're fearsome beasts and eventually we'll find a way to beat them, but first we must be able to stop them from getting into the camp."

Belle rose to her feet. "We can do it, Tasha." She looked to her three closest friends. "Can't we?"

"Yes." The chorus of Zita, Hock and Vellum was a defiant shout.

Tasha smiled. "Good, as your Queen I thank you. Here's a plan for you all to think about."

She began by listing requirements: The immediate need was for fire to provide heat for the clan and as a deterrent to dragons. She asked Sola and Situ and the gang of four to search for dry fuel, suggesting that lower layers of flattened grass might have had some protection from the rain and that on the ground among the trees there could be wood that would burn with some encouragement.

"Okay," Sola said.

The six Foragers set off.

"Meantime, Jemma, would you and Ingamo set up a spit. Use the torches to roast fish for oil. We may need plenty of it. The fish we'll eat for dinner."

The old couple rose, happy to be part of the action.

Dumperty raised his hand. "Tasha, can I go and check the snare?"

"Not now. You can do that tomorrow."

"Promise?"

"Yes. You can help now in setting up our sleeping places."

Every face was looking at Tasha, satisfied that there was a plan, eager to be active. "Let's hang out everything to dry," she said.

What had been a bedraggled, sodden group of unhappy people was up and about, busy with a purpose. The camp came into being again, furs and skins draped across wooden frames to dry. Wet sand was scraped from sleeping places to reveal the dry beneath. Dumperty assisted Jemma and Ingamo by placing clay pots below the roasting fish. Oil dripped and was transferred to larger containers. Everyone had a goal and worked steadily to achieve it.

Sola and Situ returned with a pack half-full with grass. Placed by the spit it quickly dried in the heat. In turn it was used to dry more as Belle and her crew emptied their packs and went out to refill them. As Tasha had suspected, there was underbrush, twigs and fallen limbs that had escaped a soaking among the trees. It too was laid to dry. Progressively a stock of usable fuel built up.

Mangrove and Snotty surveyed the terrain, discussing how best to protect the clan.

In the days of the Romans, generals fighting to expand the empire had been faced each night with a similar problem. Their solution was to have the men of the legions dig a ditch around the camp and use the removed earth to throw up a rampart, an earthen wall. The work was arduous and time consuming, but the Roman armies, with sentries on guard, spent their nights safe within the encircling fortifications. The barbarians could not get at them.

Mangrove and Snotty had no knowledge of Roman military tactics, but the problem they faced was no different. Komodos were the threat. How to keep them at bay was the question.

The pile of grass and timber continued to grow. Mangrove looked at it and got Snotty's agreement that at the rate it was increasing there should be enough to burn throughout the night if it became necessary.

"But we'll need to bring the sleeping places closer together." As an example he drew a circle in the sand. "With everyone inside, we can prepare our ring of fire."

Snotty nodded and pointed out that if they were attacked and the ring had to be set alight, there would need to be suitable distance between the sleeping places and the flames.

"Yeah. Let's make sure everyone understands."

Walking among the crowd engaged in restoring the camp, Snotty and Mangrove explained how defences would be set up. The plan understood, Snotty used his spear to draw an encircling border around the camp. Some rearranging of shelters was required, but once done, willing hands began to pile grass and timber along the defence line.

Among all the hustle and bustle, the fish on the spit gave up their oil, were judged cooked, set aside for the meal and fresh fish hung over the fire. Nearby the calf nudged the udder of his mother. She mooed. The calf, with legs splayed, fed.

Jemma moved away from the heat to watch. She called to Dumperty to bring her an armful of drying grass and set it before the cow. When the calf had finished suckling, the cow continued to munch. Jemma sat where the calf had stood and pulled at a teat in much the same way as the calf. Milk squirted to the ground.

"Dumperty, lie here," Jemma said.

He did so.

"Ready? I'll give you a drink." She directed the stream of milk into his open mouth.

Dumperty swallowed the warm, creamy liquid and grinned at Jemma. "It tastes terrific."

Jemma let him drink a while. "That's enough for now. If you get me a bowl, we can set some milk aside for others to try."

Rescuing the cow and calf, providing them with feed, had proved worthwhile. Fresh milk had been added to the food available.

Tasha watched the by-play, smiled at Jemma's cleverness and called Snotty and Mangrove aside. "Are you satisfied enough has been done?"

Snotty assured her they were ready for the worst. "And we'll set sentries throughout the night; four at a time, each with a torch at intervals around the inside of the perimeter."

The plan was that sentries would be relieved every few hours. Should Komodos approach, the torches would be used to ignite the ring of fire.

"Soaked with oil, the grass and wood will quickly begin to burn." Snotty demonstrated with a handful of oily grass. It burst into flame at the first touch of the torch.

"Good." Tasha relaxed. For the time being the clan should be safe. "But we can't continue to live under these conditions. We're cave dwellers. We need security from the weather and from any horrible animal that might attack us."

"Tasha, we know that," Mangrove said.

The irony of the situation was clear to the three of them. In past years, shortage of food had been a perennial and pressing problem, but in Homecave the clan had enjoyed relative comfort and the sense of belonging. The coming of the Torterats had finally forced the migration south, but in the harsh environment of an ice-cold land, Homecave had provided the perfect place to live. In a complete reversal, food was now no problem. Wherever they turned, something new to eat was found. The main requirement, a good dwelling, had so far eluded them.

"Okay," Mangrove went on. "Dram's search for another Homecave was cut short." He waved an arm at the defensive circle. "We just have to put up with this until one is found. None of us like it, but there's no alternative, unless of course we move to the crystal cavern where Cloud lost her eyes."

Tasha shook her head. Access was too difficult, the light was too dim and the place was damp and dangerous. "Just ask..."

"Tasha, you have to put the idea of a new Homecave aside," Snotty interrupted. "We'll remain besieged here until we know more about the dragons. We have to understand their habits. I want to know them as well as I knew the Trats. Until I do..." He looked at Mangrove. "Until *we* do, the dragons will terrorise us. We'll be too frightened to move."

Mangrove frowned. "What are you saying, Snotty?"

Snotty explained that as Foragers, he and Manny had been able to outwit the Torterats. Repeatedly the two of them had hunted in Torterat territory. By being vigilant they had learned how the Trats behaved. Even under the most adverse of weather conditions, they had learned to recognise the mutants travelling over the snow. They had discovered that Trats communicated and that there was a hierarchy of command.

"Yes," said Mangrove. "We got to know them, but nevertheless the Trats caught you and me, remember?"

"That was my fault, but..."

"Forget it, Snotty, but what we *mustn't* forget is that the Trats drove us from our home. Eventually they won."

"That's my point. We have to beat the dragons. We can't keep on running. Where else can we go?"

Snotty had laid the facts bare.

"How *do* we beat them?" Concern distorted Tasha's face. "You heard Dram. You heard Biscetti and Cloud. They saw one catch and eat a horse. They've seen the vomit ball. They've been up close, almost killed by a dragon. How..."

Snotty raised his hand to calm her. "I don't know yet. Manny and I have to find a way."

Dispassionately he laid out the means by which he hoped to reach an understanding of Komodo habits. Assuming they got through the night, he and Mangrove would leave the camp compound at first light, their aim to find a Komodo and observe its ways.

"That's all, Snotty, no heroics," Tasha said. "No exposing yourself to danger."

"Leave it to me and Manny. We need to know how these creatures think."

He winked at Mangrove and saw the brow of his friend wrinkle with the knowledge of what was to come. The observation of one dragon would not suffice. To get a complete picture, they would need to know if Komodos acted in concert. Did circumstance exist when they became a team of marauding monsters?

As was often the case with the Romans in ancient Gaul, the defences erected were not put to the test. The sentries neither saw nor heard a threat. The ring remained unlit and in place; insurance for another day.

Before the barest hint of light in the eastern sky, Snotty and Mangrove left the confines of the camp and made for the river. Packs on their backs carried food, weapons and in Snotty's case, the coiled rope he had made from vines.

For a short time they travelled in virtual darkness, keeping their bearings with the sound of the surf behind them and the gentle breeze coming down the valley blowing cool in their faces. It was like old times. The two most experienced hunters doing what they did best; travelling toward the unknown with no definite plan other than to gather intelligence on a declared enemy. If other opportunities came their way, so be it.

Dawn brought light to seep across the countryside, giving shape to the things around them. Slowly hills and trees became visible. Mangrove and Snotty walked on, using whatever cover offered, always alert for movement, sniffing the air for smells that could bring early warning.

"Look at the river," Snotty whispered.

Mist was rising from the surface to hang white as snow within the banks; a river upon a river, nebulously flowing toward the sea. Mangrove stood still in admiration. So much was beautiful in the new land.

They moved on, watching the mist spill over the banks and fog the valley until visibility had dropped to twenty or thirty metres.

"We'll have to stop, Snotty. We can't wander around unable to see."

"Okay, let's sit down and wait it out."

"Remember days like this. Snow would be falling, a whiteout preventing us from distinguishing anything, the snow smothering every sound. We'd burrow into a drift..." Mangrove stopped talking, thinking of patience enforced by the weather, recalling the cold.

Mist brushed by them, pushed by the breeze. Tiny drops of moisture gathered on hair, rolled down cheeks and dripped on collars. Mangrove looked up. He could not see the sky. Snotty and he were totally enveloped by the mist, blind in a silent world. Nothing much seemed to have changed from the frozen times except the temperature.

"Listen." Snotty kept his voice low.

From further up the valley a sound came to them. Dampened by distance and the heaviness of the cottony clouds, the sound drifted by like a subdued groan, tapering as it passed into a thin hiss.

Mangrove cocked his head. "How did Dram describe the dragon's roar? Wasn't it something like that?"

"It's hard to tell. You know, muffled by the fog."

"Hmm, best we stick here until we can see."

The Foragers had no alternative.

The sun was climbing higher, its heat burning into the white cocoon shrouding them. Misty wisps lifted into clear air, spiralled, evaporated and were gone. Light made its way through the thinning fog. Snotty stood, able to see, and watched it burn away completely. The interlude had ended.

Mangrove rose. It was time to move on. He stiffened. This time there was no mistaking the sound. It came as an explosive discharge, as though air was suddenly expelled to boom and to continue in a rapier sharp hiss.

"Snotty, we've found one."

"No quite, but we will."

The departing fog had given extra sparkle to the day. Sunlight reflected from every blade of grass, from every leaf. Ripples on the river stood in relief, carved by the breeze, identically, endlessly repeated. The whole valley shone.

Mangrove shaded his eyes and wished that he was wearing his hood. He sank to the ground "Snotty, it's so bright. Get down. I'd rather see the dragons before they see us."

"You're right."

From ground level they searched for the signs that Cloud had described, the movement of grass, a sight of some part of the scaly body as the Komodo covertly shifted its bulk to close on its prey. Stems wavered, but did so gently and in swathes, bending a little before the intermittent puffs of the lightest of airs coming down the valley. For minutes on end the two scanned the ground ahead seeing no hint of a dragon.

Snotty flicked his eyes toward the forest where Cloud had reported that horses had been grazing. "It must have been from about here that the girls first saw the black one."

"Well, there's nothing there now. Unless he's seen us and is waiting for us to come into charging range."

Snotty shook his head. "No. The girls said the dragons stink. We're downwind. We'd know."

"Yeah. You want to get to the wood up there?"

"We have to."

With Snotty at point, Mangrove following five metres behind, they advanced taking advantage of the longer grass and any tree that could provide cover.

With the barest warning to Mangrove, Snotty dropped to the ground.

Alarmed, Mangrove did likewise and pushing through the curtain of waving stalks, using elbows to drag himself forward, joined Snotty.

"What's up?"

A finger poked the air, giving direction. "Dragon."

Carefully parting grass, Mangrove raised his head. Three hundred metres away, the red Komodo that the girls had encountered was climbing a tree, claws like crampons – the sharp metal spikes that climbers in the distant past had worn to scale mountains – digging into the bark, leaving the scars that Biscetti had seen raked into stone.

For a moment he could see no reason for what was happening. "Why is..."

A movement of darker green among the leaves caught his attention. He strained to make out whether it was simply the breeze brushing the faces of the leaves. The greenery parted and Mangrove saw another, much smaller Komodo. The animal had the same armoured scales that Dram had described, but they varied in colour with some green, some striped and stippled in yellow and grey. Still young, the small Komodo needed the protection of camouflage.

"Snotty, there's another one, much smaller. Its skin's different; lots of colours." Mangrove stared, fascinated. "Snotty, look at this."

The juvenile turned his broad, domed head to look back at the red Komodo coming steadily toward him. The thick limb sagged under their weight.

The two Foragers watched the red Komodo lunge at the one much smaller. They saw the red jaws unhinge and the serrated teeth snap a chunk from the yellow banded tail. In quick succession, the great head tore the smaller dragon apart, swallowing lumps of flesh whole.

"Manny, the dragons are cannibals."

The Foragers could hear the snapping of bone. They could see the strings of blood and gore on the teeth of the red Komodo as her jaws gaped in the moment before they clamped and cut away more flesh. On the wind came the smell, the stink of Komodo breath passing over rotting gums.

Before their eyes, chunk after chunk, the smaller Komodo was eaten. In minutes the living, breathing animal had become the contents of a stomach, gastric juices already beginning to transform solid flesh and to separate indigestible claws and teeth and armoured scales for ejection in the characteristic bloodied ball.

The red Komodo backed down the trunk of the tree, stood at its base swinging her head, forked tongue flicking at the air. The description the girls had given, graphic as it had been, had not prepared Mangrove and Snotty for the reality.

Mangrove exhaled a long, reflective breath. "I can't believe I saw that."

"That's why we're here, Manny. Now we'll follow her and see what she does next."

"The dragons eat each other." The incredulity was evident in Mangrove's tone.

For the first time they had come across an animal so powerful, so ruthless, that nothing, not even the young of its species, was safe from it.

The Komodo dragged its head back and forth on the grass and the Foragers watched the ritual cleaning of the mess from its face.

"They eat anything, anything they want." Snotty's brief sentence summed up the power of the Komodo and hinted at the admiration he felt.

The two were still lying together in the grass. Mangrove looked into the face centimetres from his. "So what can we do against such a monster, because that's what these dragons are?"

"Manny, we have to find a way. We have to work out how to beat the dragons. Come on, she's going."

The red Komodo had begun to move toward the cliff face where it had found Dram, Biscetti and Cloud the previous day.

"I thought they rested after a kill," Mangrove whispered.

"Maybe she still has an appetite."

"Terrific!"

"That's okay, Manny. I reckon the dragons won't hunt as a team, but how do they react in other ways?"

Mangrove said nothing. On Dram's account, when one killed, other dragons hung around. They mopped up the scraps. He was pretty sure that if the opportunity offered, he and Snotty might be surprised by what could occur.

The Komodo stopped and swayed from side to side, the forked tongue regularly sampling molecules that might be brought on the faint wind. She turned on heavy legs and seemed to look toward the boys.

As far as Snotty was concerned, an opportunity was on offer. He stood up, his body above the knees clear of the grass. The Komodo's head swung toward the movement, tongue darting, trying to pick up some taste. Snotty remained still. The animal took a step forward and paused, looking toward the human.

"I don't think she can see me," Snotty said. "You stand too."

Wondering why he would accept such an insane invitation, Mangrove slowly rose. The Komodo's tongue flickered at the Foragers. That was the only reaction.

"She's upwind, Manny. She may be able to pick up a scent when the breeze is favourable, but her eyesight can't be too good. We must be a blur. Maybe she sees us as a tree."

Unmoving, they observed the animal for what she might do.

The Komodo leaned forward, the yellow tongue darting out in a vain attempt to make sense of the image in her brain.

It was only a guess, but Snotty's assessment of the Komodo's vision was correct. Evolution had developed a cunning, vicious animal whose sense of smell was superb, whose receptors in certain scales on her body could pick up tremors in the ground caused by hooves or paws or even feet. The superb ability to catch and kill meant that the Komodo feared nothing alive, but the animal's eyes were its weakness. In evolving, in growing to its giant size, armour plated, immensely strong and with an array of senses that under the right circumstances could detect prey ten kilometres distant, the Komodo had no real need for acute vision.

Human eyes, with which Mangrove and Snotty were watching, had evolved differently. They were much better equipped than the Komodo to see fine detail and she had a further weakness. Even in daylight the big animal had difficulty seeing distant objects. The Foragers were at the limit of the Komodo's field of vision.

Mangrove rejected the suggestion that standing by Snotty they might be perceived as anything but two human beings.

"Forget the tree idea. Maybe she senses that something is unusual, but I think you're right. The dragon can't make us out."

"She saw the girls. She attacked Cloud."

"They were close."

Thinking aloud, Mangrove considered the possibilities. They had found a chink in the Komodo's weaponry. The question was how far did the weakness extend? How close would he and Snotty need to be before the dragon recognised a meal? The Foragers needed the answer. Where did immunity from detection end and risk begin? "And never forget, Snotty, whatever that distance is, the safety margin only exists when we're downwind."

The point was made. Lives would depend on it, but the question remained. How close could they get to a dragon without it noticing?

The Komodo was losing interest, shifting her weight from leg to leg, looking in other directions, her hunger not satisfied.

"We'd better find out," Snotty said.

He remained where he stood, puzzling how best to do so, undecided with Mangrove beside him waiting to hear how this could be achieved.

The Komodo too was undecided, her neck stretching, the yellow fork of her tongue constantly flicking in its search for clues, but the situation was about to change.

The Earth was neither still nor undecided: a planet continuing to travel its path through space, rotating as it went, spinning the hours. In those hours, the sun had burnt off the mist and climbing higher had warmed the land. Air that had flowed as a breeze from the cooler land to the relatively warmer ocean, reversed to flow from the sea to find land and rise with the new found heat.

Manny and Snotty had grown up in a frozen, desolate environment and from experience had learned to read the weather of that ice-cold world. They had no knowledge of capricious winds that fled at night to the ocean and returned from it as the day progressed. Had they known, they would have acted sooner.

"Snotty, windshift."

The smell of salt was in the air. As one they looked to the sky for confirmation from the clouds. All they saw was brilliant blue.

"Manny, she's gone."

In the time it had taken to glance upward, the Komodo had disappeared. The tables had turned.

Mangrove felt his heartbeat rise, the pulse in his neck throbbing. He knew that his scent and Snotty's were now being carried to the Komodo. "Yeah, she'll be in the grass stalking us. This isn't good."

Snotty scanned the long grass that had separated them from the Komodo. He looked for any unusual motion, stems that stirred unnaturally. Dram had spoken of limbs that were revealed as grass parted. He strove to see some hint of where the animal might be. Nothing! And all he could hear was the soughing of the wind.

Mangrove was driving his brain to come up with some way to recover the situation. How quickly he and Snotty had lost the upper hand. He blamed himself for not taking the breeze into account. He'd known that it was the only real advantage they had. He'd said as much to Snotty. *Think. What can we do?* Simply running away wasn't the answer. The dragon would follow them. *How much time have we got before she charges?*

Snotty was searching one hundred and twenty degrees of arc, trying to find some sign of the Komodo. He reasoned that hunting patterns would be riveted by instinct into whatever intelligence she possessed. Added to that was her experience in territory that was foreign to the Foragers. *It's a battle ground she's fought on before. She knows what she's doing. We don't.*

Without taking his eyes from the grass he tugged at Mangrove's arm. "We can't stay here. I don't know where she is."

Mangrove had come to the same conclusion. "We'll have to split. With luck one of us will survive. You go toward the river. I'll take the other way, toward the mountain. Loop around so that we meet with her upwind of us."

Snotty glanced quickly at Mangrove. "The river is the better way to go. Whoever goes that way will be hidden by the bank."

"Just do it, Snotty."

But it was true. Crouched, running along the beach at the river's edge, Snotty would be out of sight. Mangrove had planned it that way. He couldn't be sure how close the Komodo now was, but the runner crossing the open field would have no cover. That was the route he would take. If Dram was right about the dragon's speed of attack, he probably wouldn't make it, but Snotty would get through.

"Manny?"

"I'll be okay."

Snotty put his arms around his friend. He tried to wipe it from his mind, but the clear picture of bloodied jaws tearing at flesh remained. "Run fast, Manny."

"Yeah, now go. She must be close."

Tears filled Snotty's eyes. He hugged Mangrove.

They both began to run.

Forty metres distant the red bulk of the Komodo erupted from the grass. The roar deafened the runners, the long, following hiss like a needle aimed to pierce their eardrums. Mangrove grimaced and held his hands to his ears to stop the pain. It would all soon be over. He was running into Endless Night. He ran hard. His death would be quick. All that mattered was that Snotty got away.

Racing in the opposite direction, Snotty sucked air into his lungs, driving his legs at the ground, seeing the river getting closer, wishing with all his might that Manny would not be taken.

But the Komodo did not act in the way the Foragers had expected. For her the river was a barrier to prevent escape. She had hunted for years in the grass of the field. Many times she had startled quarry and seen the terrified animal run toward the water. Her next move had been practiced to perfection. Every detail of the ground over which Snotty was sprinting was familiar. His pace, the course he was on, fed into the computer of her brain. With a burst of acceleration the Komodo adjusted her angle of attack toward the point where Snotty would reach the bank. Her bowed legs pounded the earth.

Snotty could hear the rapid, repeated thumping, an approaching drumbeat growing louder. He glanced toward the sound, saw sun reflecting red from scales, saw the great mass of the animal hurtling to cut him off. For a moment he weighed his chances. Should he change direction? He discarded the idea. There was no way he could outrun the dragon. His hope was to arrive at the river before she did. Maybe then he had options: the dragon might be afraid of water, he could wade out from the shore until the Komodo, tired of waiting or driven by hunger sought another victim. Alternatively, opportunity might offer him the choice to go either up river or down. Somehow he might outwit her.

Snotty increased his stride. He had to get to the narrow strip of sand below the bank, get there before the Komodo left him no way to escape.

Mangrove ran on, expecting to be clubbed to the ground, to feel for a few short seconds the first chunk ripped from his body, to see blood, to be overcome by the rottenness of infected teeth. His running was going on too long. He looked over his shoulder. There was no dragon. Mangrove stopped and bent with hands resting on his knees, panting for breath. As he dragged oxygen into his lungs, dread caused his skin to prickle. His mouth stretched wide in horror. He had sent Snotty the wrong way, sent him to his death.

"No." The scream of denial rose loud, an elongated cry of horror and of guilt.

Mangrove straightened, searching for Snotty. He saw the figures rushing on their collision course: Snotty upright, his legs pumping, using his arms with elbows bent to give him balance, propelling him faster; the dragon, head high, heavy legs moving in rapid sequence, closing the gap.

Mangrove leapt forward, sprinting toward the river, calling on the last reserves of his strength. Time seemed to drag. Snotty and the Komodo were moving in slow motion, every detail lit by brilliant sunlight. Mangrove urged himself to run faster, but he too was caught in the action so intense that it translated in his mind to treacle speed.

He saw it that way, saw so clearly that time and distance were condensing. The Komodo's path would intersect with Snotty's before he could reach the potential escape routes offered by the river. Mangrove screamed. At the top of his lungs he cried in anguish, a terrible bellow of hurt. His lifelong friend was about to be claimed by Endless Night.

Chapter 8

Dumperty was persistent. "But you said I could check the snare." He looked up at Tasha, pressing his argument. He was a Forager and she had promised. "I'm sure we'll have caught a hare-cousin."

"Perhaps you should wait a while until we know it's safe to go outside the defences."

He looked beyond the circle of oil soaked grass and brushwood to the ridge across the river. There, he had had his initiation as a Forager. He wanted to build on that, go alone to the rabbit warren where Snotty had set the snare and return triumphant with meat for the cooking pot.

"It *is* safe. Take a look, there's nothing to be afraid of."

The river, the distant hillside, every tree, every blade of grass gleamed bright in the sunlight. Tasha spent time in careful scrutiny. In her experience, serene scenes were not always what they appeared to be.

"What I can see looks okay, but, Dumperty, you can't go alone."

He argued. Tasha was adamant. Dumperty was a novice with little idea of how quickly an expedition could fall apart if things went wrong.

"Ask Dram if she would like to go with you."

"Yay." He grinned and ran to put the question.

Dram looked toward Tasha and saw the confirming nod.

"But be very careful, the two of you. Go well armed and see that he takes no risks. And Dram, your purpose is to check the snare and come straight back, okay?"

The tall girl waved that she understood.

The two crossed the bar and made for the ridge.

"This way." Dumperty was eager, urging Dram to hurry.

She cautioned him to take it easy. One hare-cousin in the trap would be a skimpy addition to the larder. By a guarded approach to the warren, she might be able to use her bow. That way they would have many. Dumperty acknowledged the sense of Dram's suggestion; another element of Forager practice for him to add to his learning.

Dumperty motioned to a thicket in the distance. "The hare-cousins have their home this side of the trees."

They took the precautionary detour, a wide parabola that would lead them well clear of the warren. Dram's plan was to use the cover to determine the lay of the land then crawl to where she could loose off her arrows.

In the shade of the trees the air was cooler, sunlight filtering through the leaves to dance upon the ground and to give the Foragers a mottled camouflage, perfect for observing the rabbits at the warren. One, caught by the hind leg, was tugging at the line in an effort to get free. The snare had done its job. Unconcerned, other rabbits were entering and emerging from burrows or simply sitting in the sun.

Dram shucked her pack. "Wait here and watch what I do."

She began to crawl toward the warren, quiver looped over one shoulder, bow over the other.

Dumperty watched her slow, careful advance. Eighty metres from the rabbits, Dram sank to the ground. Using elbows and knees, almost invisible in the grass, she continued her approach. At thirty metres distant she silently drew an arrow from her quiver and fitted it to the bow. Raising her head a little, one shoulder dipped, Dram stretched the string, the bow arching. She got off the shot, drew another arrow, fired, drew and shot again. In less than four seconds three arrows were in the air speeding at their targets. Travelling at sixty metres per second the arrows were silent. Only as the arrow pierced the rabbit did it hear ever so briefly the sound of rushing air.

Dumperty ran from the shelter of the trees. Dram got to her feet and walked. Her aim had been good. She had no need to hurry.

The snared rabbit was pulling hard at the line. Dram waited for Dumperty.

"Have you ever killed a hare?"

He shook his head.

"Watch." She drew her knife and in one quick motion slit the animal's throat. "Now drink."

As she had done with Biscetti and the snow hare all that time ago on the ice, Dram held the rabbit for Dumperty to drink its blood. He let the warm liquid run into his mouth. Any food was good, but this was another initiation to the ways of a Forager; the first taste of a kill. He swallowed and let Dram have her share. Grinning at each other they wiped smears from lips and chins and cleaned hands on their tunics.

"Four hare-cousins. Dram, you shoot so well."

She nodded. "Pick them up and let's go."

Dumperty grabbed a rabbit by the ears and lifted it. Dram began to giggle.

"What...?" But the question was answered. The dead rabbit's bladder was draining, yellow urine staining Dumperty's leg. "Ugh."

"Never do that." Dram was shaking with laughter. "Always pick up a dead hare by his back paws. Otherwise," she gestured at his wet leg. "You're going to stink."

Dumperty wiped at his leg with grass. Dram had played a trick on him, but it was another lesson learned.

"Come on, we'll clean them and stack them in our packs," she said. "Watch the way I remove the skin."

Dram held a rabbit and with her knife scored the hind legs so that she could grasp the fur. Holding the legs she pulled firmly to peel the skin from its body, continuing to drag until, in the way ancients had taken off a jumper, inside out the skin slipped over the rabbit's head. The demonstration complete, the membrane that formed the inner lining of the skin shone moist and blue in her hand.

"That's so neat, Dram."

Kneeling they skinned and cleaned, eating the still warm offal.

With her knife, Dram skewered a hole in each skin and showed Dumperty how to thread them on to his belt. "That way they'll dry."

They walked back to the trees. The pink, bare carcasses of hare-cousins were placed in their packs.

"I know what Tasha said, but do we have to go back now, Dram?" Dumperty looked at her, pleading.

She glanced at the sun. The day was young and if *she* could be the one to find the new Homecave, how good that would be.

"I guess not. Let's see if there's anything interesting in the valley where you found the cow."

They climbed the slope.

Near the summit, demonstrating the knowhow newly acquired from Snotty and Manny, Dumperty went ahead, keeping close to the ground. Satisfied all was well, he signalled Dram. She joined him lying on the hilltop and inspected the terrain below. Nothing appeared out of the ordinary. To be sure, she checked again. With a slap to his back, she gave the all clear. They rose and descended the far side of the hill.

Not far off was a small wood. They passed through it to where the open field of grass resumed. A kilometre ahead more trees were growing thickly. At Dumperty's belt the skins moved with the rhythm of his steps. Occasionally blood would drip to the ground, minute drops that lay scarlet on the grass before they darkened.

Entering the forest, the two Foragers, one tall one short, wended their way between trees enjoying the cooler air. Again, sunlight filtered by the canopy mottled everything below. Dumperty looked at Dram and laughed at the spattering of light and dark crossing her face.

With a quick grab Dram held Dumperty's arm. "Shh."

The two stood stock-still, listening. The noise that had prompted the action came again; a low whimper. Dram raised a finger, a signal to pay attention, to identify the sound and from where it might be coming.

The whimper came again. There was quiet and then another sound, a low whine. Dram jabbed the air and mouthed direction to Dumperty. He nodded and lifting his feet carefully, went that way. Dram kept him in view, alert for any further sound.

The whine sounded again. Dumperty pressed against a tree, rough bark against his cheek. He shifted position to allow one eye to check the way ahead. The whining was louder. He scanned the ground trying to pinpoint from where it came. Light and shadow interchanged, masking outlines so that shapes were hard to recognise. A movement startled him. He looked, concentrating, and saw the yellow dog and her litter.

The bitch lay resting against a fallen log, her puppies feeding. Dumperty counted. Six were sucking. A seventh, the smallest, was being nudged away by the mother. The pup whimpered and whined and tried to get close. His mother snapped at him and bared her teeth. She had too many mouths to feed. The runt would have to fend for himself.

Dumperty waved to Dram. She joined him.

"The mother doesn't want the little one."

Dram looked at the bitch, so thin that it appeared her bones would cut through her yellow coat.

"No. She probably hasn't had a meal herself in a long time. Giving birth can be difficult."

"Can we give her a hare-cousin?"

"Perhaps."

Dumperty was keeping his eyes on the dogs. The unwanted pup was persisting in his effort to suckle. The mother's teeth closed on his neck. She tossed him aside. He fell into the dirt, a small ball of dusty fur, his yelp of pain sharp and loud.

"Oh," Dumperty cried out in sympathy. "Why is she doing that?"

"She probably has very little milk and he's the smallest of the litter. A mother has to choose sometimes. She's saving her milk for the stronger pups."

"He's small like I am."

"Yes, he's the tiny one."

Dumperty looked up at the tall girl. "Was my mother like that? Did she not want me?"

Dram stroked Dumperty's hair. "She wanted you, darling, but it was a time of famine. We had very little food. Your mother and your father saved what food they had for you."

"They went to Endless Night so I could live?"

"Yes."

The boy looked at the rejected runt of the litter and drew a parallel with himself as a baby: an orphan who would not have survived without the benevolence of the clan.

"Dram, let's save the puppy. Let me take him with me."

She put to Dumperty that the pup was young, that without his mother's milk he might not live.

"We have a cow. He can drink her milk. Anyhow, his mother won't feed him. If we leave him here, he'll die anyway."

"Oh, okay, but where will you keep him?"

Dumperty laughed. "In my pocket."

Taking pity on the mother in such poor condition, Dram took a rabbit from her pack and placed it within her reach. The dog snarled at her approach, but hunger overcame fear and the dog knew that some of the meat that satisfied her would convert to milk for her pups.

Dumperty brushed dirt from the weakling and held him to his cheek. "You're mine now. I'll look after you."

The pup nuzzled him.

"Are we going back to the beach, Dram?"

"No, I thought we might go on up this valley. Manny and Snotty may not find a cave. Maybe we can."

"But Tasha said..."

Dumperty had in mind the conditions Tasha had imposed. She had allowed the visit to the warren, nothing else. His conscience troubled him. He had persuaded Dram to extend their trip, but now they really should return.

Dram told Dumperty not to worry. If they could bring back news of a Homecave, Tasha would be very pleased.

"I guess so. Yeah, that would be terrific." Dumperty patted the tiny dog in the pocket of his tunic. "I'm going to call him *Schmucky*."

"Why that?"

"Because he's a bit grubby."

Dram laughed. "Come on, let's see if we can find a decent place to live."

Involved in their acts of mercy, intent on the mission to locate a new Homecave, Dram and Dumperty were confined within the hills that defined the second valley. The Foragers were isolated from all that was going on elsewhere, with not the faintest idea of what was happening to Manny and Snotty.

The red Komodo had turned her head at the scream from Mangrove. Running toward her she saw the demented human. The monster slowed and stopped. Mangrove was charging straight at her, one arm reaching to pluck the stone axe from his pack and all the while shouting in fear that Snotty was about to die and in the hope that he might distract the monster.

Nothing had ever threatened a Komodo. In millions of years the giant lizards had gone unchallenged. The yellow tongue pierced the air, picked up the odour of human sweat tainted with emotion and conveyed the data to the animal's brain. Two new factors entered the equation: the novelty of being attacked, and, by an enemy previously unknown. The Komodo hesitated.

Snotty heard the shouting, saw Manny ready to throw his axe, saw the Komodo stop. He realised that Manny had given him a lifeline. He would get to the river, but now both their lives were in jeopardy. Snotty reached for a river stone, hurled it at the dragon, found more and watched them bounce off the armoured scales.

Manny was still screaming, closing on the monster. The Komodo's head swung, looking at one, looking at the other, unsure of which threat to deal with first.

The hail of stones continued. Snotty knew that the dragon would scarcely feel them, but the stones were a nuisance to further unsettle the animal.

At ten metres distance, Mangrove hurled his axe. It spun through the air, a balanced weapon aimed to harm, on trajectory to strike the monster's neck. Stones peppered the Komodo, she turned toward Snotty. The axe rotated in the sunlight. Itself a wedge of stone that time without number had smashed holes in ice, had served to fell trees or to cut wood, the stone axe was a tool of many uses and a reliable weapon if kept sharp. It turned end over end until the blade slammed into the long, thick neck. Surprised, in pain, the Komodo reared on hind legs, roared and faced her attacker.

For a moment the shaft of the axe stood out from the armoured scales like the rigid shaft of a banderilla, the dart meant to weaken the neck muscles of the bull in an ancient conflict with a matador. In exultation Mangrove punched the air, in disappointment watched the axe fall to the grass. Totally drained of energy, almost unable to stand, he swayed and thought that he would pass out. Metres from the Komodo, the putrid smell of bacteria filled his nostrils. Mangrove looked at the bloodied slime on serrated teeth and wondered how long it would be before his hair and his own teeth would become part of a vomit ball lying with the flies.

"Manny, run."

He heard Snotty shouting, but had no strength. Mangrove lifted a hand and waved farewell.

"Manny, Manny." The wild, distressed cries urging his friend to get away while a slim chance remained.

Mangrove fitted an arrow to his bow. With this final act of defiance, he would try to wound the dragon. It would be Snotty who could run and live.

Snotty left the strip of sand, climbed the bank and advanced, hurling stones, screaming in anger. The dragon turned again to face him, stones hitting her head, her snout. From behind, Mangrove's arrow flew to strike and to stick briefly between scales. Although but pinpricks for the Komodo, she reared again, a prehistoric monster confused by happenings for which she was unprogrammed. Roaring, the Komodo lumbered to the river, hissed and in a motion uncharacteristically graceful, sank into the water.

Snotty watched in disbelief. With its long tail sweeping, limbs paddling, the giant creature moved fast underwater for thirty metres then rose to the surface and swam strongly to the far bank.

"Manny, look. The dragon can swim."

Mangrove had sunk to the ground. Sitting with legs spread, grateful to be alive, he saw the dragon leave the water and with wet scales shining red, in her rolling gait walk away without looking back at her tormentors. The Komodo's ability in water was another thing to trouble him. Water could not be counted on as a protective barrier like some medieval moat.

Snotty grinned at him. "We made it."

Mangrove's chin sank to his chest, the possibility that he could have condemned his dearest friend to death weighing heavily. "She could have killed you. She could have killed us both. Only luck saved us."

Snotty disagreed, believing that that the combined assault from two fronts was more than the dragon could cope with. "We confused her."

"She'll learn from that experience. Next time, and there will be a next time because we're the intruders here, the outcome might be different. The dragons won't leave us in peace until they eat us or we get out of their territory."

"We beat one, we can beat them all. It's just a matter of tactics."

Mangrove sighed. "We're living on the edge, Snotty. Can't you see that?"

The crisis had passed. Snotty's crazy anger gone with the retreating Komodo. Elated at driving it off, his attitude had become one of confidence. He and Manny had found a way to defeat a powerful enemy.

"Manny, we won and to live on the edge is fun."

Mangrove did not immediately reply, occupied with the thought that the shadow of Endless Night had passed too close for comfort. At the time he had not found it fun. When he spoke it was to remind Snotty that they should pray to the stars that luck would always be with them.

Snotty held out his hand and helped Mangrove from the ground. "Thanks for all you did."

"You did the same."

"That's what I always say. We're a good team. Together we get the job done."

The Foragers resumed their journey up the valley, Mangrove already teasing his mind to find a better way to nullify the menace of the Komodos. Luck was too haphazard and eventually could prove to be an unreliable ally. *But what can we do? Nothing seems to stop them.*

Separated by the river and by the ridge that bordered the second valley, Manny and Snotty walked a course that paralleled that of Dram and Dumperty, each pair unaware of the other.

The Komodo left the river shaking water from red scales and craving food. The juvenile she had eaten, far from providing satisfaction had served to sharpen her appetite. She roared in frustration, swung her head and licked the air. The forked tongue found no trace of game. Roaring again, the explosive hiss of the Komodo, rapier-like, cut to the slope of the hill and beyond. The animal lumbered along the far side of the river, hunting for anything that would fill her belly.

Keeping to the river, the Komodo picked up the scent of rabbit and made for the warren. It was deserted. Hearing her, seeing her, rabbits had rushed into burrows to go deep underground. Not deceived, the forked tongue snaked into hole after hole, tasting the fresh odour of rabbit. In fury the Komodo ripped at the earth, exposing tunnels that met and ran on in a network that ultimately led to escape. The rabbits had prepared their bolt holes in advance. Far from the warren, they had already emerged to flee.

Red scales dulled with dust, the Komodo swung her head in frustration. Other smells touched her tongue, the smell of blood and intestines and of urine. With her snout close to the earth, she found the unwanted remnants of rabbits skinned by Dram. The Komodo took a few steps, paused and flicked the air with the tips of her yellow tongue. Molecules from a tiny drop of blood that had fallen from the skins on Dumperty's belt stimulated nerve endings.

Hunger drove the Komodo. Traces of blood led her to the grove of trees and up the slope to stand at the crest, the valley spread before her. The sea breeze had risen a little with the warming day and testing the wind brought no hint of anything of interest. Only the faint spots of rabbit blood provided some hope of a meal. She roared again and descended into the valley to travel west, crossing the grassland in her search.

Well up the valley, the pup in Dumperty's pocket tensed and whimpered. The boy fondled him, soothing him, thinking that the pup had been dreaming, frightened by some nightmare or perhaps just missing his mother. Schmucky licked a finger and dozed again.

Dram took a bearing from the sun, estimating that noon was not far off. "We'll make for the escarpment at the head of the valley. If there *is* a cave, that will be the place to find it."

Kilometres away, upwind of Dram and Dumperty, the monster paused and placing heavy legs carefully found another drop and with direction confirmed increased speed toward the first grove of trees. She was on the hunt.

Passing through the trees, the Komodo made for the second outgrowth. Closing upon it she heard the sounds that had attracted the Foragers.

The mother tried to defend her litter. Weeks of pregnancy, the effort of labour and suckling pups, the attempt to save their lives and her own all went to waste. In minutes the Komodo had swallowed mother and infants and was wiping her bloodied jaws against the bole of a tree.

The thin mother and her brood provided little flesh. The few moments of catastrophe for the dogs could be likened to a brief pit-stop for the dragon. Finished, she was on the move again, traces of blood guiding her.

Schmucky would never know how fortunate he had been, but the odour of bacteria was borne on the wind and from Dumperty's pocket the pup could smell it. He stiffened and with ears pricked whimpered and moaned. Dumperty stroked him. The pup would not be quieted. A piece of rabbit meat on which he might chew failed to pacify him.

"Something's worrying Schmucky." Dram looked into the pocket. The pup was trembling, his head raised, nostrils twitching.

Dram tipped back her head and sniffed. She too picked up the nauseating smell.

"Dragon." Her voice was shaking with fright as she reminded Dumperty of the experience she had shared with Biscetti and Cloud. "I saw what they can do. Dragons don't just eat, they gulp down every bit of their victims with jaws that spread wide and drip with bloodied slime that stinks. They're the most evil creatures I've ever seen."

"Worse than Trats?"

In the past Dumperty had listened to stories of Torterats, now he was hearing of dragons. New to foraging, he had not seen either.

Dram shuddered. "I hate them both."

"Is the dragon close, do you think?"

Dram was looking back the way they had come, the odour of the Komodo strong on the breeze. She saw movement in the trees where they had found Schmucky and screwed her eyes to slits. The shape was obscured by tree trunks and so dappled with shadow and sunlight was difficult to make out.

Dumperty could see the rapid rise and fall of her chest with each intake of breath. "Are you scared, Dram?"

"I've told you, I've seen what these monsters can do." Her eyes never strayed from searching. "Pray to the stars the dragon doesn't know we're here. Ohh..."

The Komodo had emerged from the wood, sun reflecting from red scales.

"I can see her. It's the red dragon. Run, Dumperty, run."

Fear is contagious. Dumperty felt his heart beating hard, his skin prickling. "How did she find us?"

"Does it matter? Just run." Dram pointed to the ridge separating the valley from the river. "That way."

They were off, racing to escape, racing against time. The running figures were too far away for the Komodo to see them, but the blackened blood spots, minute and sparsely spread, gave off their own odour. To the inquiring yellow tongue, the almost invisible spots of blood were potent, reliable markers. Had Dumperty dropped white pebbles from his pocket, he would not have left a better trail.

They ran across fields of grass and as best they could hurried up the hill. At the top they looked back. The Komodo had her head to the ground, not coming toward them, still following the track they had taken after leaving the wood.

"She's lost us," Dumperty said.

Dram's response was delayed, her attention focused on the Komodo. The animal's actions puzzled her. Finally, as if the answer she sought was relayed in slow motion, she spoke. "She's sensing where we've been. We must have..."

Dram examined herself for clues, some tell-tale sign that might explain their predicament and found nothing. She looked Dumperty over, her eyes running down from his head. The rabbit pelts hung from his belt. Dram saw thin, dark lines, threads as fine as cotton that ended in drops of congealing blood. There was little of the blood – practice had made Dram adept at skinning animals – but she realised that the few drops that had fallen had been enough for the Komodo.

She pointed to the pelts. "The blood gave us away."

"Should we get rid of them?"

"Yes. They may distract the dragon for a short time."

They looked at the Komodo from the height of the hill. She had changed direction and with head still lowered, unaware of their presence, was coming toward them.

"Go over the crest so that we're out of her sight." Dram said. "But don't go all the way down the other side yet, keep close to the top."

"Should we cut back toward the beach?"

"No way, she'd have our scent the moment we got up wind. Right now she doesn't know what she's chasing."

"Okay."

With Dram leading the way, the two dropped below the brow of the hill and followed the line of the ridge.

On the far side of the river, Mangrove and Snotty were progressing toward the plateau that thrust up from the head of the valley, closing it off. Vigilant to possible danger, they paused to survey the terrain ahead and behind.

Mangrove touched Snotty's arm. "Look."

They watched Dram and Dumperty running.

"Something's after them, Manny."

"It'll be the red dragon. It has to be. We got rid of her, but she's found another meal in those two." Mangrove puckered his lips and whistled.

The shrill notes came to the ears of the running pair in three short, sharp bursts; sounds at once recognisable as bearing Manny's signature. Still moving, they turned heads trying to spot him. Mangrove and Snotty were waving, signalling to come to the river.

To Dram and Dumperty the sight of their friends brought a rush of relief. No longer were they alone. Mangrove and Snotty were stalwart, reliable, able to lead them to safety. If the two fleeing the Komodo could cross the river all would be well.

From opposite sides of the river they called to one another, each knowing that none could swim. Anxiety again began to eat at Dram and Dumperty. They waded into the water until it became too deep to go further. The river was impassable.

Chapter 9

Tasha glanced at the sun. Dram and Dumperty should have returned long ago. *Where are you two?*

Biscetti saw the quick look to determine the hour of the day and the worry on Tasha's face. "What's the matter?"

"Dram and Dumperty aren't back. Checking the snare shouldn't have taken this long. Dram knows she was only to visit the hare-cousins' warren and come home; successful or not."

"Hmm." Biscetti compressed her lips. "They might have struck trouble, but my guess is that Dram is doing her own thing. She'll come back when she decides."

"Do you think so?"

"You bet I do."

Tasha studied her sister. Biscetti had not forgiven Dram for things that had occurred in the past. Memories of Dram's actions were an undercurrent that swayed Biscetti's thinking. Nevertheless she could be right. Dram was a confident Forager whose arrow seldom missed its target. She may have taken the opportunity to explore the second valley despite explicit instruction to the contrary.

The lines returned to Tasha's face. The possibility existed that the two had run into trouble. She had no way of knowing.

"So, what next, Tasha?" Biscetti pressured her sister, criticism of Dram implicit in her tone.

Tasha looked at the encircling defences, at the stockpiles of fuel held within the stockade. If attack came, all hands would be needed to maintain the burning perimeter. She should send a search party for Dram and Dumperty, but with Manny and Snotty also on expedition, to further deplete the number of defenders might place them all at risk. Tasha frowned. She was again confronted with the quandary. What was the better course of action?

Biscetti understood Tasha's dilemma and wished she had not tried to provoke her sister. "You could send a runner."

The suggestion was a compromise. Send one, not two, to find the missing pair. Even that was not a real solution. To have five Foragers absent in the current circumstances weakened defence. Tasha gazed at the hill that hid the next valley and weighed the alternatives. Sola or Situ would be quickest should she send either of them, but they would be of greater help should a Komodo appear. Kalich had run hard and long to bring the news of Dram caught in the quicksand. Perhaps for a brief period he could be spared from the camp. The pieces fell into place.

Tasha nodded. "I'll send Kalich."

"To find them?"

"Let's hope so."

In a few brief and concise words, Kalich was given his mission. He was to find the warren. Dram and Dumperty might be lingering there, hunting or setting more snares. He was to bring them back. If they were not there and he saw no evidence of a fight, he was to climb to the top of the ridge and search the valley where the cow and calf had been found. If there was no sight of the two, he was to return immediately. The assumption being that Dram had decided to travel further into the valley.

"Be quick, Kalich. We can't afford to have you gone for long."

"I understand."

He was off, forcing his way across the bar.

The rabbits had resumed their normal habits, gambolling around the warren or dozing in the sun. That some of their number were no longer present, due to the snare and Dram's arrows, had been a short lived disturbance no longer of consequence.

Kalich, with a fair idea of where the burrows were located – Dumperty had told everyone how and where the snare had been set – picked out movement when still distant. The pattern of hopping, the raised and lowered ears, the silhouettes of resting animals were so much like the hares, their cousins. Kalich looked for the figures of Dram and Dumperty and saw only rabbits. He made straight for the warren. By the time he arrived it appeared deserted, the inhabitants safely underground.

He stared at the wreck of the warren, unable to understand what could have occurred. Burrows were torn up, fresh earth flung wildly to lie scattered about in lumpy piles.

There was no doubt that Dram and Dumperty had visited the place. The success of their hunt was obvious. The intestines of cleaned rabbits were buzzing with flies. Tufts of fur, lost as Dram cut loose skins from flesh, lay on soil now darkened with blood. The stake, to which the snare had been attached, had survived to remain anchored in the ground. Kalich walked the area searching for some indication of what may have happened next. He saw no sign of a struggle that could have involved Dram and Dumperty. What he found were faint footprints in the sand surrounding the warren. They led toward the hill, but once the sand gave way to grass the trail ended. He guessed what the two had done and climbed to the ridge. The valley was deserted. Kalich contemplated going as far as the trees, but Tasha had been explicit. His task was complete. It was his duty to return and report what he had found.

He looked around once more, taking care that he had missed nothing of relevance. It was plain to him that Dram and Dumperty had carried out the normal activities of a hunt and then decided to go on. Whether they or some other creature had wrought destruction on the warren, he could not determine. He turned his back on the valley and began to run for the camp.

Tasha listened to all that Kalich had to say. There was no doubt that Dram had stepped outside the limits placed on her expedition. Perhaps she could explain the trashing of the burrows, but there was no indication that she and Dumperty were in trouble. Tasha turned her attention to the more mundane requirements of water supplies and the state of the pantry.

Sola and Situ, thoroughly reliable, had been to the spring shortly after dawn and replenished the water. Belle and Hock had caught more fish. Individuals, if they needed a snack, would feel for pipis, usually eating them raw. Grass seeds, ground to flour under Jemma's guidance, provided carbohydrate, but the seeds were small and the work of collecting them time consuming. Jemma, however, had provided a further treat by mixing the flour with cow's milk to form dough and then baking it. The biscuits though few, were mouth-wateringly good.

The big gap that needed filling was a place to live. Without a permanent, secure home the situation was far from perfect. Tasha thought of Manny and Snotty making their way up the valley, willing them to be safe and to be lucky. If they could find a decent cave, the clan would lack for nothing.

She stood by Jemma supervising the flour making. Tasha knelt and took her turn at the grinding stones, thinking that so little came from so much work. She filed in her mind the need to locate a source of nuts and a more abundant source of flour, but compared with life in the ice world they had known, food was plentiful.

Busy, she did not at first hear her name called, only glancing up as Cloud touched her shoulder.

"Tasha, there are animals on the sleeping hare. They've been there quite a while, moving about, jostling, but they seem to be checking the lay of the land."

Tasha tried to see for herself. Against the skyline she could make out figures of some sort, but the distance was too great for certainty.

"What are they do you think? How many can you see?"

Cloud counted aloud. Twelve of the creatures were at the edge of the plateau.

"Describe them to me."

Jemma and the grinders listened with interest, trying to see for themselves the figures that Cloud could see.

"Oh, they seem to be about as big as a wolf, maybe a juvenile wolf."

"Colour?"

"Light grey, really light, like slightly dirty snow."

Tasha felt the nerve endings throughout her body begin to quiver. "Can you see teeth? Do these animals have a long snout?"

Cloud stared up at the plateau. Deliberately, carefully, she wiped her glasses, placed them back on her nose and focused intently. "Yes. They have long, sharp snouts. It's hard to see their teeth. They keep running around, even climbing over each other as if they are excited."

Tasha's eyes met Jemma's. The old lady was trembling. Cloud had described Torterats.

"It can't be," Jemma said. "Please let it not be them."

"Be who?" Cloud could not understand Jemma's reaction.

"Trats, child. In the past you were never able to see one, but oh..." Jemma sighed deeply, her hands shaking as she brought them to her cheeks.

Cloud had not previously laid eyes on a Torterat, but she was well aware of them. Abandoning Homecave, the dreadful passage through Kaldor and across the desert, the privations suffered, all had been forced on the clan by the Torterat invasion.

Cloud recalled faces: Dandle, her long red hair curling to her shoulders, the boy forager Ulan, the elderly couple Tang and Janus, all of whom had been seduced by food offered by the wraiths only to become transparent floating figures themselves, dancing until the end of time in the forest of Kaldor. The loss of dear friends was all due to the scourge of the Torterats.

"I thought we had escaped the Trats," she said.

Tasha had not turned her gaze from the sleeping hare, watching what was happening at the lip of the plateau. Difficult as it was to make out single Trats, their characteristic movements were enough to identify them. In manic agitation they climbed over one another in a swarming jumble of activity. Distance dulled the impression. Rather than discrete individuals, the Trats appeared as an amorphous, pulsing mass.

"Escaped? I thought so too." Tasha shook her head, the sad realisation dawning that there was no escape from the mutant rats. Their aim was vengeance; the annihilation of the Camarilla.

Memories came in quick succession. Tasha had been in the hollow mountain. She was among those who had desecrated the Trat base by entering it and by flooding the atrium with light. She had been at the crevasse and assisted in withdrawing the makeshift bridge so that Trats had gone tumbling into the void. She, Tasha, had seen their bodies falling between walls of ice the colour of sapphire, continuing to fall until they disappeared into the pitch black of eternity.

"Yes," she murmured softly. "The Trats have scores to settle. They'll follow us to the end of the earth."

Cloud's count put the number at twelve. Tasha considered the implication. The Trats on the sleeping hare were a phalanx, a scouting party sent forward to reconnoitre. Their task was to gather information and no doubt to wreak havoc on the clan if the chance arose.

She imagined the high pitched yipping as they studied the valleys spread before them and searched for the humans. They would be sniffing the wind.

In the way of the Komodo, beyond a limited distance Torterat vision was poor. For the time being they would be dependent on scents carried on the breeze and being at altitude they would not pick up the presence of the humans. *At least that's in our favour.*

Word of the Torterats spread throughout the camp. People left what they were doing and came to hear what action Tasha would take in the light of the new and unexpected threat.

She summed up the situation. "The Trats don't know we're here. They must be wondering what to do next, whether to descend to the valley or to return and report. We don't know how far they've travelled. If the main group is still at Kaldor, we have no pressing problem. If, however, they are through the desert or are waiting in the mountains..."

She had no need to continue. Everyone knew that to contend simultaneously with Komodos and Torterats was too much to expect. Eyes swept the prepared ring of fire and gazed out upon the sea. The common thought, although unexpressed, was that the breaking waves would be the last sound heard, the death knell to accompany the tiny remnant of humanity to Endless Night.

"What do we do, Tasha?"

"We prepare. Gather wood, some shape arrows, others add to the fuel stock. We'll build a second ring outside the one we now have. If the Trats attack us, we'll fight. Somehow I don't think they will. We outnumber them by more than four to one."

"What of Manny and Snotty?"

"And Dram and Dumperty?"

Voices were raised in concern.

Tasha breathed deeply, steeling herself. For the first time in living memory, Foragers on expedition were to be left to fend for themselves in the face of danger known to the clan.

"As far as we know, the four of them are not in trouble. Dram should have Dumperty back already and I expect they'll return before sundown. Manny and Snotty could be away for two days, but they are the best of our best and they know Trats. Only an ambush would take them off guard and Trats, particularly a phalanx, don't operate that way."

Much of Tasha's reasoning was without the foundation of fact. She didn't know the current circumstances in which the absent Foragers found themselves. The conclusions she reached and relayed to the listeners surrounding her were based on the instruction she had given Dram and on her knowledge of Manny and Snotty. She had been with the boys on forays into Trat territory and she had faith in their ingenuity. Despite all that, her words to the gathering were largely an expression of hope.

Tasha waited for someone to query her logic. Instead, she was given warm support.

"Okay, let's get moving. We have a lot to do. Cloud, keep your eyes on the Trats. If they take off, tell me."

"I will."

Manny looked across the water at Dram and Dumperty. They were wading first one way and then the other unsure of what to do, but certain that if they remained where they were the Komodo would in due course catch up with them. Manny spent a moment examining the long line of the crest. There was no sign of the dragon, but inevitably it would show itself.

"Snotty, we've got to get them to our side of the river and fast."

Snotty understood the need for speed. To evade the dragon, Dram and Dumperty, all of them for that matter, had to be beyond her visual range.

"Yeah, but how?" He was studying the river, running his eyes along the water's edge, looking for possible sandbanks or evidence of shallow water that might allow the two on the far side to ford the river. "There's nowhere for them to cross."

Again, Mangrove looked to the hilltop. The bulky shape of the red Komodo stood out against the sky, her head weaving, searching the air for some trace of blood.

"She's there, Snotty. She's lost the scent, but she'll come this way. We have to be quick."

Dram was shouting to them, begging them to do something. Mangrove signalled her to keep her voice down. The dragon was too far off to hear, but there was no sense in taking further risk.

The need for urgency was rising. Mangrove searched the bank either side of Dram and Dumperty. "Snotty, if there was some driftwood, something that would float and support those two, they could swim it across."

"I can't see anything over there."

"No."

Snotty turned his attention to the bank either side of where they stood. Fifty metres away a dark shape lay on the narrow strip of sand.

"What's that?"

They ran to it. Perhaps three metres long, a log was stuck fast in the sand. Mangrove glanced to where the Komodo had been. With the breeze at her back, her bowed legs thick and ungainly were bringing her steadily along the crest. Mangrove gauged the distance to where Dram now stood waist deep in water, the much shorter Dumperty hanging back.

"We haven't got long."

They dumped backpacks and on their knees, bare hands scraping at the sand, they hurried to free the log that the vagaries of wind and tide had temporarily abandoned. Centimetres from it, wavelets lapped, came tantalisingly close and retreated.

Mangrove dug furiously, grit driving under his nails. "We won't get it out in time this way."

Snotty tried to rock the log. It didn't budge.

"We'll have to dig a channel." He began using both hands, throwing sand aside to let the water in.

Gravity and the river did their work. The log floated free. Guiding it into the stream, the boys splashed through shallow water pushing it, until out of their depth they hung with upper body on the rough wood and kicked. The incoming tide swept them smoothly along, taking them upstream, putting distance between them and the Komodo.

Dram and Dumperty returned to the beach, jogging to keep pace with their rescuers, occasionally looking back to check the progress of the dragon, thankful that they were undiscovered.

The log, propelled by current and the even beat of kicking legs, was getting closer. Mangrove whistled and used one hand to give direction. The pick-up had to be a clean, swift affair, as far from the bank as possible.

Dumperty had taken Schmucky from his pocket, stroking the puppy's head after the wild, bumping run.

"Okay, let's go," Dram said.

The two re-entered the river and waded into deeper water.

"Dram, I can't go any further." The little fellow had his head tilted, water at his chin, the pup held high.

"Climb onto my back." Dram bent and Dumperty scrambled to wrap his arms around the tall girl's backpack. Holding Schmucky in one hand, he moved awkwardly, wasting valuable time. She urged him to hurry. "Leave the dog. Let him swim."

"No. He's too small."

Dram moved further into the river, water rising to her armpits. Her feet scrabbled in the sand, only the weight of Dumperty kept her from being carried away by the current.

"Where's the dragon?" Dram was breathing heavily, fighting the force of the river, fearful of what would happen if the meeting with the log was misjudged. There would be no second chance. Timing was critical.

Clinging to Dram, feeling her unsteady, her feet slipping, Dumperty glanced toward the stretch of hilltop. With distinctive rolling gait, the Komodo continued to come their way. With water eddying by them, Dumperty saw the distance decreasing.

"She's getting closer."

The tremor of fear that shook Dram rippled through the boy on her back. Schmucky, wet and cold began to whine. Dumperty kissed him and whispered encouragement. "Don't worry. The boys will save us."

Snotty and Mangrove were steering the log as best they could. To arrive where Dram was standing, they had to take into account the flow of the river with which they glided upstream and balance against that their own kicking, which was taking them across it. Their course was determined by the combination of those forces. The log angled in, moving quite fast with the incoming tide.

"We're going to miss them, Manny."

"They'll drown if we do, or be eaten. Kick harder."

He called to Dram to be ready. She would have but seconds to grab the log. If she failed to get a grip, it would be all over.

Dram and Dumperty watched the log coming at them. Its size, its weight, its speed would surely knock Dram off her feet, perhaps fracture her ribs and break the legs Dumperty had clamped around her. As the log hit her chest Snotty reached for her, grasped a wrist and pulled her to lie gasping beside him. Dumperty slid from her back to hang beside her. Schmucky, still whining, lay shivering between his arms.

"Hang on tight," Mangrove said. "Snotty and I will come to your side. When we're there start kicking."

Dram spat water and nodded, but above the sound of splashing and the grunts of exertion as the Foragers manoeuvred, the roar of the red Komodo came clearly to them.

"She's seen us." Snotty was kicking hard.

"But we're in the river. We're safe now." Dram saw the look on Snotty's face. "Aren't we?"

"The dragons can swim. They swim like fish."

Dram felt her muscles weaken. Panic was stealing her strength.

"Kick, just kick." Mangrove spoke harshly. He could see the Komodo on the beach two hundred metres downstream. "She knows this river. She'll use the current in the same way we have."

The Komodo slid into the water, effortlessly letting the current carry her. Wherever the Foragers left the river, she would be very close behind.

The tide carried hunter and hunted. From the sleeping hare, eyes were attracted to the movement of darker objects on the sheer surface of the river. The phalanx of Torterats spilled over the edge of the plateau. To Cloud, distant in the camp by the beach, they poured down the mountainside like a rolling ball, their pale, furry bodies coalesced into a single mass. She called to Tasha that the Trats were on the move, not coming their way, heading for the river somewhere upstream.

Tasha waved her acknowledgement. The Trats were moving with purpose. She thought of Manny and Snotty, the possibility that they were the object of the Trats' sudden interest. Her resolve to retain all her forces at the camp wavered. To send five or six armed Foragers would turn the balance against the mutant rats. Should she do it? Tasha rejected the idea. In the event of a Komodo attack every one would be needed. Even then the chance of survival was slim. Wanting to weep at what might ensue for Manny and Snotty, she turned her attention to the strengthening of the stockade's fortification. The Queen of the Camarilla had to show courage. Personal feelings could not be allowed to influence her decisions. She could not waver. Her duty was to be the rock on which her people relied.

The Torterats plunging down to the valley had found their target. For months they had followed the trail of the clan. For countless days and nights in the dim confines of Kaldor they had tracked the confused, meandering path of their quarry. Scouts had found the ancient bunker that Dumperty had entered. They had seen the mummified remains of military men and women and their children, and recognised that members of the clan had been in the bunker. In its shelter, the main body of the Torterats waited. The flying squad sent to locate Tasha and her people would bring back the news of their whereabouts. Once known, the whole population of Torterats would take their revenge. They would wipe out the Camarilla.

The scouting party had followed the trail. Across the desert, through the dunes, over the mountains the evidence mounted. Careless, overburdened with equipment designed for use in the snow people had piecemeal abandoned items, trash that served to mark the passage they had taken.

Tracking had been made easy for the Torterats. The ashes of cooking fires let them know where the humans had rested, gave a measure to time and distance of daily travel and provided vital information on the physical condition of those they hunted.

Food had not been a problem for the mutant rats. The bat bodies buried by Tasha, the fruit of the gourds, even the scorpions that had terrified the clan, all had been eaten. For moisture, dew had been licked from the leaves of trees or from their own fur. Torterats were tough, adapted to survive in the extreme cold of the north. As they travelled south, heat had tormented them. This they had tried to overcome by plucking fur from their coats. To some extent reducing the thickness of fur had helped and so strong was the hatred for the humans, they willingly put up with discomfort.

Rushing down the mountainside to get at the Foragers in the river, exultant that their search had ended, a crescendo of high pitched yipping lifted into the air of the valley.

Wet, spreadeagled on the log between Dumperty's arms, Schmucky tensed, pricked his ears and looked toward the sleeping hare. Sitting up, he barked. The dog's keen hearing had picked up the sound still too far off for Forager ears.

"What's worrying him?" Snotty was kicking hard, driving the make-do life raft toward the shore.

"He's heard something."

Schmucky was straining forward, his nose pointing to the source of the sound.

Snotty swallowed and stretched his jaws to clear his ears. Faint as it was, he recognised the squeaking.

"Trats." The word came terse and harsh as he scanned the land ahead and saw the pale patch moving fast. "On the slope, Manny, see them?"

"Yeah, and they've seen us."

Snotty felt the river bottom under his feet and looked quickly toward the red Komodo. She was no more than one hundred metres distant, saving energy, drifting with the current. He saw her raise her head in the direction of the sleeping hare. She too had heard the screeching.

Dram screamed, her head so close to his that Snotty winced. She was now standing in water to her knees, her face twisted with terror. Drowning her screaming, the mighty roar of a dragon deafened them. On the bank where they intended to land, the black Komodo blocked their way.

Mangrove shook Dram, both hands at her shoulders. "Stop it, stop your screaming."

She quietened. No longer needed, the log floated off in the stream.

The Foragers, the puppy held in Dumperty's arms, stood in the shallows not far from the water's edge.

Had there been an observer of the scene, he would have expected the swift end of the humans and the dog. Cut off from escape they were helpless, marooned in the shadow of the massive, black Komodo staring down at them.

Fifty metres along the bank, the red Komodo had climbed from the river, keeping her distance from her bigger rival, but close enough to steal a chunk of human meat when the big male's attention was dedicated to tearing them to pieces.

The imaginary observer would have seen the rapid advance of the Torterats and heard their shrill squeaking. He would have pitied the Foragers, realising how short a time they had to live.

The foetid, bloodied jaws of the Komodos would close on the fragile human bodies, or the razor sharp teeth of Torterats would slice through flesh. In the final struggle, perhaps all three enemies of the Camarilla would participate in the removal of Dram and Snotty and Mangrove and little Dumperty; an orgy of killing and eating while the river ran peacefully by.

The observer would feel immensely sorry for these young people who were about to die. The sorrow he would feel would be magnified by the knowledge that the Foragers were children, whose short lives had been terribly hard. In the world of ice from which they had come, the tasks of hunting and gathering had been their duty from an early age. Death from the biting cold or from a hungry enemy had been the risk they took as they went about their daily work. Not one had ever complained. They had suffered empty bellies during frequent famine and regarded hunger as normal, yet despite it all, the youth of the Camarilla were happy.

The observer would wipe away a tear, knowing that the privations they suffered were not of their making. The Foragers' lives, their final tragic minutes had been determined aeons in the past through the greed and wastefulness of the ancients and the terrible nuclear wars they had fought.

Four thousand years earlier, at the closing of the chapter of the Good Times, the future of humankind was already cast. The story, in which Dram, Manny, Snotty and Dumperty were a thread, had been unfolding ever since. That they were about to be torn apart by Komodos and Torterats was not a matter of chance. That responsibility could be sheeted home to the ancients. Their actions in the years known as the twentieth and twenty first centuries were entirely to blame.

In the water the Foragers could hear the yipping getting louder. From where they stood they were unable to see the Torterat charge, but Dram and Manny and Snotty had seen it before. They knew that the Trats were coming headlong, climbing over each other as they ran.

Silent, frozen in shock, Dram could not take her eyes from the black Komodo. Snotty was weighing the possibilities of flight.

Mangrove was listening to the approach of the Torterats, watching the reaction of the dragons. The yipping was increasingly loud, disturbing the Komodos, causing them to constantly switch attention from humans to the creatures rushing across the grassy field. Dumperty, his faith in his heroes undiminished, waited for the plan that would take them to safety.

The indecision of the red Komodo ended. The phalanx of Torterats had become a threat. She roared and turned to face them. Her action triggered silence.

In the quiet, the barked command came clearly.

"The Trats are communicating, Snotty," Mangrove said.

"Yeah, but what's happening? I've got to know."

The barked order had its effect. As if programmed, the mass of white fur split to become two. One group wheeled toward the red Komodo. The other aimed for the black. It was enough to prompt the massive beast to turn away from the Foragers. From the water, the four saw the two Komodos follow instinct. The big animals began to move from the river. They would meet the Torterat challenge in the field.

Snotty splashed through shallow water to the beach. With his head just above the bank, he watched Torterats racing toward the lumbering Komodos. Mangrove, Dram and Dumperty joined him to observe the clash.

The no-man's-land between white Torterat and black Komodo and between white and red shrank. The yipping had recommenced. The battle cries that Manny and Snotty had heard in the snow, they heard again. This time, for the moment at least, they were spectators.

Roaring, each Komodo fronted the attackers, forked tongues licking the air.

From their vantage point, the Foragers viewed two theatres of war: two circles on the field where Trats surrounded a Komodo.

Again commands were barked and mutant rats threw themselves at the armour of the prehistoric beasts. The life or death struggle had begun.

"Let's go." Dram was pulling at Snotty's tunic. "We can get away while they fight."

He shook her free. "I have to know the outcome."

"No, Snotty, we should run while we can."

"I have to stay. You three can go if you want."

"Go, Dram," Mangrove said. "Take Dumperty with you."

Dumperty shook his head. "Schmucky and I are staying with you and Snotty."

Dram saw jaws dripping red with mucous, smelled the stink of rotted gums, heard the high-pitched screeching and shuddered as the incisors of Torterats slashed between armoured scales.

"You're all mad," she cried and ran.

Komodos reared on thick hind legs, pierced fur with stiletto claws and clamped serrated teeth on Torterat bodies. One by one, Torterats were torn apart and swallowed.

Hidden at the bank, the boys watched the carnage; the bloody annihilation of the cohort.

The last remaining Torterat retreated from the red Komodo as she gulped the body of a brother. The survivor waited a moment, saw that from the twelve that had flung themselves into battle, only he had not entered a Komodo stomach. He fled.

The savagery had ended. Quiet replaced the pandemonium. The Foragers watched Komodos wipe jaws on grass, scrape hollows in the soil and lying in them close their eyes. Warmed by the sun they slept and in their stomachs indigestible teeth and fur began to form the vomit ball that before long would be expelled on the very field where the Torterats had made their charge.

On the plateau of the sleeping hare, the sole survivor looked down on the battlefield. He had more to do before he could begin the journey to the forest of Kaldor. He settled to the ground and waited.

Mangrove inhaled deeply and in a long breath expelled the air. He, the three of them, had witnessed the defeat of the Torterats. With the exception of one, whose silhouette had stood briefly against the sky, the Foragers had seen the phalanx removed from the face of the earth.

Mangrove looked at the Komodos in their hollows. They are invincible, he thought, but the sun glinted from blood that trickled from wounds amongst the scales. *Perhaps not.*

Dumperty broke the silence. "What do we do now?"

"We could go back to the camp, or we do what we set out to do, continue our search of the valley." Snotty looked to Mangrove for concurrence.

Mangrove nodded.

The three Foragers, the pup again in Dumperty's pocket, walked along the thin strip of sand beside the river. The tide had turned. The log, their life raft, passed them by on its way to the ocean.

The imagined observer, scarcely able to believe that no harm had come to them, would have admired the courage of the Foragers. In his judgement, that the humans had avoided death was due solely to chance. Either enemy, Torterat or Komodo, could have and should have wiped out the four. Instead, the animals had fought: Rattus rattus versus Varanus komodoensis. To the observer's surprise, the real target, Homo sapiens, had lived and perhaps learned.

Chapter 10

People extending the depth of fortification around the camp saw Dram stumbling through the thin fringe of trees some distance behind the dune. Work ceased, bundles were laid down as the eyes of everyone fixed on the figure of the girl. Stark in the minds of all was the fact that she was alone. The small figure of Dumperty, who should have been by her side, was missing. A tremor of anxiety murmured through the camp.

Distressed, Dram crossed the developing second ring of defence and sat with her head in her hands.

Tasha squatted by her. "Where's Dumperty, Dram?"

The tall girl began to weep. "Dumperty, Manny, Snotty, I think they are all gone."

"Gone where?"

"To Endless Night."

Tasha shuddered and for a moment her eyes closed. "You think they have gone, or are you certain? Tell me what happened. Tell me *exactly* what happened."

In halting sentences as she tried to control her sobbing, Dram described how she and Dumperty had been snatched from the red dragon by Mangrove and Snotty, only to be confronted by her and the black male.

"Then the Trats came and I said we should escape, but Snotty and Manny wouldn't leave and Dumperty stayed with them and, Tasha, the Trats attacked the dragons."

Dram was shaking. "The boys and I would have been next. There were so many Trats."

"There were twelve. Cloud counted them."

Tasha's precision did nothing to ease her worry. Torterats, or dragons, would be too strong for the three boys.

"But when the fighting began what happened?"

Dram admitted that she had run away. She had left the boys. "They were crazy to stay."

Tasha persisted. She had to know the facts. "But when you ran, the boys were okay?"

"Snotty said that he had to know who would win the battle. Manny and Dumperty stayed with him."

"Dram." Tasha was shouting, trying to force a true picture of events from Dram. "Were they hurt?"

Dram shook her head. "They were watching."

Tasha relaxed. Bad as the scene may have been, Snotty had made the right decision. Knowledge of enemies was invaluable. To be able to see one pitted against another was a rare opportunity. There was no reason to believe that the boys' lives had ended. Tasha put herself in their position and concluded that if they did not soon return, they had resumed their mission of discovery. To be certain, in the morning she would send a runner to examine the battlefield.

"There is one more thing, Dram." Tasha looked directly at her. "You were told to visit the warren and return. Why did you disobey me?"

Dram turned away to stare at the bar where the river met the sea. "Dumperty wanted to go on. He thought that we might find a cave."

"Really?"

Dram continued to stare at the broken water running over the bar. The log that had ferried her and the others across the river was rising and falling in the short, rough waves on its way to the sea.

Tasha knew that Dram had lied.

Snotty was jaunty. Luck had not deserted him and Manny. "How about that? The dragons ate the Trats." He still found it hard to believe. "We won't see a Trat again."

Mangrove held in his memory the silhouette gazing down from the sleeping hare. That animal would take with him the story. When the main body of Torterats learned of the disaster, it was Manny's belief that retribution would be planned. The Trats had not followed the clan for months over innumerable kilometres to ultimately find them and then be denied vengeance.

"They'll be back, Snotty. Trats don't give up."

Dumperty listened to his idols. Each viewed the situation from a different viewpoint. Neither asked him for his opinion, but as the discussion progressed the newly fledged Forager understood that Snotty's optimism coloured the way he saw the world. But his optimism gave Snotty a cheerfulness that was contagious. It was a pleasure to be with him and maybe the luck Snotty said would always shine on him was not simply good fortune, but his ability to find a way to succeed, no matter what the odds.

Manny was different. Dumperty knew that's what made them such a fine team. Manny liked to consider the facts and weigh the alternatives. He took into account everything that had a bearing on what might transpire. If fortune favoured them that was okay by Manny, but luck was not something on which he relied. He preferred the certainty of control, or at least the opportunity to know what he was up against and if possible to influence the outcome.

For Dumperty each approach had its appeal and that's what made being with the two such a wonderful experience.

Mangrove was still thinking about the fighting. "The Trats got through the dragons' armour. They drew blood."

Snotty nodded. "Yeah, I saw that."

"So if we could find a weapon sharp enough, strong enough not to break and had the force to drive it between a dragon's scales, maybe the dragon could be defeated."

"A lot of *ifs*, Manny."

"I was thinking of the spear you found, either that or some variation of it."

Snotty agreed that it was an idea worth thinking about.

Dumperty smiled. He stroked Schmucky. Life couldn't be better.

At Mangrove's suggestion they stuck by the river. Walking on the bank provided an easy path and gave them a view of the grassy fields and woods that lay between the river and the plateau. The rock face of the cliff was clearly visible, solid and unbroken, giving no indication of possible habitation.

In bright afternoon sunlight the expedition had taken on the nature of a picnic. The boys ate cooked pipis and pieces of rabbit that although raw, had a pleasant tasting, chewy quality. Dumperty told of the rabbit he had held by the ears. The others laughed. Most Foragers had been caught in that way the first time they had held a hare. Hare-cousins had proved to be no different.

Schmucky began to whine a little time before the boys heard the noise, a noise that put an end to laughter. It was as though hail was falling not so far away and coming closer, yet the sky was clear. The breeze that had blown for hours from the sea was suddenly still, but it was the river that caused them to look in wonder. In a frisson of dancing droplets the water's surface erupted. The river had come alive, quivering, the surface popping as though aerated, giving the appearance that rain was jumping from it for ten centimetres or so before falling back to repeat the dance.

The noise grew louder. To be heard, the boys had to raise their voices, full of concern, questioning what was going on.

It was then that the earth began to shake. Firm ground on which they had always trod no longer gave reliable footing. Mangrove shouted that they should sit before they fell. Sitting, looking at each other with eyes wide, their bodies shook with the earth. Sand was slipping from the bank to the beach, grains streaming in columns to form small piles below. Trees trembled, their branches losing leaves that fluttered to the ground. Trying to hold steady, the boys spread arms and with fingers grasping tussocks of grass tried to anchor themselves. It was futile. They rocked with the rocking ground.

Into the confusion and the noise came another sound. Faint at first, it grew in intensity; a rhythmic drumming that grew to hammer at the ears of the Foragers. Unable to stand, limbs spread in the effort to still movement, they searched the sky for clouds from which the thunder could be coming. The sky remained startlingly blue, free of cloud. Organs in their bodies began to quiver, teeth chattered as the new noise translated into another wavelength that moved the ground they sat upon. Then bursting into view, the Foragers saw the herd of galloping horses.

Panicked by the earthquake, hides foam-flecked, the horses thundered toward the Foragers. Struggling to stand, lurching about, Snotty raised his arms and like some unbalanced scarecrow waved at the horses hurtling across the grassland toward them. They were so close, coming so fast.

Snotty could see big, brown eyes wide with fear, manes flaring as the horses raced straight at him and at Mangrove and Dumperty still sitting, still holding tight to stalks of grass; drowning men clutching at straws.

"Yah," Snotty shouted. "Yah." His arms flapping, urging the herd to see the humans in their path.

Huge frightened eyes stared from the galloping horses, registered the new threat and flying hooves drove the terrified animals to veer away. In a great wheeling arc the thundering herd was gone.

Snotty fell to the ground. All he now had to contend with was land that would not stay still.

A final rumble sounded and as quickly as the shaking had begun it stopped. The river flowed serene once more.

"What was that?" Dumperty appealed for explanation.

Snotty had no answer. In all his life he had never felt the ground tremble under his feet.

From the mountain far to the south dark smoke was rising. Mangrove watched thick, billowing clouds that seemed to be alive rolling high. He wondered if there was a connection between the great outpouring from the mountain and the moving land.

He did well to ask the question. From the magma near the centre of the earth, molten rock had migrated upward, boiling its way to the volcano from whose cone smoke was belching. That seismic event had brought on another.

Twelve kilometres below the feet of Mangrove, Snotty and Dumperty, at a fault in the earth's crust, there had been an abrupt shift of rock. Over centuries, slow movements deep inside the planet had brought pressure to bear on its outer, hard shell. The hard but brittle rock had resisted the pressure until the movement of magma brought further force to bear. The stored energy broke loose. In seconds, great areas of subterranean rock had succumbed, fractured and moved, shaking the earth above.

Mangrove would never have tried to explain why the earth trembled. Nothing in his experience, nothing in the folklore of the Camarilla, gave any inkling that the interior of the earth was molten, that the solid, stable surface of the earth was in fact a series of plates that shifted continents and threw up mountain ranges. What Mangrove had done was ponder whether there was a relationship between the sulphurous clouds that were spewing from the mountain on the horizon and the quaking of the ground. The quake had indeed been brought about by events more than one hundred kilometres inside the earth. In turn those events had an effect on rock far less deep and in the wild release of energy, shock waves rippled through the mantle until the ground rose and fell and the river gave its display. The smoke and ash rising from the volcano and the moving ground were closely related. How and why, Mangrove could not explain, but the coincidence was enough for him to put the two together.

He drew Snotty's attention to the smoke, much more active than it had been in the morning. "The smoke thickens, the ground goes up and down and the river dances. Why did that happen, Snotty?"

Snotty shrugged. "Who knows?"

"Hmm." But the more Mangrove thought about it, the more convinced he was that all the events were connected and perhaps part of the same inexplicable phenomenon.

Snotty took Schmucky from Dumperty and held the pup in his hands. "What I *do* know is that this little dog knew the Trats were coming. He must have heard them, because he started to whimper and he knew what was going to happen before the ground began to shake. Each time he tried to warn us. In future we should take notice."

Dumperty listened, his expression serious as he recalled his flight with Dram. "Schmucky knew something was wrong when the red dragon was following us. We didn't know it, but he was trying to tell us we were in danger then."

"Yeah, he's smart."

The boys sat for a while, unsure, fearing that the motion might return. In the aftermath of the earthquake there was total quiet, as if a giant hand had stilled every noise. They waited.

With a single call that was followed by another, which encouraged many, the silence was broken by the renewed singing of birds and the soughing of the breeze in the grass and among the leaves of the trees.

Snotty got to his feet. "The ground is still now. Let's get going."

Peace had returned to the afternoon, but as they walked Snotty was thinking of the horses and how fast they ran. He held the image of pounding hooves, of haunches whose muscles rippled and manes that streamed like the spray blown from waves. The fact that he and the others could have been run down no longer bothered him. He could not forget how wild and free the horses were. *If I could run like that?* The question had no answer, but another thought kept coming into his head. *What if I could sit on one when he ran?*

He imagined the exhilaration he would feel as he swept through the countryside. High on a horse he would see far and cover distances in no time at all. He would share the power of the animal, guiding it to go wherever he wished and going so fast that time would have a different meaning. Days would become hours, hours turn to minutes because instead of walking he would ride. How long, he wondered, will it take to travel from the ocean to the head of the valley? Perhaps two days on foot, yet on a horse I could leave at dawn and be there before midday. He pictured himself and Manny mounted. They would be able to do so much. Time would magically expand for them. In a day they would achieve what had once taken two or three. If the hunting here or there proved unsuccessful, they would ride off to another place where game might be found. In his fancy he saw this mobility as life changing. With a horse, nothing would ever be the same again.

If I could be on a horse... The opportunities created would be without number.

There and then, walking by the river, he determined that he would ride a horse. Unable to contain his excitement, he put the thought to Mangrove.

"What do you reckon? And it would be such fun."

"Wow," Dumperty said. "Can I have a horse too?"

"Why not?" Snotty was grinning.

Mangrove was quiet. The proposition had merit, but how would they catch a horse? How would they manage to sit on one if it could be caught? "And how would you make him take you to those places you wanted to be?"

"We'll work it out."

"Hmm."

But Mangrove was intrigued by the boldness of the idea. Astride a horse his own hair would blow in the wind in the same way as a mane. To have hooves drumming the earth as he flew over fields of grass, to be in one place one moment and in another the next he and Snotty would be like clouds driven by a gale.

"Snotty, it won't be easy, but yeah, we ought to figure out a way. A horse, that would be..."

Mangrove needed to say no more. He, Snotty and Dumperty were dreaming of flying hooves and speed and power.

At the stockade, shock waves from the earthquake tumbled shelters to the ground. People fell. The loads they were carrying spread untidily around them. The cooking pot rocked until it crashed from its support, spilling its contents to extinguish the fire. Some tried to run, but they too soon fell, unable to keep a footing on earth that fluttered. The flour, so painstakingly milled, remained safe in its container, but the milk pot broke under Jemma's foot as she staggered, her balance gone. From among the ruin of the camp, human cries of fear competed with the bellowing of the cow and her calf.

Tasha thrust her fingers into the sand, her hands seeking support, trying to still the wild motion. As she watched, the front of the dune where it faced the ocean began to crumble. Sand slips poured like liquid, streaming to the beach below. All that had seemed reliable was in flux. She feared that the dune would collapse into the sea, taking the camp and all within it. The clan would drown and be no more.

But the quake ran its course. The noise ceased and the earth resumed its old stability.

Yet again, Tasha asked her people to bring order to their temporary home. Shelters had to be re-erected, the encircling defences needed to be repaired, the cooking fire re-lit.

What else could she do? Asked why the ground had shaken, she could give no reason. However of one thing she was certain. The clan could not remain on the dune. As soon as Mangrove and Snotty returned, whether they had found a cave or not, the band would strike camp and go. To where they would go, for the time being she had no idea.

Dumperty borrowed the Swiss knife from Snotty. The rabbit meat for Schmucky had to be cut into pieces tiny enough for the small pup to swallow. Dumperty knew that milk was the best diet for the dog, but until the group returned to camp and the cow could provide, rabbit cut very fine was the alternative.

Mangrove watched the pup trying to chew. "We'll light a fire tonight. I'll make a rabbit broth. Schmucky should enjoy that."

Dumperty thanked Mangrove and said that if there was to be rabbit broth, he'd like some himself.

The Foragers continued their progress by the river. The terrain did not vary; grassed fields with a few trees and the occasional copse or wood. The straight face of the cliff went on unbroken. Apart from the cave of crystal formations where Cloud had lost her eyes, no other openings existed in all the length they had examined.

Snotty raised a finger toward the sun. "It's getting late. We should find a place to rest for the night."

The decision was made jointly that they would stay by the river. The expanse of water was no barrier to Komodos, but with a sentry keeping watch throughout the night any approach from across the river would be readily seen. Swimming also created splashing. The noise would give them warning.

They chose a shallow gully, a dip in the bank where they would be out of sight of predators. There they lit the fire and, after eating the promised broth, prepared to sleep.

Mangrove took the first watch as the moon rose. Its light lay on the river to form a silver pathway that tracked away from Mangrove in the direction of the ocean. He gazed at the moon, no longer round, but waning, and thought of the regularity with which its shape appeared to change; the thin wafer that grew to be a ball before shrinking again and for a few nights not showing itself at all.

Philosophically he pondered the sky. The waxing, waning moon, the sun which daily rose and set, were reliable heavenly bodies that looked down on the Camarilla seeing all that went on in their lives. The sun and the moon gave a beginning and an end to each day, yet remained impassive to the trials undergone by the clan. From dawn to sunset, from sunset to dawn, the sun and moon were simply onlookers in the sky.

In the river a fish jumped. The noise startled Mangrove. He looked for a Komodo, but the fish jumped again and ripples spread in the moonlight.

Mangrove knew that below the silver track reflecting from the river, another battleground existed. Leaping into the air – that brief escape from the water – would be futile. Life, he thought, ended in death with the same inevitability that the sun and the moon sailed across the sky. Wherever we are, whether we happen to be dumb animal or human, the fight for survival is constant. It was the life he had always known. He and Snotty hunted for food, or they themselves were being chased down. Mangrove did not see it as unfair. That was the way it was, the way it had always been. Torterats, dragons, whatever else might come to threaten the clan were simply part of the chain. To stay alive, you had to be nimble and although the Camarilla held dear the tenet that killing should only be for the purpose of eating or when under immediate threat to preserve one's life, Mangrove could see that this philosophy might no longer serve his people. The aim of the Torterats was clear; to wipe out the last of the human race. To prevent that happening, the clan would need to take the initiative.

Mangrove stood and in the quiet of the night, in the weak light of moon and stars he slowly turned in a circle, his eyes searching for movement. He saw none. For the time being he and his companions were safe. What the following days and months would bring, he could only guess. He was sure, however, that at some time in the future, he and Snotty and all the clan would be fighting for their lives.

As stars wheeled in the bowl of night, Dumperty stood his watch. For a short period the baying of dogs came from somewhere in the next valley. Schmucky poked his head from the pocket and grizzled. When the howling stopped, he snuggled down again and slept.

In the early hours Snotty relieved Dumperty. By then, cloud had rolled in from the south to obscure moon and stars. In the blackness, apart from fish that leapt from the river, there was no sound. The night passed uneventfully.

A little before dawn, rain began to fall. Unable to make out detail in the dull light, the Foragers left the river and headed for the escarpment. If there was an opening in the cliff face, they would need to be close to see it.

The three had taken jackets from their packs and walked with hoods covering their heads. Despite the protection, rain ran in runnels, dribbling from hood to jacket. Bare legs were sleek with rain that found its way into their boots softening the leather so that it squeaked and squelched. The Foragers sloshed through the grass until arriving at the base of the cliff they made their way west. Without the sunshine of the previous day, the search for a home had become a miserable mission. The temperature had dropped with the rain. Wet and now chilled for the first time since arriving in the new land, the three trudged on, hoping for a gap in the rock wall that would prove large enough to be the clan's new home. As the hours passed, their disappointment rose.

"I don't think we'll find anything," Dumperty said. "Do you, Manny?"

Mangrove shrugged. The movement caused more rain to trickle down his neck. He turned his eyes briefly to the clouds and the falling rain. "If we do, at least we could shelter from this."

The plateau that marked the northern boundary of the valley began to curve southward, enclosing its western end. The direction in which the Foragers were travelling changed from west to due south. They had left the open fields and were among trees that hindered the view ahead, yet with leaves weighed down and dripping, gave no protection from the weather.

"Where are we going, Manny?" Dumperty wondered how they would find their way.

"Oh I'd say we'll hit the river before too long. Then we'll head back to the dune."

"Yeah," Snotty said disgruntled. "And we've found nothing."

They continued along the base of the cliff, searching for an opening in the rock, a split that might be the doorway to a roomy cave. The cliff remained a solid rock wall. When the course south brought them again to the river, the survey of the valley was complete. No home for the Camarilla could be found. The three turned east and headed for the camp on the dune.

Chapter 11

Through the night, Dram had slept little. She had lied to Tasha and Tasha knew it. Restless, guilty, Dram rose from her sleeping place at first light, slipped on her pack and adjusted bow and quiver at her shoulders.

The touch on Tasha's shoulder woke her. "What do you want, Dram?"

Dram put a finger to her own lips. People around them were still sleeping. She wanted to talk to Tasha without waking them. Whispering, Dram apologised for her lie and volunteered to go back to the place where she had left the boys. She would be the runner.

Tasha considered the request. Dram was quick over the ground, almost as fast as Sola or Situ and by being the runner, Dram could atone for the lie.

"Very well, but go no further than there immediately you've got some idea of what happened."

"Thanks, Tasha." Dram was off and running.

In the grey light of dawn, the lone Torterat opened his eyes and recommenced his observation of the valley. He would be asked how many of the clan still existed. The phalanx, now destroyed, while following the trail of the migrating Camarilla had seen no ashes from cremation fires, no bodies left by the track, but the humans he had seen the previous day were too few. The main body of the tribe had to be found and counted.

The Torterat watched Mangrove, Snotty and Dumperty leave the gully where they had spent the night. They were of no interest. He scanned the coastline, but the distance was far too great. His eyes drifted back to the valley, seeing trees and grassland that spread to the river. He saw the Komodos in their scrapes waiting for the warmth of a fully risen sun and knew that in their bellies, being dissolved by gastric acid, were the now unrecognizable remains of his brothers from the phalanx. Somehow, in due course, the Komodos would be dealt with.

Dram was moving swiftly along the riverbank. Against the smooth backdrop of the river she was easily seen; a tall figure, her long strides as fluid as the water beside her. The Torterat watched her, saw that she was alone, checked that no other person was ahead of her, that none was following. He rose, slid from the edge of the plateau and sure-footed, mindless of stones and earth that gave and slid from under him, plunged down the mountainside.

Intent on her running, looking a few metres ahead for variations in ground level, anything that might cause her to stumble, Dram kept up her pace. Occasionally she glanced at the river or with a quick scan of the valley sort reassurance that her way would be free of danger. All was clear. The only sounds were the thud of her feet on the grass and birdcalls welcoming the day.

Taking stock of the immediate vicinity was a ritual. Never a guarantee, it nevertheless increased the chance of remaining alive. On the river gulls flapped about and cormorants bobbed into view to swallow a fish before diving again; nothing unusual happening. In the quick snapshots of the valley Dram saw no reason for alarm. She concentrated on speed and on maintaining her footing.

Speed was also in the armory of the Torterat. Leaving the slope to cross the floor of the valley, making little use of the cover offered by the few scattered trees, relying on being low to the ground, the Torterat made for Dram. Racing over the grass, veering only when necessary to avoid an obstacle, eyes never leaving his quarry, his head holding still while his body flexed and stretched, bone and muscle in perfect co-ordination, the Torterat closed on her.

Dram repeated the cycle of safety checks. Her brain processed the cues from the rise and fall of the ground and guided her feet. The idyll of the river lay peaceful for as far as she could see. Again her eyes ran ahead of her, selecting where each foot should fall. In turn she reconnoitred the valley, seeing patches of grass waving in random gusts of the breeze.

A glimpse of white caught her attention, appearing, disappearing among the bending, rising, grass. Her stride faltered, the quick-fire subliminal images setting alarms ringing in her brain. She concentrated. The momentary sighting was enough. *A Trat.*

Dram stopped running, frozen, unsure what to do, trembling with fear. The Torterat was coming for her. She loathed them. Past events flashed in her mind. Torterats would have killed her had they caught her in the snow. She saw bodies falling into the blue depths of the crevasse. She saw sharp snouts with lips curled back in hatred, teeth that would cut her to ribbons. On that occasion only Snotty's ingenuity had saved her. She cried out his name. Over and over she screamed *Snotty, Snotty,* begging for help. But Snotty was kilometres away, unaware. All the while the Torterat was racing toward her. Unable to move, she watched him coming.

Fear immobilised the circuits of her nervous system. Forgetful that her bow was at her shoulder, that a quiver of arrows was strapped to her back, Dram stood defenceless. She knew that she should run, but paralysis gripped her legs.

Moments passed.

The Trat, now close, locked his eyes on hers. Each looked into the mind of the other and the animal saw that the human recognised his dominance.

Dram saw triumph shining and the thought that she was about to die jolted her. She turned away, drove one foot hard into the ground and ran, heading for the camp where she would be one among many and the arrows of her friends would put an end to the Trat.

Her action came too late.

The Torterat had the advantage. Already travelling fast, there was little need for him to accelerate. Dram had to propel herself from stock-still to high speed. Given time and distance she may have succeeded, but the Trat allowed neither.

Dram could hear him close behind her. She could hear the animal noises he made, the high pitched grunts that came involuntarily from his throat with his effort. As she dragged oxygen into her lungs she could smell the characteristic pungency of the creature, the smell she associated with the hollow mountain and Torterats intent on killing her. Dram knew that she was about to die, that the Trat would leap on her and knock her to the ground from which she would never rise. She offered a prayer to the stars that her end would be swift.

She heard the shrill screech. The Torterat was beside her, nipping at her leg. Dram shied away. He had turned her.

Dram was now running toward the sleeping hare. Direction didn't matter. Her aim was to outrun the Trat. He had dropped behind. She ran hard. Like a dream the possibility floated before her that she might escape. The whistling noises of exertion still came from the Trat and he appeared at her left side, nipping again. Dram was forced to the right and the Trat was there, his teeth snapping. She dodged, but he rounded to her other side and when she glanced down the Trat was grinning. He was playing with her.

Dram spurted, feinted with a twist of her shoulders as if she would go left, stepped from left foot and shot right. The Torterat had seen the movement telegraphed in the ripple of her muscles and the placement of her feet. Teeth bared, he anticipated her move and was there to head her off, driving her toward the mountainside.

It was a game with the mutant. He toyed with Dram, letting her think with each turn that she could succeed then cutting off any line of escape. The Trat was like a cowboy from ancient times, treating Dram as if she were a rogue steer and he the camp drafter. He cut from side to side, never letting her stray from the course that he wished to follow.

While crossing the valley, Dram continued to believe that the Trat would tire, that with luck she would mislead him and dodge to freedom. Only when she was on the slope did she realise that she was the victim of his cruel amusement. She called on all her reserves of strength, darted to her right where far off were the dune and the camp and salvation, but the Trat was quick to block the move. One way only was allowed; up the slope to the plateau of the sleeping hare.

Dram gave up. She slowed and would have stopped completely, but the Torterat was at her heels, nipping, driving her up the hill. Head down, gulping air, stumbling as she went, Dram obeyed.

The slope steepened. At times she fell and scraped knees and the palms of her hands on the rough ground. There was to be no stopping. The Torterat was always behind her, chivvying her to rise, not letting her rest.

Scrambling up the mountainside, fearful of Torterat teeth that threatened to tear her flesh, realisation of what was happening hit Dram. The Trat was not intent on sending her to Endless Night, not yet anyway. He had taken her captive.

"All right, all right," she muttered, turning to let him know that she understood she was his prisoner.

The words may have been unintelligible to the Torterat, but Dram's body language – her drooping head, the despair on her face – gave a clear message. He understood that she had succumbed. The Torterat had become the master.

She pulled herself over the edge of the plateau and would have lain there to get back her breath and her strength, but the Trat snarled and nipped her foot. Dram rose and looked toward the coast where Tasha awaited her return. She could make out the dark rings of the defences and the shapes of shelters within them. The sight gave her no comfort. Her predicament was unknown to those who were working there. They would await her return in vain.

Heartache weighed cold and heavy as stone in Dram's breast. She had been abducted and had no idea of what her fate might be.

Teeth snapped again. She sighed deeply, all hope gone. The Torterat screeched and slashed at her leg. Dram hurried across the summit of the sleeping hare, recalling the moment when she and Tasha and the others had first stood there looking on the new land, the joy of that occasion so different from her current condition. Dram could see the range, the way ahead that led to the cleft, and much further off, row upon row of sand hills. Beyond them, impossible to see at the distance, was the desert plain.

The exodus from the north was vivid in her memory. The privation, the horror of sinking in quicksand, the many things of which she was ashamed, and which she would rather not think about, flooded her mind. The Trat was driving her north. She would be walking over ground on which she had already trod and which had brought her misery. Dram's eyes welled with tears. With her captor urging her on, she passed between the ears of the sleeping hare, descended from the summit and weeping began the long march north.

The search of the whole valley had yielded nothing suitable in which the clan might make a home. However, exploration over two eventful days, whilst unsuccessful, in Mangrove's view had not been wasted. In fact, the information gathered was vital to the welfare of them all. Uppermost in his mind was that the Torterats had located the clan. All but one of the phalanx had been wiped out, but it was the picture of the survivor looking from the sleeping hare that Mangrove could not forget. It worried him. If that was his chief concern, it was not the only one. The presence of dragons would be a perpetual threat. Encounters with the beasts had revealed no weakness that Foragers might exploit. The clan was vulnerable and if caught without warning... Mangrove shook his head in vain attempt to erase the thought. The movement dislodged rain that clung to his hood. A tiny rivulet ran wet and cold down his neck to find his chest. *And we have no Homecave.* The lack of shelter would grind away at group morale, wearing it down. Exposure to the elements for too long would bring sickness. On top of it all, the new land for frightening moments had shaken, shaken so much that none of them had been able to keep his feet.

Walking in steady rain, Mangrove wished that the troubles facing his people would go away, or that each might come alone. Problems were more easily dealt with singly.

Such wishes had been made by mankind from the beginning of time and had Mangrove known of writing and reading – if books had still existed – he might have learned that in ancient times a great playwright had written that *when sorrows come, they come not in single spies, but in battalions*. In all the intervening millennia nothing had changed. Troubles usually arrived in company, never alone.

Mangrove realised the futility of his wishing. Maybe the luck that Snotty relied on would be around, but Mangrove would not count on luck. He believed that only ingenuity, his and perhaps that of others, would find the answers to the threats they faced.

"What are we going to do, Snotty?"

"What are you talking about?"

"Sorry." Mangrove listed the dangers menacing them.

Dumperty looked on and listened. It didn't sound good. The way Manny spoke, a grim future was in store.

Snotty thought for a while before answering. He wiped rain from his face. "If the Trats come back, we'll work something out. We always have."

"And the dragons?"

Before Snotty could reply, Dumperty shushed him and pointed to the river a couple of hundred metres ahead. Horses were standing on the strip of beach, some rolling on the sand. Others were in the water.

"Get down," Snotty whispered.

Lying on sodden grass, the three watched the horses at play.

"Why are we doing this?" Mangrove was ready to rise.

"Because I'm going to catch one."

"Oh yeah."

"Yeah."

Mangrove reminded Snotty that they should to get back to the camp without delay. Tasha had to be informed of the situation.

"We can't stay in this valley. You know that. The quicker we leave the better."

"I know, but this is a great opportunity. Come on, Manny. We should try to get one."

"Manny, please can we try?" Dumperty's eyes were bright with the prospect.

"Okay, okay."

The pleading had its effect, but Mangrove recalled the sight of flying manes and his ears filled again with the thunder of hooves. He couldn't find fault with Snotty, because he too, Mangrove, was gripped by the same wild desire to sit astride a horse and race the wind.

Snotty opened his pack, laid the length of plaited vine on the grass and stared at it. He would make a running noose in the same way he had made the snare to catch the hare-cousin. If he could get close enough he could throw the noose over the head of a horse. Snotty, the boy of the seventh millennium, planned to do what had been done in the wild west of America in the nineteenth and twentieth centuries. He would lasso the animal.

Snotty tested the rope by jerking it tight between his hands. It seemed strong enough. He let Mangrove and Dumperty know what he planned to do.

"Can you get close enough?" Mangrove looked at the mob. Some stood up to their hocks in the water. Others appeared to be swimming.

Snotty explained that he would use the river. He would stay in the shallows and virtually lying down, with his hands on the bottom to keep him steady, he would use the current to drift toward the horses. "All they'll see will be my head."

"Too risky. You need some sort of camouflage, something to float in front of your face."

Dumperty volunteered to find a leafy branch and went off. Within minutes he had returned with a clump of kelp that had been cast up on the beach. Long, thick, brown strands dangled from his hand.

"What about this? You can cover your head with it."

"Good one, little guy."

Mangrove was looking at the way the horses were behaving. Some gambolled on the beach, galloping a little way along the sand, tossing their heads, trotting back.

"Snotty, these animals are pretty big."

"The bigger the better. They run faster."

"Hmm."

Mangrove continued to look the horses over. One, that he reckoned was probably the youngest in the mob, had not moved and appeared to be resting a hind leg, the hoof tilted forward, the rounded tip just touching the sand. Jostled by those around him, the small horse lifted the hoof before placing it gently down again. Mangrove thought that the leg had been injured and drew the horse to Snotty's attention.

"Yeah, he's a juvenile. He must have hurt himself."

Snotty's interest did not lie in the yearling. He had his eyes on a stallion that had rolled into the water and lay on his side resting.

Snotty crawled into the river, the kelp draped over his head, the rope wound around his shoulder. The current, lazy close to shore, carried him slowly toward the mob and the horse he had chosen to be his.

Snotty peered through the curtain of kelp. It was old, long wrenched by some storm from its anchorage. The kelp stank of lying too long out of water. The vegetation had begun to rot, and where it touched his face he began to itch.

"Come on, come on." He muttered to the current, wanting the drifting to be ended, wanting to be able to fling off the seaweed, to stand and rope the stallion.

The current would not be hurried. At its own speed it took him closer.

Impatient, sick of the scratchy, stinking, itchy weed, Snotty forced himself to wait and when the moment came he stood in a great splash, tore the kelp from his head and whirling the rope hurled the noose at the stallion.

Watching, Dumperty and Mangrove saw the spooked horse roll as if to avoid the rope. It appeared that way, but the reason was simple. The stallion, like all horses – with heavy body and slender legs – had difficulty rising. Rolling provided the momentum necessary to get the weight of the animal on its feet.

Not expecting this, Snotty's aim was astray. The noose flopped over the horse's ears, but short of falling over his neck. Eyes wide with alarm, the stallion stood and reared high, tossing back his head to rid himself of the fetter. Hanging tight, the vine suddenly taut, Snotty was jerked from his feet to splash again into the water. Head still high, the horse backed, dragging Snotty like a fish on a line. Water was forced up his nose and into his mouth. He held on. His weight, the added resistance of the water tightened the rope to press hard on the stallion's head and ears. In a wild swing, the horse dropped his neck. No longer taut, the noose slipped, slid down his nose and dropped into the water. Freed, the big animal turned to join the panicked mob galloping away.

Coughing, spitting, Snotty stood in shallow water and wiped his eyes. Mangrove and Dumperty ran to him, shouting that the half grown foal was still on the beach, limping, favouring his hind leg, unable to be with the herd.

"Catch him, Snotty. He can't run."

Snotty waved that he had heard, coiled the vine as he ran from the water toward the small horse and ballooned the noose. He didn't need to hurry. To bear weight on his hoof was too painful for the horse. Deserted by the mob, he stood alone on the beach and watched the human approaching.

Snotty stopped running and walked very slowly toward him, speaking softly, his arm extended, the noose ready. The young horse shied away, whinnied with pain and lifted his hoof from the sand. Snotty murmured words of comfort, edging closer. He sniffed the wet horse smell. The still falling rain was dripping from the yearling's mane and tail. The horse had his head to one side, holding it as far as possible from the human. A frightened eye stared at Snotty.

"It's okay. It's okay. Take it easy. I won't hurt you." Words of comfort repeatedly whispered.

The yearling tried again to go, whinnied and stood trembling.

"There, there, it's okay." Snotty carefully laid the noose over the horse's head for it to slip on to his neck. His hand moved with the rope, stroking the horse's mane, smoothing the hair, feeling the nervous warmth of the animal. "See, I won't hurt you."

Dumperty and Mangrove stood nearby, listening to the horse whispering.

"Manny, take a look at his foot, see what's wrong."

Snotty kept up his charming; whispering, stroking, feeling the trembling lessen. Mangrove approached quietly, bent and examined the rear hoof. The way the horse favoured his leg, he could see the broken river stone jammed into the soft tissue at the back of the hoof.

"There's a piece of rock stuck in his foot. It must have been lying on the beach and he trod on it. It must be really sharp."

"Can you get it out?"

"I don't know. It's really deep in his foot."

Snotty looked down. Mangrove had his finger just above the spot.

"Listen, get the knife from my pocket. Maybe you can use it."

Mangrove felt for the knife held by its chain to Snotty's belt. He released the clasp and using a thumbnail prised each blade and implement from the snug slot in which it lay. He looked at the array, needing a tool that would do the job without inflicting more pain on the horse. Wanting to know exactly how the stone had lodged, he selected the magnifying glass, wiped rain from his eyes and peered through the lens. Strands of ragged tissue surrounded the site of the injury.

"It must really hurt. No wonder he can't run."

"But can you get the stone out?"

Mangrove shrugged. "I'll try."

Once more he examined the dozen or so possibilities offered by the Swiss knife and decided that he must first cut away the shredded tissue. He folded the magnifier, the blades and saws and everything else into their slots but the scissors. With these he cleaned up the wound until he could see clearly the sharp contours of the stone.

"Okay, I can see what I have to do."

Mangrove returned the scissors and opened the smallest blade. Narrow and coming to a fine point, he touched it lightly, dimpling his finger.

"The tip of this blade is really sharp."

Talking to the horse, one hand stroking its neck, the other holding tight to the halter, Snotty nodded to Mangrove to begin and like a surgeon of old, the blade of the Swiss knife a scalpel, the beach by the river his operating theatre, Manny gently inserted the point of the blade between stone and tissue.

The horse remained still.

With great care, knowing that if he penetrated the hoof the horse would shy, Mangrove pushed the blade deeper. Judging that the tip was in position, he applied a little pressure, testing whether the blade could lever out the stone. He saw the slight movement.

"Snotty, here goes." With a turn of his wrist, Mangrove flicked the stone from the wound.

The horse tried to rear, Snotty held tight, still talking, still stroking. The horse whinnied.

Dumperty had followed every step of Mangrove's surgery. He imagined the stone in his own foot, the hole that its removal would leave and the pain he would feel. He knew that if it had happened to him, Jemma would bathe the wound to clean and soothe it. Dumperty suggested to Snotty that for these reasons he should lead the horse into the river.

"Hey, good idea."

Snotty walked the yearling into the shallows. The cool water had its effect. Snotty took his time, seeing the difference in the horse, the flashing eyes calming, the straining at the halter easing. He kept walking around in the river for more than an hour. Feeling his own feet chilling, he led the horse to the bank and the grass beyond. It bent and began to eat. He let it feed until it ate no more.

"Can I lead him home?" Dumperty asked.

"If he'll let you, you can ride him."

Snotty held tight to the halter. Mangrove lifted Dumperty to the yearling's back.

"Here." Dumperty handed Schmucky to Mangrove. "Mind him for me."

The weight on his back was unwelcome. The horse bucked.

"Hang on." Snotty was taking his own advice, wrapping the vine around his wrist.

Dumperty grabbed a handful of mane and clung.

The horse bucked again, reared, came down, sidled away from Snotty and did all it could to dislodge Dumperty. The little fellow, both hands gripping hair, bounced repeatedly, but stayed put.

Snotty got as close as he could to the horse, began his whispering again, talking sense, persuading, explaining to the horse that he would not be hurt, reminding him that without their aid he would not be able to walk.

Sedation came in the gentleness of Snotty's voice. The bucking, the rearing, became less frequent, less violent. The young horse tired and began to understand that the load on his back would not go away and that the humans were doing him no harm. He stood still, breathing heavily, his sides heaving.

Snotty ran his hand down the long head and across the soft muzzle. He felt the draughts of warm air expelled from the horse's nostrils, put his face close to an ear and softly said, "I told you it would be okay."

The horse snorted and showed his teeth.

Legs astride, Dumperty sat upright and placed his hands at the base of the yearling's neck, which riders in ancient times had named the withers.

"What will you call him, Snotty?"

"Well, from the way he carried on, how about *Bucky*?"

"Yeah. Bucky and Schmucky, that's really good."

Bareback, Dumperty rode the yearling as Snotty led them back to the camp.

Rain fell without ceasing, a grey blanket masking the valley, giving anonymity to every feature of the landscape. By the side of the Foragers and their animals, the river had begun to rise.

Chapter 12

At the camp little was happening. People huddled under shelters seeking protection from the rain. Aware that Tasha had made the decision to leave the valley, they waited for the word to go. Little talking went on. The few words that were spoken were complaints about the rain and how unpleasant it was going to be trekking through it. Occasionally someone would get out from under cover, walk to the outer ring of the sodden, useless defences and look into the curtain of rain. Mangrove, Snotty and Dumperty had not returned, nor had Dram. Until they appeared, the clan was tied to the dune.

Tasha sat with her thoughts for company. Dram, the runner, should have returned hours ago. Her task had been simple; review the site where Komodo and Torterat had fought, observe whatever evidence lay about, from it conclude what had happened to the boys and return with the information.

Tasha chewed at her lip. It was the second time that Dram had been late returning. Perhaps she had again stepped outside the limits of her mission. Every runner was despatched with a specific purpose. Without Dram's report, Tasha and the whole clan could not know the fate of the boys. By not returning promptly, Dram had compounded the problem. She too was missing. For all Tasha knew, the four had disappeared piecemeal into the bellies of dragons. She dismissed the idea as too horrible to contemplate and drew her hood closer to keep out the rain. All that she and her people could do was wait.

Dram looked back. She could see swathes of rain falling in the distance. The sky above her was clear. The rain, and the cloud from which it fell, influenced by the rise and fall of the valleys and the surrounding plateau, had not spread further north. Dram was thankful that she was dry. To be hunted along by the Trat was bad enough. To be soaked and forced to travel over wet country would have been unbearable.

The Torterat kept her moving. An understanding had developed between them that there was a speed beyond which Dram would soon falter. She no longer ran, but Dram's legs were long and when walking her strides were also long. She covered the ground quickly and kilometres gathered behind her and her captor.

The route they travelled held no unknowns. Dram had experienced the pitfalls and dangers during the clan's exodus. The prospect was ugly. She could not alter what lay ahead, but knowing what to expect, when, and where, allowed her time to think. An opportunity to escape from the Trat might come up. She doubted that it would and if it did, whether she would have the courage to take it.

Courage; she dwelt on the word and all that it meant. Her face puckered with the unpleasant thought that she lacked true grit. Tall, strong, the best shot in the clan, bravery should have come naturally to her as it did to all the Foragers. Others she knew experienced fear, but they faced it down and took on whatever threatened.

The self examination of her character caused her to grimace again with the realisation that in the face of danger she either froze or ran. Dram recalled the scene in the desert, the night of the scorpions when Dumperty had been attacked. She had choked then, failing to act in the crisis that could have taken his life. The memory came like a shadow, passing through her being, causing her to shudder. So many other instances had shown her in poor light. Following those occasions she had always tried to justify her actions, giving plausible reasons for her behaviour. Ashamed, she closed her eyes momentarily. The truth was she could seldom overcome fear.

She dwelt on the fact for a little while and then turned her attention to her survival. Of immediate concern was water and something to eat. Once she had negotiated the cleft and left the ranges, sources of food and drink would not exist. She sighed, the departing breath heavy with dread and sadness. The days to come would be a nightmare and she might not live. Inwardly she screamed, telling herself that she shouldn't be the captive of a mutant rat, she shouldn't be in the ranges hurrying toward the desert where starvation awaited. *Why did I lie to Tasha?* Over and over again, the question hammered in her head. The answer was plain. Dram recognised that she had told the lie to protect herself from Tasha's displeasure. It was another example of her cowardice. Making it worse, she had attempted to exonerate herself by blaming little Dumperty. She had tried to lay the responsibility on him, yet she loved him dearly. *Why did I do that?* Dram also knew the answer to that question. Sliding down hillsides, climbing to ridge after ridge, she looked inside herself and saw the weaknesses in her character, knowing that they had always been there and always would.

Hunger rumbled in her belly. She had left the camp early and without eating. The flight from the Torterat and the subsequent non-stop travelling had used energy. Dram's blood sugar levels had dropped. She needed food and she needed to drink. She recalled that when Tasha had rescued her and brought her back to the clan in the chain of mountains she was now recrossing, she had been offered fish and fresh goatmeat. *Goats would rely on a stream for water and where there's water there are fish. Yes, we crossed a creek.* When she and the Trat came to it, somehow she would have to convince him that she had to eat and have some water.

Dram had slowed a little, the Torterat screeched and nipped at her heel. The reminder was enough. She hurried on.

The monotony of the ranges, their sameness, got to her. The slopes she climbed, sometimes falling to her knees, were unvarying, a repetition of brown earth, rock layers, and sparse trees. From the top of each ridge all she saw was another and another yet to be crossed. Behind her the Trat followed, nipping whenever she slowed.

The tired sky was a washed out blue, unfriendly, faded by sunlight. Dram looked up at it and at the molten disc of the sun and prayed for nightfall and respite from heat that pressed like hot stone upon her skin. There was no stopping, just the never ending climbing to a ridge and the sliding, slipping descent on its far side.

Dram wiped sweat from her eyes. A new anxiety fluttered its wings. The creek she expected to see each time she looked down from a new height refused to appear. Continually disappointed, Dram wracked her brains in an effort to reconstruct the days that followed after Tasha had brought her out of the canyon of rock pillars. *We got to the top of the cleft. We started across these awful ranges and ...* Time fell into place. Dram realised that after leaving the creek, where food and drink was abundant, the group had travelled for another four days before arriving at the sleeping hare. Now making the journey in reverse, she faced days of forced march, the Trat always at her heels. Much worse, she would not be able to eat or drink for all that time. *I can't do it. I'll never be able to do it.* The residue of hope that had somehow remained, evaporated. Her tongue was thick and dry in her mouth. The Torterat screeched. Dram stumbled on.

For hours the human prisoner and her animal escort mounted the spines of the range in an ongoing up and down trekking. With each hour Dram's torment increased. Only with dusk did the Torterat indicate that she could stop. She fell to the ground. Neither hunger nor thirst could overcome the aching tiredness of her body. Dram's eyes closed and she slept.

At midnight she stirred. Every bare part of her body was cold. Dreaming, she believed that she was again in the snow, polar air frigid on her skin. Still sleeping, her hand reached for furs into which she might snuggle. Her hand groped blindly and found nothing. Dram woke, sat up and shivered, questioning the enigmatic land where the temperature of days and nights could be so different. She reached into her pack for her hooded jacket and could not find it. Opening the pack wide she saw that the jacket was not there. It would still be lying at her sleeping place on the dune, left there when she had gone to wake Tasha.

Reality stared down from a cold sky cluttered with cold stars. Dram's arms, her legs ached with cold and her face was stiff. She moved her jaw with difficulty and tasted blood as a split opened on her bottom lip. Her mouth was totally dry, her tongue wooden and devoid of feeling. She worked her jaws more, felt the pain of her damaged lip, but slowly saliva dampened her gums and the lining of her cheeks and gave some feeling to her tongue. I must drink, she thought.

Her movement had woken the Torterat. He licked at his fur. Dram saw that dew had formed. The Trat was getting moisture by drinking the dew. He looked at her and snarled and satisfied that she could go nowhere, he went to the nearest tree, ran up it and licked dew from its leaves. Dram followed him and reaching for branches pulled them lower. Each leaf had a thin sheen of dew upon it. Dram put her tongue to a leaf and licked. Leaf after leaf gave up its dew to her. Pinpoints of distant suns shifted in the sky and planets moved in their orbits while little by little Dram slaked her thirst.

The Torterat had drunk his fill long before Dram and was again sleeping where he had lain. Dram looked at him. She rubbed her hands over her arms, trying to warm them. They stayed cold. She looked again at the sleeping Torterat, at the fur that retained his body heat so that he slept soundly. She crept close and lay beside him. The smell of the Torterat was repulsive, but a little of his heat radiated to touch her. Dram edged closer. With one eye her captor watched. He did not move. Torterat custom was to sleep close packed in order to retain heat. Shivering, Dram bent her body in a half circle to lie centimetres from the Trat. She blamed herself for her stupidity. Bone weary or not, she should have lit a fire.

Eventually, the Torterat's warmth enabled her to sleep.

At the camp, rain fell steadily throughout the night. At first light, those restless people who were anxious to get moving left their sleeping places to walk a little way from the camp. Their hope was that through the rain they would see Dram and the boys returning.

When the dim outlines of the cavalcade appeared, no one could explain what it was. The image coming through the grey curtain of rain was like nothing ever seen before. Hands reached for arrows and with bows taut, the few knelt and took aim. Gradually shape took on definition. Toward those kneeling, came the yearling led by Snotty, Dumperty sitting astride with Mangrove walking at his side. Some ran to greet them, amazed to see a horse, more so that Dumperty was comfortably sitting on it. Others went to Tasha, shouting for all to hear that the boys were back.

"Is Dram with them?" Tasha asked.

"No, but they are not alone. See."

Tasha looked in the direction of pointing fingers. The boys, the horse were making their way to her, a growing number of people crowding around them.

Dumperty dismounted and with the lead in his hand held his listeners spellbound, recounting to them all that had happened since he and Dram had crossed the river to check out the warren. The story was exciting, but the message was clear. The clan was facing extinction.

Mangrove and Snotty went immediately to Tasha. She was given the same story, much of which she had heard from Dram. Everything she heard reinforced her decision that the clan had to leave the valley and go further south.

"There's no alternative. We'll be wiped out if we stay." Tasha's statement was a blunt assessment of the situation. "And Dram, she's not with you?"

"No," Mangrove said. "We haven't seen her since the Trats made their attack."

Tasha shook her head. "Dram was ashamed of herself. She volunteered to be the runner sent to find you."

"Ashamed of what?"

Tasha told them of the lie.

"Sometimes I don't understand Dram," Mangrove said.

"Me neither, but she's okay really." Snotty was remembering the good hunting he and Dram had enjoyed in the past.

Mangrove was not so sure, but the unanswered question was where had she gone?

"We covered the whole length of the valley, Tasha. If Dram was there we would have seen her."

There was no need to say more. Silently each accepted the fact that Dram, now missing since the previous morning, had been eaten by a dragon. There was no other acceptable explanation.

Tasha walked to the crowd listening to Dumperty, called for quiet and announced that Dram would not be returning. There was little doubt that she had gone to Endless Night.

Gathered together, with the rain falling, the clan thought of the beautiful girl who had been the tallest among them. Tears filled the eyes of many. Without Dram's body there could be no funeral pyre, no ritual of goodbye.

Tasha saw the hurt in her people and began to sing the lullaby Dram had loved. One by one, voices joined to honour Dram and with the hope that she would forever sleep soundly.

The last words of the song floated into the rain.

Tasha announced that it was time to leave. The dismantling of shelters began and final packing got underway. All were happy to quit the camp, the dune, the entire valley. Too much had gone wrong.

Mangrove took Tasha aside. "The river's up, Tasha. Crossing may be difficult."

"To stay is impossible. I thought we'd rope ourselves in small parties and go over one group at a time. Perhaps we should use a rope back to shore for the sake of safety." She looked hard at Mangrove. "Can it be done?"

He thought for a few moments, looking around at the bustle of people making ready. The small, the old, would have difficulty getting through the water. He watched Dumperty leading Bucky to where the cow and calf were grazing. Manny kept looking at the horse, juggling ideas that competed for attention. Although young, the animal was much bigger and stronger than any of the clan. With a rope attached, he would provide a secure lifeline, one that would prevent a group from being swept away as it struggled to get across the deepening river. Mangrove put the proposition to Tasha. She called to Snotty to join them. He listened and laughed.

"Yeah, sounds good. When we're all on the other side, Dumperty can ride Bucky across."

It was agreed. That's what they'd do.

Groups of ten, roped together like the mountain climbers of ancient times, would enter the river. Each group would be a mix of old and young and at least four Foragers. Some of the Foragers would make the crossing a number of times; their responsibility to carry the little ones and loads too heavy for others and to assist the elderly. From well back on the bank, the line that Snotty had made from vines would be tied to Bucky and linked to the rope that held those wading. As the group progressed, Snotty proposed to lead the horse closer to the water, careful all the time to ensure that the vine remained taut.

Mangrove knew that standing in the rain devising a strategy for the crossing was easy. The plan was simple and readily understood. In the final analysis, there was no better way, but like all well laid plans, its worth would be proved in its execution.

The first group entered the water walking tentatively, Kalich, the leader, feeling ahead with one foot for the sandy bar, the ford that would allow them to cross. The tide was running out, but the swollen river was not only deeper, the water was now muddied with the run off from fields and hillsides and gullies scoured by the rain. Kalich could not see the sand under his feet. He had to put faith in his memory of his earlier crossing and in the hope that the bar would not suddenly wash away. Behind him, Hock carried Elga, one of the small girls. Following Hock, strung to him and to each other, came older members of the clan, then Zita also carrying a child, the boy Kew. More elderly came next, some of whom bore loads. Last was Biscetti. Her task was to keep watch on those ahead and to ensure that the anchor line did not part. Without the rope secured tight to Bucky, the possibility existed that all would be swept away.

Step by step, keeping pace with Kalich, Bucky, under Snotty's care kept the line taut.

The group moved toward mid-stream. There the river deepened even more and ran faster. The sand took on a wave pattern of hummocks and holes. Kalich was up to his waist in water. For those not so tall it was even higher. At the rear, the water rose to Biscetti's chest.

Kalich called to those behind that the bar had become very uneven. On the bank, the people waiting to cross, intent on what was happening, could hear the concern in Kalich's voice.

Tasha and Mangrove stood together watching those in the river, switching to look at Snotty and Bucky control the line on which so much depended.

The ebbing tide, sped along by the flooding, pushed hard at the ten who were finding it difficult to keep their footing. Buffeted by the strength of the flow, one of the elderly was knocked from her feet. The others braced to hold her. With the rope rigid, she pulled herself upright and went on.

At the half way mark Kalich was in trouble. He leaned into the current and shouted a warning that he had struck the worst section of the river. "Get through this and the going will be easier."

It was not so easy for Hock and Zita carrying children, nor for those loaded with possessions. Kalich had the dual responsibility of finding the best passage and making sure as the leader that if trouble occurred, he would remain rock solid, but those looped to the rope behind him were handicapped by size, by age or by their burdens. They began to slip, the sand unstable below their feet, the pressure of the water increasing.

Kalich turned as the rope jerked. He saw the danger and dug his feet into the bar, compelled to do it over and over again as the flowing water washed sand away. With both hands he held hard to the rope. He might have prevented the group from washing away, but his feet found no permanent purchase. Kalich was losing ground.

Watching from the bank, Tasha was the first to grasp the situation. She shouted to Snotty to hold Bucky still. "Stay where you are. Don't let the line slacken."

Her fear was that, strong as he might be, the young horse could fail to prevent ten of her people from being swept to the open ocean where they would surely drown.

Tasha entered the water, wading as rapidly as the current would permit; her aim to get between the group and the sea and then join Kalich. She would be the last resort that would assist them to remain where they had some hope of keeping heads above water. Alone she would have no chance of success, but if the line to Bucky did not part and Kalich had sufficient strength until she arrived, those roped together would have stronger anchors, one on shore the other on the bar.

Mangrove followed Tasha's progress as she fought against the current, willing her to succeed, believing that just being there, by the side of those endangered, would give them added strength.

Kalich yelled to those on shore that the sand was giving way. He was becoming a victim of forces he could not control. If unable to stand firm on the bar, the line with its human attachments would swing with the outgoing current and he would be with them. Like so many kites on the one string, the group would be taken into deep water and drown.

No longer wading, Tasha made her way along the rope to Biscetti, offered words of encouragement and went on. Biscetti nodded and tightened her grip.

On shore, Snotty was whispering to Bucky that he had to be strong. The horse seemed to understand and stiffened his forelegs, angling them at the ground, rigid girders to hold him steady. Should he fail, there was no hope that anyone in the water would survive.

Tasha had to be quick. She pulled herself hand over hand along the rope to Zita. "Give me Kew."

The boy climbed on to Tasha's back and clung tight. She continued along the line, urging people not to panic, promising them that they would all cross safely. When she reached Kalich she placed herself at his back, grasped his tunic and dug her feet hard into the sandbar. The extra muscle power stabilised the situation.

"When I give the signal to Snotty, we'll walk backwards. Okay?"

"Got it."

He and Tasha would be the engine at the front of the line. Snotty would recommence leading Bucky toward the river and so allow the group to proceed. With a quick raising of her hand, she indicated to Snotty what he should do.

The party resumed its crossing, a dangerous stop start affair that had all those watching holding their breath, but Tasha and Kalich dug deep into reserves of strength and at last the group reached the far bank.

Tasha, Kalich and Biscetti re-entered the water and holding the rope were pulled back by Bucky to the dune side of the river.

Mangrove had watched it all unfold, thinking how they might improve upon the method. His conclusion was that ten people were too many. With six there would be less resistance to the current and so less drag on the leader. The shifting of the clan from one side of the river to the other would take longer, but it would be far safer. Tasha and Snotty agreed.

Sola and Situ sat waiting to take the next group across. Manny joined them with Belle. Some of the people who would ford the river later in the day busied themselves collecting pipis. Where they were going, food might not be so easily found. In the shell, a pipi would stay fresh for at least two days. The fresh seafood would supplement the smoked fish that had been accumulated and packed for the journey.

For another three hours Foragers crossed and recrossed, taking their charges to safety. Almost the last to enter the water was Dumperty, Schmucky peeking from his pocket. Thinking that Bucky would take the same route as that taken by all who were now on the far side, he guided the horse to the bar. Bucky did not trust the shifting sand. He whinnied and chose to swim in deeper water.

On the bank, holding the tethered cow, Snotty looked on. That horses could swim surprised him. Perhaps the cow and calf could do the same. He led the cow to the water. She resisted and would go no further. Snotty yanked at the tether and the cow with head held high entered the river, the calf at her heels. Holding on to one horn he urged the cow on until she too was swimming with Snotty clinging to the horn.

Throughout the entire operation the rain fell without ceasing. Wet from rain and the water crossing, the clan ignored the discomfort, pulled up bone toggles to draw hoods close to faces and were on their way. The exodus had recommenced.

At the head of the column Snotty chose to walk alongside Tasha. Rather than ride, he led Bucky who had the cooking pot and other communal gear strapped to his sides. For the time being Bucky had become a packhorse.

The second valley had been largely explored. Tasha rejected wasting any further time on it. Her plan was to push on until something of interest was found, in particular a place to live.

Pilgrims again, the clan marched with a purpose, always hoping that in the next valley the new Homecave awaited them. To take their minds from rain that found its way inside clothing, people discussed the events at the river, making the point that without Tasha's intervention the crossing might have ended in tragedy. She was generally acclaimed as a Queen who would put her own life on the line for her people. Some admitted that they had had doubts when the old Queen Avon had chosen Tasha rather than Dram to succeed her, but time and time again Tasha had proved that she had the qualities to be their Queen. The river episode had been another example of her worth.

The conversation moved to discuss the other extraordinary events at the river. All agreed another lesson had been learned.

There were not only dragons that found water no barrier. It seemed that all animals were probably good swimmers. Frequently heard were the claims that if a calf could cross a river, it must not be difficult. Here and there an individual boasted that given the opportunity, he or she would show the others how easy it was.

For a time, joking in this way raised spirits, but the rain fell without pause. The talking grew sporadic and finally ceased. The only sounds were the slosh of feet over sodden ground and the drumming of the rain.

Chapter 13

Far away in the ranges, Dram climbed yet another steep slope. The rough, dry earth was stony and often gave way causing her to slip and sometimes fall. Spindly, undernourished trees gave some shade, but they did not grow thickly and Dram had little protection from the sun. The dew she had drunk during the night had long since sweated from her body and toiling in the heat her one desire was to drink.

The Torterat, usually at her heels, would pause to eat insects that were in their path; a grasshopper or a beetle. In this way he replaced some of his energy. Occasionally he would screech at her when she stumbled, but for most of the time his panting was little different from hers.

A crow flapped lazily above them, cried his harsh, unlovely call and chose a tree on which to watch the human and the mutant rat. Dram looked up at the bird with feathers so black that the sun glinted green from their sheen. The crow cocked its head and with one white, blue ringed eye looked back at her.

Dram dropped a shoulder and removed her bow. The Torterat yipped. Dram glanced at him. His head jutted toward her, teeth bared. The thought flashed in her mind that in the time it took the Torterat to blink she could load her bow and fire. One arrow would kill her captor and she would be free.

The Torterat lunged forward, his eyes locked on hers. He was centimetres from her legs. The moment had passed.

Dram raised a finger, pointing at the crow. The Torterat's lips came together, the threat gone. Dram wiped sweat from her eyes, reached for an arrow and fitted it to the bowstring. Curious, the crow continued to look at her. As the arrow flew at him he saw danger. His wings lifted ready for flight.

The crow's claws were still touching the branch when the arrow went through his breast.

Dram picked up the bird and yanked out the arrow. She plucked shining feathers from the crow's neck, bit into its throat and holding the crow above her head let its blood run into her open mouth. She swilled the warm liquid, letting it moisten her mouth before she swallowed.

The Torterat yipped and snarled and with his own mouth open made clear to Dram that he too needed to drink. She held the crow close to the Torterat's upturned mouth and let the blood drip.

They shared the blood of the crow. There was little of it. The drinking did not take long.

Dram plucked more feathers until the crow's poor, nude carcase lay in her hands. The Torterat jumped to snatch it from Dram. She lifted it higher, out of his reach. The Torterat bared his teeth again.

Hunger gave her the courage she thought she did not possess. "No," she shouted. "We're sharing."

The Torterat kept snarling, but did not attack.

Taking her knife from its scabbard, Dram slit the crow from breastbone to where its tail had been. Liver, heart, lungs, all the edible offal was shared. When that was eaten, Dram cut the remains of the bird in two.

Sitting on the stony ground Dram chewed at the flesh of the crow and when only bones were left she nibbled from them whatever bits of meat remained. Those gone, she cracked bones with her teeth in search of marrow.

By her side the Torterat stood over the half she had given him and ripped at bird flesh and bird bone and chewed all. He left nothing and when Dram discarded bones, the Torterat ate those too.

The crow provided a small meal, too small to satisfy, but the level of co-operation established the previous night lifted another notch.

The reasons for mutual assistance were totally selfish. Dram's survival depended on eating and drinking and sufficient rest at night. Staying alive was all that mattered to her. The Torterat had no such fear. He had travelled all the way from Kaldor and found enough nourishment to keep him going. It would be no different for him on the return journey, but if he could supplement his diet with game that Dram provided, that suited him fine.

The Torterat's chief concern was not food for himself. His purpose was to bring Dram alive to the Torterat king. She was to be the informant who would tell all, reveal the number of the Camarilla who had made it to the new land, where they were and to where they might be going. Dram would also provide intelligence on the abundance, or otherwise, of food in the valleys and she would report on the Komodos. Only Dram could explain how the humans had resisted them whereas the huge lizards had annihilated the phalanx with ease. When Dram had talked, she would be forced to lead the Torterats to the Camarilla. Then she, along with all the clan, would be killed and eaten. Until the grand plan had run its course, the Torterat's task was to keep Dram alive.

The meal over, the Torterat made to nip Dram's leg. The routine of mounting ridges, heading down gulches only to climb again, recommenced.

Human and mutant rat maintained a solid pace all day. Climbing slopes, descending the far side, Dram searched for twigs or branches that she might collect for a fire. There was little to find. The barren soil remained dry and stony under her feet, but throughout the afternoon whenever near trees, Dram would quickly bend to pick up small pieces that had fallen; dead wood that would burn.

Not until the sun had set and light was fading, did the Torterat allow Dram to rest. She dropped to the ground and lay unmoving, too tired to light the fire she had planned.

Shortly after midnight she woke to the sound of licking. Dew had settled. Rising, Dram again got moisture from the leaves. As she drank, she repeatedly massaged her arms and hugged them close to her body in an attempt to get warm. The night-cold had seeped to her core, chilling her tired and aching body. Dram's teeth chattered. Her lips quivered uncontrollably. She looked at the Torterat eyeing her from where he lay ready to resume sleeping. Dram approached him, lay down and moved close. Needing warmth she moved even closer and finally she was touching the Trat and his warmth was flowing into her. Curled on the ground, fitting together like two spoons, they slept.

Dram woke before the Torterat. She lay still in the darkness, thinking about the events of the previous day. The opportunity to be free of him had been short lived, but had she acted impulsively the arrow would have ended the Torterat's life. Freedom had been one second away. Why had she not acted? The answer was the same as it had been when she first saw the Torterat in the valley. He had been able to look into her soul and see that he was the master. The Torterat saw a human too scared to raise a hand to him. Dram flushed with shame at her cowardice.

Rolling away from the Torterat, Dram stared at the river of stars that ancients had named the Milky Way. *But I didn't let him have all the bird.* She relived the scene, proud that she had opposed the Trat, a counterbalance to her indecision with the bow. Dram consoled herself with the thought that nobody is perfect.

The eastern sky paled and the misty river of distant stars dwindled to nothing. Looking up at the empty sky, Dram felt terribly alone.

Daylight came, edging across the peaks and valleys and woke the Torterat. He looked at Dram and made his threatening noises. Another day of thirst and hunger and the climbing of numberless ridges had begun.

Wish as they might for the rain to stop falling, the downpour went on. People questioned how so much water could be held in the sky. Nothing in their experience had prepared them for grey days and dark nights of never-ending rain. It fell without wind, fell straight down, drowning the land.

For three days Tasha led with Snotty and the horse. Behind them the line straggled in the wet. They crossed valleys and saw little because the rain blotted out anything beyond a few hundred metres. Where they could make out the landscape, fresh gullies were forming as rain eroded hillsides. The further south they travelled the more obvious it became that in the valleys, lakes and waterways were forming where none had previously been.

At the end of the third day, on a ridge, with the light worsening – guessing that the sun was getting low because she had no way of really telling – Tasha called a halt. She thought that the few trees growing on the crest might give some protection from the rain.

Shelters were erected beneath the trees in the attempt to keep sleeping places dry, but branches hung heavy with water and everyone knew that the night would be long and miserable; exactly as every night had been since the trek began. Fires for cooking or warmth were impossible. The meal of pipis and smoked fish was again eaten cold. People then lay down or sat hunched under the inadequate shelters and tried to sleep.

In the small hours of the night the rain ceased. Tired, irritable, those who were awake looked up and for the first time in days smiled at stars that peeped through the ragged plumes of departing clouds. Within an hour the sky had cleared and stars and planets shone with renewed brightness through air that was clean and crisp.

In the morning when the sun had risen, the sun's heat drew steam from the skins of shelters and from damp clothing and put sparkle into eyes that had been dull. Happy to see the sun, people took kindling from packs and the cooking pot was soon bubbling over a fire.

Tasha winked at Mangrove. Hot food had a remarkable ability to lift sagging morale.

They sat together eating and surveyed the countryside. The creek that ran through the valley had burst its banks and was running strongly in the direction of the sea. Directly below them, and for as far as Mangrove could see up the valley, the swollen creek was more than fifty metres wide. The flood had swamped trees so that they appeared to be rooted in water and not soil. Manny spent some time looking at the trees. He had not seen their like in the valley of the Komodos. The branches of the trees in the water were dotted with colours of red and yellow. He thought that the trees may have been in flower and remarked to Tasha that they should investigate when the water had subsided. One thing was for sure, the trekkers would not be crossing the valley while the creek was flowing so wide and so fast.

Tasha agreed. In any case, after days of trudging in the rain a day or two of rest in sunshine would be welcome. The delay was also a chance to dry clothing and every wet thing they owned.

Mangrove turned his attention to the hillside that sloped to the valley from where they sat. Runoff from excessive rain had gouged such a gash that further down, part of the hill had slumped into a depression. This hollow was deep, so deep that he could not see into it. He pointed it out to Tasha.

The minor watercourse that had cut into the hill had ceased to run, but the altered formation of the hillside, the power of nature to cause such damage, intrigued Tasha.

"Let's have a closer look."

"Okay."

Tasha led the way, Mangrove a little distance behind her. She slid down into the dip and he lost sight of her.

"Manny, come and look at this."

The vibrant excitement in Tasha's voice spurred him on. He stopped at the lip of the depression. Tasha was four metres below in the centre of the collapsed section of the hillside. While the eroded gulley continued to the valley floor where a great quantity of soil spilled out like some river delta, that was of no interest to Tasha. She was looking at what the washaway had revealed.

At their feet was a concrete wall two metres high running at right angles to the gulley. It was obvious that they were seeing only part of the wall. It went on into the hillside either side of the rough bed of the eroded gulley. Mangrove and Tasha had not seen concrete, not even in the stomach of the mountain carved by ghosts, but they recognised that what they were now looking at had been made by man.

The thick slab of concrete appeared to bridge a hole. Tasha knelt and poked her head and shoulders into the hole. Her body was blocking the light. She withdrew a little so that she might see better and for ten whole seconds Manny watched her head turn as she examined whatever was within the hole.

Tasha drew back and looked at him. "You'd better see this."

Mangrove knelt, and allowing sunlight to shine over and around his shoulders peered into a cavern larger than any he had ever come across. Looking down he could see that the hole was not simply a cavity created by erosion. Water cascading down the slope had exposed the upper part of a doorway. The concrete that had drawn their attention was in fact the external face of the wall of the cavern. Mangrove drew breath sharply, realising that the doorway was an opening through a wall at least two metres thick. He tilted his head to look upward and because of the thickness of the wall saw only the ribbed marks left long, long ago by the formwork used in the construction of the building. Mangrove gazed around. The understanding dawning that he was looking into a concrete box of huge dimension. He scraped away more earth, opening up the doorway a little more to improve his view. The lower part of the building was layered. At its base was a square with sides of some thirty metres long. With so little light he was unable to see far into the chamber. What existed in the darkness he would explore later, but from what he could see, around the central square and a metre higher was a platform three metres in width. Around this and higher again was another platform also of three metres width. Mangrove was looking at layers that rose from each side of the central square and that at each higher level got closer to the walls of the giant concrete box until the last and highest platform met the wall. The pattern was one of ascending sides of a square, pleasing to his eye.

He withdrew from the cavity and turned to Tasha.

"Well," she said. "What is this place?"

"I'm not sure. I can't see enough. We have to get in and really look around." Mangrove scraped away more earth to enlarge the opening. "This has gotta be the entrance."

Together they dug down until enough dirt had been removed to allow Tasha to step from the open air of the valley into the strange creation she had discovered. Mangrove shifted more earth from either side to let in more light before he too passed through the doorway in the massively thick walls.

They stood in awe. The giant chamber rose high above to a ceiling that Mangrove imagined must be almost at the height of the crest of the hill.

"The ancients built this place," Tasha said. "Remember the pictures we saw in the hollow mountain. Do you think this was another attempt to survive?"

Mangrove was looking at the pattern of platforms, noticing that steps led from one level to the next. The platforms had been intended to have a function. "Yeah, I'm sure it was." He ran his eyes up the flat walls, marvelling at their height, knowing how thick they were. "But I think this place was really just a shelter. The ancients built it as protection from the weapons that ended the Good Times." He smiled and pointed at the levels that rose from the central square. "Doesn't this remind you a bit of Homecave? You know, how we had some of our sleeping places on ledges."

Tasha looked and nodded. There was a similarity. The fire with its cooking pot would be in the centre of the floor.

"So the ancients came in here to escape being killed?"

"That's my guess."

Manny's intuition, prompted by the scenes recorded on the disc in the hollow mountain, had found the answer. He and Tasha were standing in a concrete bunker, not a military command post such as the one Dumperty had entered in the forest of Kaldor, but an air-raid shelter built in the hope that it would withstand the nuclear missiles that ancient nations had rained upon each other. The people of the surrounding district would come to the shelter whenever danger threatened and would stay until it was safe to return to their homes. During the times they lived within the massive walls and under the even thicker roof, the frightened people would sleep on cots or on bedrolls set up on the raised platforms, the areas designed for their sleeping places. Four thousand years later in Homecave, sleeping arrangements had changed little.

Constructed in a section of the hill that had been excavated for the purpose, the strength of the concrete fortress had been increased by its location; the earth that covered it above and hugged its sides. The shelter had been a protective shield on countless occasions, but that good fortune had not saved the population. Every person – those who had put their faith in the tonnes of concrete and those who had hidden in the cellars of their own houses – had died. Either radiation or starvation had taken them all. Only the bunker had remained; a relic of a distant and terrible past.

During the many centuries that followed the end of the Good Times, wind had blown soil to gather at the one exposed wall of the bunker. These windblown grains of earth had finally covered the wall and the doorway through which so many people had passed. Grass spread its roots and eventually the hillside was restored to the way nature had intended.

Rain and erosion had laid the entrance bare again for Tasha to find.

The two continued to look around.

"We need more light," Tasha said. "Maybe there's another way in at the back. It's too dark to see, but, Manny, you're right. This place does remind me of Homecave, except maybe it's better." She grinned at him. "We've found our new home."

Mangrove smiled. "I think so."

They laughed at their good fortune and the sound of laughter echoed from concrete walls that had heard no human voice for so many silent years.

"Let's get the others," Tasha said.

Moving in could not really happen until the doorway was totally cleared of earth and stones. This was accomplished by filling packs and passing them along a chain of willing hands until the earth was tipped out where it would be in no one's way.

Jemma stood by and when the last of the heavy dirt was gone, she swept the doorway clean of dust.

"Let's keep it this way," she said.

Some of the younger ones frowned.

Jemma noticed. "Do as you're told, or you won't get any more of my biscuits."

"Okay."

The far reaches of the shelter – the tiers farthest from the door – were in darkness and not desirable, but the tiers on either side of the door and to the right and left of the square floor were occupied as the afternoon progressed.

As people moved into the new home, Mangrove noticed that they chose for their sleeping places much the same spots as those they had occupied in Homecave. In these personal spaces they would keep belongings such as food bowls, backpacks and weapons, clothing and furs. The stuff of each member of the clan was placed just as it had been in Homecave. Neighbours then, were neighbours again.

We are creatures of habit, he thought, and smiled to himself. He and Snotty were no different. They had made their sleeping places alongside each other, exactly as they had been in the old days.

There was another reason for Mangrove to smile. One sleeping place was not in its Homecave position. Dumperty, now a Forager, had moved to be close to him and Snotty.

The bunker took on a lived-in air. Belle and Zita, with Hock's help, set up a fireplace in the centre of the floor and mounted the cooking pot on stones. To check the way smoke would behave, Belle kindled a fire. Mangrove and Snotty stood nearby watching what would happen.

Smoke spiralled upward, readily rising on the column of heat from the fire until, as Manny had suspected, the smoke drifted through slits high in the concrete walls, slits put there for the purpose of ventilation. He watched the way the fire burned, appreciating that the ancients had constructed their safe house very well.

Light from the fire flickered on the walls of the new home.

Snotty was looking at the doorway, almost a tunnel so thick was the wall. "You know, Manny, if it comes to it, if we are attacked I mean, we can easily defend ourselves here."

Mangrove nodded, not quite convinced but thinking that Snotty might be right. Marks and indentations in the walls either side of the entrance suggested that a door, something large and much heavier than those they had seen in the huts inside the hollow mountain, had once been used to close the opening when all were safe inside. Even without the door Manny agreed that the passage would give defenders the advantage. He had no doubt that one day it would be put to the test.

"The Trats *will* come after us, Snotty. *And* the dragons."

"I reckon we've got away from them, but if they follow, there could be no better place than this to show them who's boss." Snotty was grinning.

Mangrove sensed that Snotty was almost wishing for a showdown with their enemies. "I hope you're right."

"Don't worry. Nothing can touch us here. We'll be sweet."

Mangrove smiled at Snotty's confidence. "A safe haven, huh?"

"It is. Nothing alive could break through those walls and nothing can come through this entrance if we don't want it. Yeah, it's a safe haven."

Well, from now on, Mangrove thought, this is our safe house. He walked to where Tasha was preparing her sleeping place. "We have to give our new home a name."

"Yes."

"How about Safe Haven?"

Tasha repeated the name. "Hmm, or maybe just Haven? Haven has a nice sound."

"Suits me."

Cloud who was nearby heard the word and called to others. Everyone was happy with the name. It had a fine ring to it, a good omen for the future.

Tasha called for quiet. The safety of Haven could never be guaranteed even if the entrance gave advantage to the clan when under attack.

"We must gather brushwood and store it inside. If the Trats come, we may need to keep fires burning for a long time so let's be well prepared."

For the next few hours the work of gathering fuel went on. Fire would be the means to hold back an enemy. Fire would be for the clan what the moat and drawbridge were for the knights and dukes of the era known as the Middle Ages. Fire would give the besieged clan time; time to think and to plan a counter offensive.

Excused from searching and gathering, Dumperty was busy ramming pegs into the ground about thirty metres from the entrance. Satisfied that they would hold, he tethered Bucky and the cow where they could graze. The calf stayed close to her mother, occasionally nibbling grass, but more interested in nudging the cow's udders for milk.

Schmucky was running about, trying to get the calf to play, making high pitched puppy barks and often falling over. As the serious work of preparation against a possible disaster went on around them, the young animals played.

Tasha did not stop moving, carrying loads to dump them within Haven. She laughed at the antics of Schmucky and thought how contradictory the scene was. That's our life, she mused, always the mixture of life happily going on while a terrible threat hangs over us. And she wondered if that would ever change.

When the piles of wood, and anything that would burn, were judged to be sufficient, Tasha, Cloud, Snotty and Mangrove came out into the sunshine. Schmucky ran to them. Tasha lifted the pup and held him in her arms. She looked at the creek. Already water was receding from its high point.

"Let's walk a bit."

Walking on grass that had not long before been submerged by floodwater, the four chatted about their good fortune in finding Haven.

Snotty interrupted, suddenly holding up his hand. "Look."

Ahead of them was what remained of a vomit ball. It no longer had the characteristic shape. Rain and water from the swollen creek had broken down the slime that held the ball together, but the indigestible bits that had been ejected from a Komodo's stomach had not washed away. They lay spread on the grass. Hooves, teeth, coarse hair, a knee bone, were easily recognisable. At some time a Komodo had eaten a horse.

"Horses must roam all over these valleys," Snotty said.

"Yes." Mangrove was examining part of a jaw bone with two teeth attached. "So must the dragons. I told you."

Snotty looked up and down the valley, seeing only the waters of the creek, and the trees with splashes of colour in their branches.

"Well, there aren't any dragons here now." He pointed to the trees. "How about we take a closer look?"

"Okay," Tasha said. She put Schmucky down and he ran back to Dumperty.

With the peak of the flood now passed, the colourfully spotted trees were no longer standing in water. As the four got nearer to them, the colours became more vibrant and took on definite shape.

Snotty narrowed his eyes, trying to better focus. "Are they some sort of nut?"

Mangrove shook his head. "Too big. Maybe they're gourds like the ones growing in Kaldor."

Getting closer still, it became apparent that the rich shades of red and yellow, even green tinged with yellow, were globes. They hung from branches as solid, round balls of colour.

"What are they?" Snotty was curious.

Impatient to find out, he climbed among branches with spikes that caught at his tunic and scratched his bare skin. He pushed aside dark green leaves and took hold of a globe of red and yellow tones. Warmed by the sun, round and smooth to his touch, the globe was firm and yet with a softness. Snotty tossed the globe to Manny. He found more and dropped them to Tasha and Cloud. With one in his pocket, he climbed down.

Tasha held the globe to her nose and sniffed. "Hmm."

Perfume tantalised her senses. She picked at the globe with her thumb and saw that it had a thin outer layer. Fluid ran over her fingers. Tasha sniffed again, the others watching her. The perfume came to them.

"Weird," Snotty said.

Tasha licked her fingers, looked at the globe and bit into it. Sweet juice flooded her mouth. She chewed yellow flesh, swallowed and chewed with juice running down her chin. Tasha ate her first peach until the flesh was gone and she held a rough stone in her hand.

The others saw the delight in Tasha's eyes and they too bit into the peaches they held. When those peaches were eaten, Snotty climbed the tree again. He, Tasha, Cloud and Mangrove ate peaches until their stomachs would take no more. Stuffed with fruit, they sat in the sun and looked with wonder at the trees around them.

If by some magic means they had they been able to travel into the past, Tasha, Cloud and the boys would have seen that in the Good Times farmers had planted orchards in the valley. Rows of peaches and pear trees, apricots and oranges, apples, plums, all had been cared for, watered from the creek and carefully pruned. When the fruit was ripe, crops were stripped from the trees and the cycle of care begun again.

Abandoned, left without farmers to tend them, the trees unpruned grew in wild shapes. Over the years, old trees died, but fruit that had dropped to the ground sent down roots and grew to bear peach or pear or plum. The fences that had surrounded the orchards mouldered away and the rows planted in parallel lost their orderliness to spread at random.

With the passing of centuries the untouched trees became less productive. They no longer bore as much fruit and what did grow became smaller, but for the young people, who had never tasted the like of it, who had never imagined that such a thing as a fruit tree existed, the peaches they had eaten were a taste of paradise.

The Foragers with bellies full sprawled on the ground. The warm weight of the sun pressed down on them. Their eyelids drooped and in a haze of contentment they thought only of the newfound riches.

Cloud's cry shattered the quiet of the sleepy afternoon.

"What is it, Cloud?" Tasha sat beside the girl and held her hand. Cloud was staring into the distance. "Cloud?"

But Tasha's questions went unheard. Cloud was trembling, tiny sounds coming from her throat, the sort of sounds she might make if she were in peril. Tasha tried to calm her. The sun was shining brightly, water burbled in the creek nearby. There was nothing to fear. But Tasha and the boys looking on knew that strange things could enter Cloud's mind.

Cloud's grip tightened on Tasha's hand. Her lips moved as if she was groping for words and then the words came, clear enough for all to hear. "Past and present come and go, but past is future even so, future's past we'll come to know."

Snotty put his face close to Cloud's, asking her what meaning they should put to the words, that none of what she had said made sense. Cloud did not respond. Her eyes closed and she fainted away.

"Manny, get some water for her," Tasha said and as Mangrove ran to the creek, Tasha cradled Cloud in her arms.

With water dabbed on her cheeks and forehead, Cloud eyes opened. She blinked a few times, as if she had been on a journey and unaware of where she was.

"It's okay, Cloud." Tasha stroked the girl's hair and saw understanding return.

Snotty came close again. "What does it mean, Cloud?"

"Don't, Snotty." Mangrove smiled reassuringly at Cloud. "Cloud sees these things in her mind. They may be real. They may be imagined. In time we'll come to know which. Until then..."

"Yeah, okay." It's true, Snotty thought. That's the way it always is with Cloud.

Chapter 14

From the top of the ridge Dram saw the creek. Hot, hungry, thirsty, she tried to run. Weak, dehydrated, Dram was a caricature of a human being. Her legs seemed to be filleted, boneless legs that had lost their purpose. They bent in odd directions, joints folding contrary to the way they should, unable to support her weight. Dram stumbled a crazy meandering path to the stream.

Her first thought was to throw herself into the water, to feel it flow cool around her skin and through her hair. She would open her mouth and let water run down her throat, then she would use her bow to provide the meal she craved.

The Torterat ran with her. He, no different from Dram, was driven by hunger and thirst.

Like allies, not enemies, they lay in the water, cooling and drinking.

A shadow flitted along the surface of the creek. For one brief moment Dram felt it pass over her then it was gone. Dram turned on to her back, resting on river stones, gazing upward, looking for the cloud. She found no cloud. Rising on thermals in the baked and faded blue, were raptors, three of them, spiralling into the sun, now and then blotting it out to cast a shadow. Dram watched them soar higher until they became small specks. She rose from the water. Now she would eat.

With an arrow fitted to her bow, Dram stepped slowly, deliberately, like some wading bird, along the bank of the creek.

She scanned the water for fish. The first she saw was lazily moving its fins, holding steady against the gentle current. Dram fired. The fish arched and quivered in the rigor of death. Dram lifted the arrow with fish impaled, and bit into twitching flesh. She took a second bite, juggled bones with her tongue and spat them out as she eased the arrow from the wound and threw the now disfigured fish to the Torterat. He gobbled it down. She shot another, gutted it and ate.

As the Torterat watched, Dram shot fish after fish, piling them on the bank. Every now and then she would take her eyes from the water to look at the rocky outcrop where Biscetti had shot the goat. With a stock of smoked fish and, if she was lucky, dried goat meat, Dram hoped to be able to feed herself during the days to come.

From their height, almost invisible to Dram had she bothered to look again, raptors were switching focus. In their bird eyes, lenses that gave wide perspective were exchanged for telescopic. The broad view of all that lay below was no longer needed, replacing it in close up was Dram and fish and Torterat. The raptors peeled away from the column of heated air and began a slow controlled descent.

Dram counted fish. Ten lay on the bank. She estimated that most were a kilogram in weight. Perhaps two or three were half as big again. The number of fish was short of what Dram needed and the Trat had pulled one aside, busily eating. Dram didn't care. Plenty more could be taken from the creek.

The arrow struck again. Dram pulled the shaft free and looked toward the outcrop. A small goat, just a kid, was climbing daintily, nibbling at greenery that had taken root in cracks in the rocks. Small as it was, the kid would be tender. Dram could almost smell goat meat roasting on the spit. She swallowed. Her mouth was watering.

The little goat, alone, inexperienced, had his head down, tugging at plants, chewing as he took another step to another sprig of green.

Dram waded across the creek, never taking her eyes from the goat, an arrow loose on her bowstring. Once on the far side she stalked the unsuspecting animal, needing to be closer before she could fire. A movement distracted her. Above the kid a python was winding between rocks. Dram had no knowledge of snakes. She could not name the creature that slithered so smoothly around and over whatever was in his way, but she recognised the python's purpose. Its eyes were fixed on the feeding kid.

"No." Dram softly mouthed the word.

In her mind she was shouting *He's mine, he's mine*. But the python was also silent, part of his thick body in the air above the kid. The flat triangular head held steady. Dram watched the python sliding closer, and saw muscle ripple under the camouflage of browns and yellows and black of satin snakeskin. The python was defying gravity. He should have fallen so much of the great tube of his body was in mid-air, his head a metre from the kid.

Dram looked for reason and for the first time saw the full length of the snake, his body coiled around rocks, all of it sliding forward like a stream, yet never losing grip.

In the air above the kid, the python's body kinked and folded on itself like a spring. As Dram watched the snake struck without warning. She scarcely saw the kink unfold. She saw the flat head flash like lightning, jaws wide, and the goat caught between fangs. Then flowing from above, the python's body wrapped around the goat. Dram heard the piteous bleat, heard the goat's cry strangled as pressure squeezed his life away. Head first, the goat was swallowed by the snake.

No, Dram thought, not swallowed, the snake was moving his body over the kid. She could see the outline of the body within the snake. The body wasn't moving. The python was inching forward, enveloping the goat, bringing his stomach to *it*.

Dram began to run. The goat was rightfully hers. She could see its bulk outlined quite clearly inside the snake, still whole, still untouched. Dram climbed, climbing until she stood above the rock ledge where the python with convulsive movements was dragging himself like a stocking over the goat. She pulled on the bowstring, the bow arching under tension. Dram aimed and heard the sharp twang as the bowstring sent the arrow on its way.

The flint tip of the arrow went straight through the flat head, taking most of the snake's brain as it went. The python coiled upon itself, rolling and rolling yet going nowhere.

Dram watched until the coiling ceased. She lowered herself to the ledge, took her knife and sliced open the belly of the snake. The kid lay as if asleep. Dram held a leg and drew it from its snake-gut cocoon.

"Yay." She held the little goat high. He was hers.

Happy with her kill, engrossed in the prize now in her hands, Dram was unaware that the python had not been alone. Sliding soundlessly among the rocks – the very rocks where Dram had recently stood and fired to kill – the python's mate had witnessed his death. The big snake did not mourn. She had no urge to avenge the mate whose head had been torn apart by the arrow and who had been ripped open by a flint blade. The python could see and smell the goat that Dram was holding with such triumph. The snake wanted the goat. To get it she knew that she must first get rid of Dram.

Wanting praise for her achievement, Dram shouted to the Torterat and holding the goat above her head, waved the body for him to see. The mutant rat looked up briefly before resuming his eating. A number of the fish were already gone.

Covering the ground without a sound, the female python aimed to come at Dram from behind. Moving quickly, taking an indirect route that would put her within striking distance, the snake lowered herself to be on the same ledge. She came closer, moving with silent stealth, her raised head weaving with the motion of her body.

In ignorance of what was happening, Dram shouldered her bow and prepared to go. She heard nothing. The blow hit her back with such force that she was knocked down. As she fell, she saw arrows scatter about, spilled from their quiver. The bow flew from her shoulder to lie useless on the ground.

A heavy weight held Dram flat to the rock. Questions flashed in her mind: what had hit her? What was pressing her down? In a split second she knew. Satin skin was winding around her.

Patterns of olive-brown and black and yellow were tightening like a vice to squeeze her chest. Dram screamed, screamed again, hoping to bring the Torterat to her aid, the picture of the kid in her mind, its cry choked off.

The quiver, still strapped to her back, had one lone arrow remaining. Dram heard the quiver crush under the pressure that was building. She could feel her ribs constricting, pressing in on her lungs. One last strangled yelp was forced from her throat.

The Torterat interrupted his eating, to look toward the noise. He did not see the strangling of one human being. He saw the girl being taken from him, saw the end of his plan for extinguishing all human life. Dram, the hostage for whom he had expended so much effort and from whom information would be extracted, was about to die.

The Torterat crossed the creek and ran to her, emitting high pitched screeches that pierced the air, bounced from the faces of rocks and rang in the ears of the snake.

Glittering eyes saw the Torterat. Coloured patterns wound around Dram, a corkscrew of pressure crushing her, never ceasing, continually increasing.

A darkening film passed across Dram's eyes. She knew that Endless Night was approaching. Her hand reached for her knife and stabbed and stabbed at the coils squeezing her life away. Blood spurted to wet her face, an insignificant squirt that meant nothing to the python. The pressure increased. Dram used the blade to saw at python skin, to cut through black and yellow and slice at python flesh. Her efforts were futile. The black curtain of Endless Night began to enfold her.

The Torterat was in front of the snake. He moved like a dancer, tempting, goading. The glittering eyes followed the movements, gave no inkling until in a lightning flash, the broad, flat head struck, jaws wide, for the Torterat's throat.

The Trat skipped to one side, leapt high and from behind seized the back of the python's head. Torterat teeth sank deep, probing for the spinal column.

In a wild, erratic way, the snake twisted and turned, uncoiled, coiled again, thrashing on rock to rid herself of her attacker. For one short moment Dram was able to fill her lungs, thought that she was free and was then wrapped again in the compression of the snake's embrace.

Dram's knife was still in her hand, frozen in a grip of fear. She plunged the blade into the patterned coils that held her tight. *Somewhere there must be a heart.*

The snake was rolling, Dram thrusting the knife over and over again, the Torterat being banged to the rock, not letting go, sharp teeth digging deeper. Screaming, screeching, the thump of bodies hitting rock: all mixed with a dreadful hissing. Human, mutant rat, python, each was fighting for life.

Dram struck at the snake, sinking the blade to its hilt. She gasped for air and drove the knife in again. Great coils squeezed her hard. Dram swung the blade backhand, driving it with all the force she could muster, aiming higher toward the snake's head, seeing the blade go into the paler markings of underbelly. She felt the tremor that shook the snake, felt coils grip her more tightly, felt them relax so that she could breathe freely again. Blood was pulsing from the python's ruptured heart, running over Dram's hand and down her arm. She withdrew the knife and pushed at the windings of black and yellow and olive until she could step from them. She looked at the Torterat lying with his teeth still sunk into the snake. The Trat's eyes were closed. Dram thought that the bashing he had suffered had killed him, but the eyes opened and the Trat stood and snarled at her.

Crushed in the wild melee, the small body of the goat lay under the length of the snake.

Dram held her aching ribs. She coughed, grimaced with pain and examined the dead animals. She coughed again and rubbed gently through her tunic at bruises on her chest. Hurting as she was, Dram managed a smile. The goat was hers again and the two snakes would provide many, many meals. Her eyes travelled along the length of the pythons, the annoying thought intruding that she would never be able to carry so much meat. *Well, better too much than too little.*

The Torterat was screeching. She turned to him. He was facing her, but looking above and beyond her, his cries of alarm continuing shrill and loud. Dram twisted to see what was causing his concern. The raptor was freefalling, wings tucked in a dive, angled straight at her. Dram stared, disbelieving. She watched the raptor thrust his legs forward, claws extended. The bird of prey was just four metres away, a fast moving projectile about to slam into her.

Dram threw herself to the ground. As she went down, claws tangled in her hair, pulling out hanks as the bird went by. Dram screamed with pain, the raptor crying in frustration at missing his catch. She watched the bird begin to climb, wings expanding, contracting, pumping the air. He was gaining height rapidly, but other raptors had seen his failure. One was already intent on Dram.

Automatically, Dram's left shoulder dropped to un-sling her bow, her right hand reaching behind her head for an arrow. The bow did not slip from her shoulder. It lay where it had fallen when the python had struck her. Her hand felt the damaged quiver and the single arrow. She tugged at the arrow. A broken feathered shaft came free, the flint head no longer attached. She hurled the useless thing to the ground.

A spasm shook Dram, the chill draught of fear that she was unarmed. She looked upward. The second raptor was coming for her, wings folded, streamlined to perfection, dropping from the sky as if made of stone. Dram glanced at her bow, too far from where she stood, no time to get to it. She bellowed in anguish at the cruelty of being alone and about to die. Dram wanted to live. Without taking her eyes off the bird she bent and felt for a stone, anything that she might throw at the raptor in one last defiant act that might save her life. Her fingers scraped at bare rock and found no stones. She touched the broken shaft and rose with it in her hand, the bird closing on her. She watched it coming, saw death and threw.

The feathered shaft turned end over end, a Catherine-wheel of colour and sound, a harmless stick. But the raptor had been put off, swerved from the path of the shaft and making the same harsh cries of frustration, flapped away.

Dram ran for the bow, held it while she gathered arrows from the ground and placed them at her feet. She looked up to check on the raptor that had made the first attack. Two hundred metres above, it was flying in tight circles, head down, looking at her. In a moment that changed. Dram saw the wings fold, saw the bird transformed into a deadly projectile.

The final act of life and death played out: the bird falling from the sky, Dram fitting an arrow, raising the bow, drawing back the string, the bow bending, energy building, the raptor a meteor heading for Dram.

Each had eyes fixed on the other. Dram held the bow steady, the bowstring almost at full draw. She waited; one foot planted back a little to provide balance. The bird was nearly upon her, finally angling to hit with talons extended. Dram pulled hard on the bowstring, aimed, held the bird in her sights and released.

Raptor and arrow met in mid-flight, each travelling immensely fast so that the flint arrowhead shattered the raptor's breastbone. So hard was the impact that the flint itself broke into pieces and shrapnel-like inflicted further wounds, piercing the bird's heart, puncturing its lungs. The raptor died instantly, hit the ground and skidded to a stop. Feathers fluttered down to lie beside the body.

Dram stood over the bird and saw strands of her own hair caught in its claws. She bent, took a feather from the ground and stuck it behind an ear. Hair for a feather, a feather for hair; the score was evened.

She looked upward. Where there had once been three raptors there were now two. The birds had rejoined the thermal, spiralling against the faded blue of an infinitely distant sky. One of the birds Dram had already met. The other had seen how the human behaved. He had his head down, watching Dram and the Torterat.

They'll come again, Dram thought. They're just biding their time.

It worried her that the raptors could fall on her without warning. They would come from above. She would not see them and would not hear them. The fact was that Manny had been attacked and that without Snotty and the ancient poster that she and Snotty had seen in the military bunker, Manny would have died.

Dram gazed at the parched, brown earth, at the hills and ridges of rock over which she still had to travel. The raptors would follow her and the Trat. If they hit in a surprise attack there would be no Snotty to revive her. For an awful moment she pictured the mummified figures in the bunker, the leathered skin of shrunken faces, dark hands with bony fingers that poked from the sleeves of ancient military uniforms. She feared that lying lifeless on the baked earth she would be like them, a blackened, shrivelled figure, but then realised that it would not be like that at all. The raptors would tear at her flesh, eating everything until she was just a skeleton, her bones bleaching in the sun.

Dram looked again at the high soaring raptors. For the time being she appeared to be safe. She tried to console herself with the possibility that the birds feared a bow and arrow in her hands. They had seen what she could do!

Whatever the truth was, she expected that she would find out within the next few days. It would take her that long to smoke the meat on which she would depend during the coming journey. If ever she was to make it, that is.

Dram looked at the Torterat. *His body must hurt. Mine does.* The Torterat was looking back at her. He hadn't moved since warning Dram of the raptor attack. She was grateful. The Trat had also come to her aid when the python had held her. *If he hadn't done that I'd now be in Endless Night. Trats are strange, but he must like me.*

She could not have been more wrong, but the thought consoled her.

Work stared Dram in the face. She squared her shoulders and breathed deeply. The fish lying on the bank had to be smoked and more caught. Kindling had to be brought from her pack across the creek and firewood picked up from wherever she could find it. The goat she decided would be a treat. She would roast it. At least one of the pythons had to be cut into medallions of big, flat steaks that would smoke easily. Some of the steaks, she thought, could be dried in the sun.

Throughout the afternoon, Dram worked hard at her tasks. To get the Trat to share in the workload, she went through the charade of fetching wood, using her hands and facial expressions to indicate what he should do. To some extent she was successful. The Torterat did a little, but mostly he watched.

The physical labour was repetitive, a cycle of cutting, drying and smoking, topping up the fire with wood, adding green leaves to thicken the smoke – the same greenery that had attracted the goat. Such work required little thought. Dram had time for introspection and yet again she dwelt on her actions when under stress.

She questioned why she had first submitted to the Torterat. Twice she could've killed him with an arrow and didn't, but against the raptors she had finally stood firm with deadly effect. Dram shook her head, not understanding the contradictions in her behaviour. Months before, she had run from the monster that had come out of the lake, but when the monster had attacked Tasha, she, Dram had driven it off with fire. It was a puzzle for Dram. At times she had courage, on other occasions fear filled her with cowardice. Why am I like that?

She lived again the moments when Tasha had told her to thrust the flaming branch at the crocodile. Did I need her to command me, to be by my side and give me confidence? "I don't know," Dram muttered the words, thinking of being on the ledge with Manny and Snotty, terrified that she would fall. The boys had been right beside her. They had tried to allay her fear and failed. "What is it with me?"

The thinking, the questioning, did not interrupt her work. The Torterat occasionally scouted for wood and dragged a broken branch to the fire, Dram scarcely noticed, totally involved in preparing provisions and thinking about herself.

There *were* times when she had been too scared to act. Tasha and Biscetti had seen her frozen with fear. They had accused her and she had denied it, but Dram knew that it was true. Dram sighed. There had been so many incidents in her life when she had been overcome by fear. I'm not like Tasha. She's probably just as scared as I am, but Tasha never flinches from doing what's right because she sees it as her duty. And I'm not like Snotty. He's never afraid, not of Trats, not of dragons, not of anything. Manny sees dangers. Manny likes to know what he's up against before he makes a decision. He calculates the odds and does the wise thing, but he's different from me. Even Biscetti, who admits to being frightened, she doesn't back off when it matters.

Dram saw herself as a good Forager, one of the best. I'm strong, I'm big and I shoot so well. I do my share, maybe more than my share. Those other times when I wanted to run away... She sighed again and it dawned on her that bravery was not part of her character. On many measures she was equal to or better than other Foragers and they acknowledged her ability. There were times, even if few and far between, when she could confront danger, but she had to admit that in most ugly situations she was usually overcome by fear.

"That's the way I am." Dram spoke aloud, making the admission for the first time in her life and she saw the irony of speaking to meat that had been cut from a python she had fought to the death. "And I can't change what I am."

She put down her knife and sniffed. Fat was dripping from the kid on the spit. The smell of roasting goat filled the air. Dram carved a slice from the rump and put it in her mouth. She closed her eyes and chewed at the hot flesh. The flavour was all that she had imagined it would be.

The Torterat screeched, ran to Dram and bared his teeth. She carved another slice and tossed it to him. Over the next hour they gorged on roasted goat meat.

For the next two days, Dram carried out the smoking and drying of python flesh, caught more fish and smoked them too. The chores were almost a holiday, a break from the grinding labour of climbing and descending ridges, but late in the afternoon of the second day, the reality of what lay ahead could not be avoided. If she was being taken all the way to Kaldor, sand dunes and the bleak flatness of the stony desert would take weeks to cross.

Dram packed the now shrunken fish into her pack. Alongside them, she laid dried discs of snake. She reckoned that by rationing what she and the Trat ate each day, the food would probably last the journey. Tired, hot, Dram put the last of the snake in the pack and walked to the creek. Lying in the cool water she washed smoke from her hair and grease from her fingers. The creek rippled by, soothing heated skin, lulling Dram with gentle, watery sounds. She laid her head on a river stone and closed her eyes.

High above a raptor watched. From the time he had witnessed Dram's arrow take the life of the first python, the raptor had followed her every movement. He had seen the female python die and seen Dram kill his own brother. These experiences had made the raptor wary of the human.

The big bird spiralled downward, adjusting his focus, seeing Dram lying with eyes closed, seeing the Torterat resting in the shade of a rock, but the centre of the raptor's attention was the pack so carefully filled with food.

Still high, with wings stretched wide, the bird banked to the west, gradually losing altitude. He flew away from Dram and the Torterat, but with his head turned, always intent on what they were doing. When he judged that he was in a position to attack, the raptor banked again. With the sun behind him, he began the long glide that would take him to his target. The upturned flight feathers at the end of the raptor's wings ruffled. They were the only indicator that the bird was moving fast, not plummeting to hit and break the back of his prey, but a carefully controlled descent that would take him to the stash of food.

Like an osprey plucking a fish from a lake, the raptor without pause in flight would dig talons into the pack and carry it away; gone before the human and the mutant rat were aware of what had happened.

Dram dozed in the water. The Torterat looked at her and gazed around. The raptor held to his glide path. One hundred and twenty metres above the ground, he was closing fast on his objective.

The earth, baked all day by the sun, radiated heat to warm the air. At sixty metres the raptor flew into the heated, rising air.

The extra lift took the bird by surprise. He fluttered wings to correct his course, and dropped lower again.

Stealth was lost. The movement roused the Torterat. He saw the raptor closing on the pack and ran to it.

Strong legs thrust forward, the bird readied to snatch the food. With a loud, angry screech, the Torterat leapt at the raptor. Talons gripped the pack as the bodies of bird and mutant rat clashed together. In a jumble of stretched wings and creamy fur and back pack, the animals tumbled along the stony earth. The raptor slashed with his great curved beak, tearing at fur and flesh. The Torterat snapped at feathers, digging sharp teeth into wings, into any part of the bird's body on which his jaws could fasten. Fish and snake meat scattered across the ground. Bird cries and Torterat screeches filled the air. Fur and feathers flew from the tumbling creatures and dust rose over and around their brutal fighting.

Jolted awake by the racket, Dram sat up, water dripping from her hair. It took her a moment to understand what was happening. She could see the animals locked together, the raptor's talons sunk into the Torterat, gripping hard so that he could strike with his beak. The animals were rolling. At times the raptor held the Torterat down and appeared to be winning the battle. Then that superiority vanished. The mutant rat suddenly above, raking at the bird with his claws, tearing feathers free so that in a quick flash Dram saw naked skin and blood running from the raptor.

From the melee came the harsh cries of attack and of pain, dirt and stones and dust scattering all around.

Dram left the creek and with her bow ran toward the confusion. Once close, she saw the meat and fish that had been flung from her pack, the clue that let her put together what had happened. *Yeah, the raptor must have tried to pinch the food. Good one, Trat.* Dram fitted an arrow to her bow, shifting around the tumbling bodies, stepping back or to the side as they came too close. She needed the animals to be still for a moment.

The fighting continued, a wild screaming, screeching, crying for blood.

Dram drew back the string of her bow. C'mon, she thought, looking for the chance to shoot. But shoot what? The questions worried at Dram. What was she to do? She could shoot the Trat. She could shoot the raptor. Without risk to herself she could put an arrow through both. The way would be open for her to repack the supplies and make her way back to the clan.

Dram thought how easy it would be, but the idea of freedom was pushed aside. If she killed the Trat she would be alone, and to retrace her steps across the ridges would expose her to raptors and to pythons and to whatever other danger. Should any one of them attack, there would be no Trat to come to her assistance.

The raptor had the Torterat pinned to the ground, jabbing at the mutant rat's eyes. Thoughts streamed in Dram's head: the blinded Trat would be useless to her; without him the python would have squeezed life from her; did she owe him the favour in return? In contradiction, the Trat was her master, a tyrant forcing her into what could be permanent captivity. Her head filled with the fear of loneliness and the need for protection. In this vortex of conflicting emotion, Dram's forearm flexed exerting more force on the bowstring. She let the arrow fly.

Chapter 15

Mangrove held the torch in the communal fire. To explore the dark recesses of Haven, their new home, he needed light. The torch flamed and he held it above his head and forward. Shadows danced on the floor and on the walls of the sleeping platforms. Tasha stood behind Mangrove. They were alone in the silence of the atrium, the great space that towered above and all about them. Everyone else had gone with Snotty to see the marvel of fruit trees and to eat the delicacies he had described.

"That's better." Mangrove moved the flame and light arced high on the wall ahead. He and Tasha walked toward the pale patch, watching it grow as they approached.

The fourth side of the square was now visible. Its tiers in a way completing the pattern of the other three sides, yet there were more platforms rising higher.

"It's different, Tasha. I wonder why?"

They climbed the steps to the first platform and saw that not only were there more tiers, they were wider and higher than those that the clan now occupied.

"Bring the torch closer, Manny." Tasha was at the wall of the second tier, peering at a metal plaque with marks inscribed on it. She ran her hands over the metal, feeling the grooves that had been etched into it.

Mangrove held the flame so that the inscriptions could be clearly seen. Line after line of print had been worked into the plaque, which shone silver and brightly reflected the light into the dimness of the immense chamber. Unable to read or write, the words meant nothing to Tasha and Manny. However, from their experience in the hollow mountain, they were able to guess that the grooves did have meaning. The ancients had left a message for those that might one day follow.

Tasha walked slowly, keeping her hand on the shiny metal plate, looking with wonder at the inscription, wishing that the strange marks would make some sense to her. She stopped. The writing had come to an end. The metal plaque now bore illustrations.

Mangrove held the flame close to the drawings, moving the torch up and down, trying to make out what they intended to convey, but hindered by the limited light. The pictures, which were cartoons etched with simple lines in the metal, extended for quite a way on the wall.

"It's no good, Manny. We really need to see the whole lot and one torch isn't enough."

"Yeah." Mangrove walked a little way, the pool of light moving across the illustrations. "Remember when we were in the mountain carved by ghosts?"

"Who could forget that?"

"Well the ancients left the moving pictures for someone to see. They showed us how the Good Times came to an end. They knew they were doomed, but they left the record and we found it. In the pictures we saw the sea rising and then ice creeping over the earth." Mangrove walked back, still intent on the cartoons. "I think that wherever they were in the world, the ancients knew that their end was coming. These marks, these pictures, have been left to tell us something."

"But, Manny, we can't understand what they say."

"Maybe we can work it out."

"I don't know."

But Tasha looked at Mangrove, thinking that he would have gone to Endless Night if Snotty had not seen the diagrams in the bunker in Kaldor. Snotty had understood the message they were conveying and from memory had followed the instructions to bring Manny back to life.

She smiled at him. "We can try."

"Yeah. When the others come back we'll really light up this wall. Then we might get lucky."

Their stomachs stretched from eating peaches and plums, packs laden with fruit, the clan walked home, laughing and joking. The flood waters had receded, run with the creek and gone to sea. The creek itself was again within its banks and flowing gently. For the clan, life had taken another turn. They had a new home and found a wonderful food that grew on trees. Somewhere not too far away the creek would meet the ocean and there would be fish and pipis for the taking. Even better, the creek was not tidal. Wherever and however it emptied into the sea, salt water was not flowing back. Fresh water ran by their door. All were agreed: the clan had everything it could possibly need.

Biscetti burped and those around her laughed. "Sorry," she grinned. "Hey, look. Tasha and Manny are waving to us."

Tasha and Mangrove were waiting at the doorway to Haven.

"We've found something," Mangrove said. "Something the ancients left."

Curious to see what Manny was talking about, Biscetti, Snotty and Belle prepared torches. Others did the same. The great atrium of Haven glowed with light as Mangrove led them all to the tiers rising at the back wall.

The metal plate shone. The letters were fully visible, yet with no one able to read them, remained as mute as they had been during the millennia they had rested in darkness.

Cloud cleaned her glasses, came to the wall and looked closely at the inscription. She touched the grooves as Tasha had done, but at the end of it shook her head. Deep in her sub-conscious Cloud had words for things never previously seen, but that gift did not extend to the written word.

Baffled, she said, "I don't know what the marks are saying."

"That's okay, Cloud." Tasha touched her gently. "None of us do."

The crowd shuffled on to stand before the etchings. In the glare of so many torches, more detail was visible. The pictures were grouped within panels. Standing in a semi-circle, the clan could see every line of every panel. Mangrove counted the panels. There were twenty-seven. They had been drawn in blocks of nine; three blocks made up of three rows each row having three diagrams or cartoons. Every one of them was numbered. Mangrove had no knowledge of printed numbers, but the ancients had anticipated that whoever finally looked upon the cartoons might be like Mangrove. To make doubly sure that each was examined in strict sequence, an arrow linked one to the next. Provided each cartoon got across its part of the message, by following the arrows full understanding would be gained.

Mangrove called Snotty to join him. "You've seen this sort of stuff before. What do you reckon these pictures are trying to say?"

Snotty spent a little while examining the first of the diagrams. In it were depicted a boy and a girl that Snotty guessed were about his own age. To distinguish male from female, the boy was shown with short hair and the girl with hair to her shoulders. Snotty pointed to the boy and everyone laughed. Every Forager, boy or girl, had hair that fell beyond shoulder length. The ancients had also included the universal signs for male and female beside each figure.

Snotty went to the next cartoon. The figures of boy and girl had been repeated many times.

Manny counted. "Twenty-five girls and twenty-five boys."

"Yeah."

The third cartoon showed boys and girls at play: running, dancing, swimming, obviously healthy.

Snotty nodded and went on. "Hey, look at these, Manny! We know what these pictures are saying."

In the full light, Manny had no difficulty understanding what was drawn. The cartoons from four to eight showed the sea rising, islands lost under the waves, riverbeds empty of water, fields of wheat dead and dying, cities destroyed and finally ice creeping over the globe. The cartoons told the same story as the film in the hollow mountain.

It was just as he had said to Tasha, the ancients in all parts of the world had seen their civilization disintegrating and had recorded it for whoever might still exist, or who one day might visit the earth from another galaxy.

The next drawing was not so easy to understand. The boy and the girl were shown lying in cylinders or capsules. Low on the side of each capsule was a circular fitting. Biscetti made the comment that it looked like the children were resting in ice coffins.

Tasha nodded. "That's what I was thinking."

It was true. The cylinders were that shape, and were open like an ice coffin. A number of machines with dials stood around each capsule. Above the chest of boy and girl, lines had been drawn to indicate that they were breathing. The next cartoon was similar except that masks covered the mouth and nose of the boy and girl. A tube ran from the mask to one of the machines and various tubes were connected from their bodies to other pieces of apparatus.

Snotty touched the figures and shook his head.

"What are they doing to those children?" Tasha was caught up in the drama, upset that she was seeing young people being tortured.

Everyone looking on felt the same emotion. The pictures were revealing something inhuman happening.

"I don't know," Snotty said. He moved to the next cartoon.

The boy and girl lay face up in their capsules, the tubes no longer present. The artist indicating that their chests were now still.

"They've stopped breathing," Mangrove said.

Snotty followed the arrows, moving from drawing to drawing. The story unfolded for all watching. They saw lids being bolted onto each cylinder. Each lid had a transparent window through which could be seen the face of the person inside. Boy and girl lay peacefully, eyes closed.

In succeeding cartoons a tube or hose was connected to the fittings on the side of the capsule. The letter O and an arrow together with curly lines had been etched alongside the hose to indicate that oxygen had been removed from the capsule. To be certain of understanding, the artist had sketched the oxygen atom. None of the chemistry was recognised by Tasha or the others, but the arrow and the icon for wind got across the message that the children, who no longer breathed, now lay in an airless chamber.

Another hose was attached and the arrow and icon reversed. Gas was being pumped into the capsules. The symbol for carbon dioxide and its molecular structure was shown. Again the chemistry was meaningless to the onlookers.

Drawings of a room filled with the human cargo containers were shown: five rows of ten; a total of fifty; half male, half female. Next was a picture of a cylinder with the valve on the side being opened to allow the carbon dioxide, being heavier than air, to escape. Air was shown flowing in to take its place. More pictures showed the capsules being opened by the people they contained. It seemed that whoever found the preserved children had only to open the valve. Once the atmosphere in the cylinder had returned to normal, it appeared that those sealed inside revived and were capable of releasing themselves. A smiling boy and girl stood beside the containers in which they had lain. Each had a drink in one hand and food in the other. From the way the picture was drawn, it was obvious that drinking and eating was a matter of urgency once out of the capsule.

Biscetti laughed. "I reckon you'd be hungry and thirsty if you'd been in that coffin since the end of the Good Times."

Others laughed with her. It was incomprehensible to them that a human could lie without breathing for all that time and still be alive.

The final cartoon showed a handprint set inside a circle that contained etchings of fifty capsules.

"What's this one mean?" Snotty, who had so far kept pace with the story, stood looking at the last of the drawings.

"Well," Tasha said. "The person who drew the pictures went to a lot of trouble to tell us that somewhere there are Foragers in boxes that look a bit like ice coffins. He showed us that they can be brought back to life."

"Yes!" Biscetti was impatient. "But where are they?"

Tasha looked at her sister. "That's what I'm saying. The hand must tell us something."

Mangrove had walked further along the tier, examining the wall as he went. "Here."

The crowd moved to where he stood. A large circle was set into the concrete. All could see that it was the model for the final drawing.

Mangrove placed his hand within the outline that had been etched thousands of years earlier. Neither his palm nor his spread fingers filled the profile of the original adult hand.

He looked to Ingamo. "I think we are meant to press it. You try. Your hands are bigger."

Ingamo shook his head. "No." He stepped from the crowd so that all would hear what he had to say. "We should let these sleeping children be. They come from a different world. They lived in the Good Times. They are not as we are. They will not like it here." Ingamo looked into the faces lit by flickering flames, appealing to them to heed his advice. "I'm old, I've seen more than any of you. To waken the Sleepers will bring trouble. We don't need them. Let them lie in their coffins."

Voices muttered that Ingamo only ever saw the dark side, that so little pleased him and that he was always gloomy.

"You can say those things, but believe me no good can come of this. Let the Sleepers be."

"That would be cruel," Biscetti said.

Belle and others echoed her words, but some in the gathering had been swayed by Ingamo. Whichever side was taken, the young people in the capsules were referred to as *the Sleepers*. Ingamo's label had stuck.

Tasha listened to the arguments, trying to weigh them one against the other, but one thought dominated her mind; the

Camarilla had always believed that they were the only humans on earth. If that were no longer true, if the Sleepers were found and brought back to life, how would that affect her people? Tasha pushed and pulled at the question. She was the Queen of the Camarilla. Would the Sleepers accept her? Would they fit into the tiny society in which every member relied on the other in the battle for existence?

She found no answer.

Snotty had laid his hand in the outline on the wall. It fitted like a hand in a glove that was far too big. He grinned at Tasha. "I could press anyway."

"Let me think," she said.

Tasha looked again at the cartoons. *The Sleepers are just like us.*

Although only line drawings, she saw them as young people who really could be Foragers. Scenes that had played on the screen in the hollow mountain ran through her mind. She and Snotty and the others had been made aware of so much that had happened long ago. They had seen men and women suffering and babies starving, but what the Foragers had looked at were images, not real people. If the Sleepers were woken, the clan would be confronting living flesh and blood. She, Tasha, would be inviting strangers to become part of the clan. Okay, the Sleepers were probably of her own age, but nevertheless strangers would step out of their coffins and out of the past to enter the world of the Camarilla. *What are they like? What would they think of us? What would we think of them?* Tasha frowned, grinding her teeth, thinking of how difficult it might be for the Sleepers and for the clan. *Perhaps Ingamo is right.*

Whether to act or to do nothing was Tasha's dilemma. She thought of the adults who had made the decision to save their children from starvation or a violent death. Those parents had put those they loved into the capsules, entrusting some race in the future to find and release them. Knowing this, wouldn't it be wrong to deny the children a new life?

Tasha imagined herself encapsulated, imagined rows of coffins with transparent windows through which she could see the faces of Biscetti and Manny and Snotty alongside her own. She, all of them, would want life to be given back so that they might work and play and laugh together again.

Tasha looked at her people as they waited to learn what her decision would be. There is really no choice, she thought, and raised her hands for silence.

Speaking firmly, loud enough so that no one missed a word, Tasha put the arguments for and against waking the Sleepers. "All things considered, I think that what we must do is clear."

The gathering stood in silence, waiting.

"We should open the coffins and welcome these people to the clan."

Cheers came from many, but there were some who remained unconvinced.

"Listen to me," Tasha said. "If *you* had been imprisoned for so long in a coffin, what would *your* wish be?"

The expressions on faces changed and heads nodded.

Only Ingamo disagreed. "We'll regret this. No good can come of it."

By his side, Jemma shushed him, but she did so quietly because she too had doubts.

"Okay." Snotty put his hand on the print. "Now, Tasha?"

"Yes."

He pushed, wondering what magic he was about to reveal. Everyone watching moved forward in anticipation.

Nothing happened.

Snotty applied more pressure. He expected the handprint to give and an opening to appear through which he would see the faces of the Sleepers lying within their coffins. No reaction answered the weight of his pushing. Using both hands, one upon the other, he applied all the force he could. There was no response.

Turning to Tasha, Snotty shrugged. The look on his face saying that he had done all he could and asking whether this was what the cartoons intended him to do.

Mangrove saw the question in Snotty's eyes and put his own hands over Snotty's to add more pressure. The result was no different. No movement occurred. No room was revealed. No secret passage opened to lead them to the Sleepers.

"Perhaps the pictures are just drawings, decorations that people made to amuse themselves?" Snotty was asking for answers.

"I don't think so," Mangrove said. "The pictures tell a story. Whoever drew them wanted the Sleepers to be found." He pointed to the final frames. "Look, you can see here how the children can be woken and that they should then be given food and drink."

"Maybe that has happened already." Tasha said. "Maybe they were released ages ago. Someone pressed the handprint, let them out of their coffins and then disaster wiped out everybody; the Sleepers, their rescuers, everybody."

Mangrove nodded. "It's possible. Anyway there's nothing more we can do."

The excitement fizzled away. There would be no meeting with strange, new people. Clan members turned their backs on the story inscribed in the metal plate and went about the business of settling into Haven.

Flashing in the sunlight, Dram's arrow was a tailed comet hurtling through space.

Desperately the Torterat swung his head to avoid the beak hooking at his eyes, his screeches loud with pain and the knowledge that he was losing the battle.

The sound of the speeding arrow was like a quick intake of breath and then came the soft thud as it went through the raptor's throat, the force of the arrow so great that it knocked the raptor backwards. The bird died instantly and fell with talons sunk into Torterat flesh, clinging to his enemy even in death.

Dram put down her bow and as gently as possible removed claws from fur. They might have been fishhooks, so carefully did she extract them. The Torterat bared his teeth, but let her complete the operation. She kicked the raptor aside and left the

Torterat to lie recovering. There were other things she must do. Food for the journey might prove to be insufficient, but it was all that she could carry. Water was the problem.

The remains of pythons lay around Dram. She stood thinking, looking at python tails that slimmed to their ends. *Yes. They'll do.*

The satin skin peeled from flesh that was already beginning to rot. Dram tugged, separated skin from body until she held two snakeskin bags that would serve as bladders.

The last thing Dram did before she and the Torterat set out again, was to fill each skin with water. To provide a handle she ran an arrow through the rim of each. She admired her handiwork. The water bags with patterns of red and black and yellow were very pretty. They soon lost their appeal. Once the trek had recommenced, the skins loaded with water were not things of beauty, but an added burden.

Wounds inflicted by the raptor caused the Torterat to limp. He could not keep up the hurry of previous days. In a way it suited Dram. Her muscles tired, but they did not ache with the same intensity. On the other hand she knew that unless the pace quickened, days would be added to the journey. Her worry was that extra days on the dunes and in the desert would put greater demand on the supplies of food and water.

A further irony tormented Dram. When she hurried, her mouth dried with thirst and food was always on her mind. Somewhere in the middle, she thought, would give the best result, but as the Torterat improved he demanded that she go faster.

A day later, they climbed down through the rocks of the cleft. Dram shuddered. Rows of sand dunes rose up before her and beyond them she knew was the desert. She thought of the opportunity that had offered and wished that she had put an arrow through both Trat and raptor.

The Torterat nipped at Dram's heels. It was too late for wishes.

Chapter 16

Dumperty squatted by the cow and watched milk squirt into the bowl. The cow stood patiently, well used to the routine of twice daily milking. Dumperty rose and whistled for Shmucky. The dog came running to him.

The clan had been two months at Haven, a time during which they had got to know the surrounding countryside. The vaulted chamber of Haven itself and the valley had become home, a place in which they felt secure. As it happened, the clan had arrived in the new land in early summer. As the warm weather continued and certain fruit ripened, the crop was harvested and eaten. When that was gone, another variety came into season. It seemed to the newcomers that there was no end to the bounty provided by the trees that had spread from the ancient orchards. Fish were plentiful in the creek and by following the course of the creek as it wound through hills Foragers could be at the ocean in less than three hours. Food was in abundance. The clan had never before experienced life to be so good.

Dumperty heard his name called. Sitting on the slope above the entrance to Haven, Cloud was waving to him. "There are horses among the fruit trees."

"What are they doing?"

Cloud laughed. "Eating of course."

The horses were enjoying the sweetness of fruit fallen to the ground, or with their heads high, tugging peaches or pears from the branches. From where he stood, Dumperty could not see what was going on. It didn't matter to him. There were horses in the valley. He wanted one and so did Mangrove.

"Manny, Manny." Dumperty ran between the thick walls of the entrance to Haven.

Mangrove, sitting talking to Snotty, looked toward the light and Dumperty running toward him. "What's up?"

"Horses, they're here in the valley."

"Where?"

Dumperty told him.

Mangrove jumped from the platform and turned to look up at Snotty. "Can we take Bucky?"

"Sure, we'll all go."

Bucky was grazing near the cow. Snotty untied the tether from the peg in the ground, looped the rope and slipped it over his head so that it lay like a sash over one shoulder and across his chest.

"C'mon. We can all ride."

"Wait a bit." Mangrove ran to get the vine that Snotty had fashioned into a rope.

With Dumperty and then Mangrove sitting astride behind him, Snotty tapped his heels on Bucky's flanks and urged him to go.

They stopped a hundred metres from the feeding horses.

"Which ones do you want?" Snotty was looking the mob over. There were probably twenty or thirty horses. Some were fully grown, big animals. Others he recognised as yearlings. A few were foals sticking close to their mares.

"Forget the big ones, and the mothers won't let us get close to the babies," Mangrove said.

"Okay." Snotty pointed. "Check them out."

Two identical yearlings were nosing for fruit in the grass. They could have been twins, with coats of light brown, but marked by white mane and white tail. In appearance they resembled the breed the ancients had named Palominos.

"One's a boy," Dumperty said. "The other's a girl."

"Yeah."

The Foragers saw that the boy had a white stripe running down his head from ears to nose. On the head of the female horse, a white star was between her eyes.

The two pale horses were near to each other and as one advanced in his search the other took similar steps as though not wishing to be separated from her twin.

"How about those two? We'll only get one shot at this." Snotty explained that he would walk Bucky slowly toward the mob. "When we're close enough, I'll lasso one, you take the other."

"You make it sound so easy, Snotty." Manny was sceptical.

"How else do we do it?"

Manny shrugged. "Okay."

Sitting between them, Dumperty laughed. "This is so good." He could already see himself riding a golden horse with white mane and tail.

Snotty nudged again with his heels and Bucky began to walk toward the mob.

Not so long ago, Bucky had been one of them as they freewheeled their way around the valleys. Now, with Snotty riding him, Bucky was a different horse, trained and responding to his rider's wishes.

Bucky walked slowly. With deft touches to the horse's neck, Snotty guided him toward the yearlings. The mob went on eating. A horse here or there would turn his eyes to Bucky and the strange sight on his back, but they recognised him as one of their own and went on feeding.

"This is pretty easy," Snotty whispered to the two sitting behind him.

"We haven't got one yet." Mangrove's scepticism remained. The distance was still too great to heave a noose.

Snotty slowed Bucky even more. They had reached the fringe of the wild-grown orchard and could smell the ripened fruit. Snotty let Bucky raise his head to pick a pear from among the branches. The blonde-maned yearlings continued to snuffle at the ground, finding windfalls, overripe and juicy. The rest of the mob paid no attention to Bucky and the Foragers.

"We're nearly there." Snotty lifted the coils of rope over his head. The big noose hung from one hand. Behind him, Mangrove held the looped vine.

Snotty steered Bucky toward the two Palominos. "Ready?"

"Yes."

Rope and vine circled in the air. The long necks with their white manes lifted and liquid, brown eyes turned toward the movement. Mangrove's noose dropped neatly over the head of the colt and tightened.

The second Palomino was a little further away, giving the horse the fraction of time she needed to sway her head. The rope dropped harmlessly to the ground.

Panic sparked the mob. Throughout the orchard horses shied, neighed in fright and rushed away. The air filled with the booming of galloping hooves.

Manny had his hands full. The lassoed yearling had reared. On hind legs he teetered backwards, came down, lowered his head and tried to shake free the noose. Manny held firm.

The Palomino pig-rooted, bucked and reared again. The noose tightened.

Snotty slid from Bucky and with both hands on the vine walked toward the cavorting horse, talking to him in the same tones he had used to quieten Bucky at the river. Disappointed that he had missed with his own throw, Snotty consoled himself that at least Manny had been successful. One horse was better than none. He approached the bucking yearling, whispering, talking him down, letting the horse know that he meant no harm.

"Snotty, look," Dumperty called.

The second Palomino, the female, was standing alone sixty metres distant, watching. As the Foragers looked, the filly took a few steps, coming closer. Snotty glanced that way, but his attention was centred on the horse captured by Manny's vine. Talking didn't seem to be working.

Snotty whistled and Bucky trotted to him. "Good boy."

Manny, with a tight grip on the vine, jumped down. Dumperty followed.

Snotty patted Bucky's rump. "Okay, Bucky, you show this nervous boy how he should behave."

The horse moved close to the Palomino and whinnied. The rearing and bucking ceased. Bucky nuzzled the Palomino. The two rubbed necks, old friends saying hello after some time apart.

Dumperty was watching the second Palomino, every little while she took a few more steps, coming closer all the time. "She wants to be with them."

Dumperty was right. From the moment of her birth – a few minutes after her brother had breathed air for the first time – the Palomino with the star marking on her head had not left his side. She was his double and without him felt alone and vulnerable. Imprinted on her mind from the very beginning was the idea that she was not a single animal, she was one of two, the girl half of brother and sister. They were a pair that could not be split.

The Foragers watched what would happen.

Forty metres separated the female from the two male horses. She whinnied and her twin whinnied back. Bucky too called to her. She took a few tentative steps and then trotted to join her brother and Bucky. In turn the three horses snorted, heads bobbing in ritual greeting and in recognition that all was well.

"What do we do now?" Dumperty looked to Mangrove.

"I think we get back on Bucky and lead the other two to Haven. What do you reckon, Snotty?"

"Sounds good."

In slow and careful motion, not wanting to spook the Palominos, the three mounted Bucky. The tether remained around the neck of the male, Mangrove holding its other end.

Snotty patted Bucky's neck. "Let's go home."

For a moment the female did not move. She watched her brother being led away. He seemed unconcerned. She cantered after him to walk by his shoulder.

The procession of three Foragers and three horses made its way along the bank of the creek. Like Snotty, Mangrove and Dumperty had achieved their ambitions. Each now owned a horse.

"Manny, can I have the girl?"

"Sure, little guy. What are you going to call her?"

"Star."

Mangrove laughed. "That's a great name. I'll call the boy Stripe."

In the warmth of the afternoon, happy with their achievements, the Foragers talked about the wonderful things they would do now that they had horses to ride. The hills, green after all the rain, shone in the sunlight. From the creek the sounds of water running over rocks came tinkling and gurgling. All was at peace.

The tether in Mangrove's hand jerked and tautened, almost pulling him from Bucky. "Hey."

Stripe was straining to get away, his eyes wide, staring at nothing. He whinnied and reared, desperate to shake the halter. Star sidled from him and in blind panic galloped away.

"What's wrong with them?" But Snotty felt the tremors passing through Bucky, so strong that he and Dumperty and Manny were shaken. "Easy, boy, easy," he said.

Then the noise came, noise similar to one they had heard once before. This time it began as a harsh whispering that grew in volume until all around them a roaring filled the air, a roar that had no location, but issued from everywhere, surrounding the boys, pressing upon them as if to crush them.

Mangrove blinked to clear his eyes. The blinking changed nothing. The ground was rippling, rising and falling as though solid earth had dissolved and become an ocean.

Bucky rose on hind legs to become almost vertical.

"Get off him," Snotty yelled.

The three had no choice. They slid across the horse's rump and fell tangled to the heaving ground.

"This is worse than last time." Mangrove pulled Dumperty to sit between him and Snotty. "Hold on to us and hold on tight."

Dumperty linked his arms through those of Snotty and Manny. The three watched Bucky gallop to join the Palominos.

"What's happening, Manny?" Dumperty looked at him.

Mangrove's mouth opened and his lips moved as words formed. Dumperty heard nothing but the blast as the sun disappeared. The bright, shining day was no more.

Cracks split the earth, the quake shearing the valley from hill to hill. Manny prayed to the stars that the ground they sat on would not suddenly open up and swallow them.

"Look at that. Look at the mountain." There was alarm in Snotty's voice.

Neither Mangrove nor Dumperty had ever heard him speak in that way. They looked, and knew why. The volcano had come alive. In the turmoil of smoke that rose in rolling waves from its cone, they could see the burning magma, chunks of red molten rock thrown into the air, so plastic they changed shape as they roiled in the billowing smoke.

His arms hooked into those of his friends, Dumperty pulled them closer. He was terrified, yet there was nothing he or Manny or Snotty could do. The three of them stared at the volcano, at the reddened, tumbling smoke that had climbed ten kilometres into the sky, at the bits of molten rock that kept spewing in a glowing fountain to be flung high and fall and where they fell to ignite new fires.

For almost a minute the Foragers rode the roller coaster of the moving ground, all the time fearing that the splitting earth would take them to Endless Night. Enduring this fear, they watched the awesome spectacle of the planet on which they lived throwing its burning innards at the sky.

In the distance the dark cloud grew larger as heated gases lifted ash and cloud into the stratosphere. It seemed to the Foragers that there could be no end to the clouds boiling from the volcano. The giant column, driven by its own heat and by the jet stream, drifted an ugly plume, stretching further, always replenished. The boys watched it spread and saw coming from it a grey curtain, a gauzy drapery that quickly thickened and darkened. Ash, cooled in the frigid temperatures of high altitude, had begun to fall; grey powder that fell without a sound.

In the cauldron of fire that is inner earth, magma had burst through the weakened conjunction of rock plates that had shifted months before. The molten rock, driven by expanding gases had in turn melted and blown away every obstruction in the substrata, hit the main vent of the volcano and blasted its way to the heavens. What Mangrove and Snotty and Dumperty were seeing was the exploded heart of their planet.

"Listen," Snotty said.

The rumbling had ceased. The roaring that had hurt the ears of the Foragers had faded to nothing. The ground on which they sat huddled together no longer moved.

"It's over."

"Yes, until the next time." Mangrove was looking at the ash falling like silent rain.

The grey curtain was far off, but he could see that it was moving, dropping from the drifting plume of smoke and where the ash fell, the green hills and valleys turned to grey.

Dumperty looked for the Palominos and Bucky. They stood together two hundred metres away. "The horses are over there. They didn't run far."

"There was nowhere to go," Manny said. "And the cracks in the ground... the horses had to stop."

Snotty got up and whistled through teeth scarcely apart. Three short notes pierced the silence. Bucky began to trot toward Snotty. Stripe and Star followed. The boys walked to meet them.

"I hope Tasha and the others are okay," Mangrove said. "We've got to get to Haven as quickly as we can."

The earthquake, the terrifying fissures that had rent the ground, had frightened everybody. In the aftermath, those who were not already inside had run to Haven. There they hoped its sturdy walls would keep them safe.

Tasha did her best to calm her unsettled people. She walked among them, giving assurance, overcoming their fears until panic had gone.

The strength of the quake had shaken bedding from platforms and upset the cooking pot.

"Look around, there's plenty to do." Tasha helped this one and that to return order to the mess.

"Tasha." She turned at the call of her name.

Mangrove was coming through the doorway, Snotty and Dumperty behind him. "Is everything all right?"

"Yes."

Mangrove looked around the great space of Haven. Apart from the untidiness of belongings, there appeared to be no real damage. He walked across the central square, inspecting it as he went, happy to see that the seismic forces which had opened up splits in the valley floor could not crack the man-made structure.

Wanting to be sure, he lit a torch and went on into the dark depths of the chamber. He threw light on the walls and on the tiers, the flame dancing as he went. Mangrove could see no evidence that the integrity of the shelter had suffered. He walked on.

The torchlight reflected from the metal plate. Mangrove could see the line drawings.

"Hey." The word issued in a quiet, exhaled breath.

Where he should have seen a handprint within a circle, there was a void, a black gap in the wall. He hurried to it. Part of the wall had swung open. The flame shone on heavy hinges.

"Tasha, Snotty," Mangrove yelled. "Grab a torch and come here."

The three of them stood at the opening. "The door must have shifted when the earth moved."

Snotty shook his head. "But, Manny, we pushed on the handprint and..."

"We weren't strong enough. After all that time, the door was stuck hard, too hard for us to budge."

"You're right," Tasha said.

She looked at Biscetti and Cloud, at Belle and Kalich, at the whole crowd that had followed and now stood peering at the hole in the wall. The problem that had faced Tasha was presenting itself again. On the earlier occasion the decision she had made, right or wrong, had not mattered. Now with the door swung wide, it was Tasha's call. Should they enter and wake the Sleepers, or should they close the door, turn their backs upon it and forget that an opportunity had ever existed?

Ingamo sensed what Tasha was thinking. "Close the door, Tasha. Leave the Sleepers in peace. They can do us no good."

Biscetti gave him a look. "Be quiet, Ingamo. What you're saying is wrong."

Tasha turned to Jemma. The old lady was shaking her head and making a motion with her hand. "Close it, Tasha."

The arguments replayed in Tasha's head.

Snotty gave his cheeky grin. "Come on, let's go in, Tasha."

She turned to Mangrove. "What do you say?"

"I think we owe it to the Sleepers and to the people who entrusted us with the duty to wake them."

"Those people didn't know that we'd find the Sleepers." Ingamo's voice was raised. "We owe them nothing."

Tasha held up her hand for quiet. "Ingamo is right. The ancients had no idea who would find their children. But they placed their trust in whoever it might be." She smiled at Ingamo and Jemma. "It just happened to be that we are the ones who came along. I really think we have to wake them..." For a few moments Tasha stared at the black opening. When she spoke her voice was low, hardly to be heard. "Lead the way, Manny."

With torches flaming, Mangrove and Tasha at the front, the whole crowd passed through the doorway and into the wide corridor the ancients had constructed.

The passage was quite lengthy. Mangrove counted his footsteps. He could see a glimmer of light way down the corridor. As he walked, the light ahead grew larger and around it other spots of light appeared.

"What's going on, Tasha?"

"I don't know." She could see the bobbing lights ahead in the darkness and then made out the dim the figures of people.

Biscetti was also looking at the growing light ahead. "This is weird."

"We are walking towards ourselves," Cloud said.

"You can't be serious?"

"I am. Those people we can see, they have torches. We are looking at ourselves."

Mangrove stopped walking. "What did you say, Cloud?"

She repeated that among the lights ahead she could see him and Tasha, Biscetti, herself, Snotty, many of the others. "I see us here and I see us there."

"I don't understand." Tasha was trying to make sense of what Cloud was saying. "Do the Sleepers have guards who look like us, who are our doubles?"

In the concrete corridor with the flames of torches flickering over them, behind only darkness and ahead the scene repeated, anything seemed possible.

Ingamo's voice was shaking. "I told you this was wrong. We should get out of here, close the door and forget we ever heard of Sleepers."

"No," Snotty said. "I'm going on." He looked at Tasha.

She nodded.

Snotty joined Mangrove. They led, with Tasha and the others close behind. Jemma and Ingamo, unwilling to be alone were last in line.

The lights ahead became brighter. The figures Cloud had described took form and became recognisable.

"That's you, Manny." Snotty said.

"And that's you."

Tasha waved her torch and the torch held by the figure of Tasha also waved. "It's my reflection."

None of the clan had ever seen a mirror. On odd occasions their faces had looked back at them from a stream, but a mirror, a looking glass, such a thing was unknown. Tasha was seeing herself from head to toe. She approached her image and tried to touch the face in the glass. Her fingers slid across the hard, smooth surface. Tasha smiled and the mirror answered her smile. She stood back a little. The mirror extended for the full length of the crypt into which the corridor had led them. Tasha could see rows of cylinders reflected in the glass.

Mangrove and Snotty were looking about. On Manny's calculations the vault was sixty paces from the entrance to the corridor. A concrete cavern, it lay directly below the crown of the hill in which Haven had been built. Yes, he thought, the ancients went to great lengths to protect their sleeping young. The space, in which the capsules had been stored, was the safest spot within the thousands of tonnes of concrete and the natural shape of the land.

There was no mistaking the purpose of the capsules. They were arranged exactly as depicted in the drawings. Walking among them, looking at the bodies lying within, every one could see that girls were in one group and boys in the other.

Biscetti stopped to look through the face piece of one the cylinders. Beneath the plexiglas, the hardened acrylic window much stronger than glass, she could see the face of a girl. Biscetti stared at the face, trying to comprehend how the girl could have lain unmoving from the time of the ancients. The girl, Biscetti thought, was about her own age, perhaps a year older, yet she had lived in the Good Times and known that they were coming to an end. *Well, she's gunna find our world a whole lot different.*

The accuracy of the cartoons, the message they relayed so specific, the clan knew precisely what had to be done next.

"Let this girl be the first one, Tasha," Biscetti said.

"Okay, but she'll want to eat and drink when we wake her. All the Sleepers will." Tasha asked Belle and her gang to fetch fruit and fish and water.

Biscetti waited until everything had been brought into the vault. She rehearsed in her mind the steps she would take to rouse the Sleeper.

"Okay." Biscetti placed both hands on the spoked wheel of the valve. She applied pressure. The valve did not budge. "Snotty, help me."

He gripped the wheel, his hands alongside Biscetti's. Their knuckles whitened and the wheel slowly turned.

Gas that had held the girl in suspended animation for four millennia, rushed from the open valve. The window fogged so that the girl's face could not be seen. As fresh air entered the capsule to replace the gas, the fogging cleared. Biscetti and Snotty bent their heads over the capsule. Through the transparent window they watched the girl's eyes open. Expressionless she looked at the Foragers.

Within the metal capsule the Sleeper pressed a lever. The top of the capsule lifted and fell away. More than ever it seemed to the whole clan that the Sleeper lay in an ice coffin.

The girl gripped the edge of the coffin and pulled herself to sit. She looked at the people gazing at her, looked at them with a face that conveyed no emotion. Raising one hand, the girl beckoned Biscetti to assist her in climbing from the capsule. She stood beside it. Tasha offered her two bowls, one with fish and fruit the other with water. The girl drank, draining the bowl, handing it back to be refilled. She held a peach, pressing it lightly to test its ripeness and then bit into it. She smelt the fish before taking any into her mouth. Alternately she took mouthfuls of fruit and fish until the bowl was empty.

The girl had not spoken nor had her face given any indication of the thoughts she might be having.

Tasha smiled at the girl. "Hello, I'm Tasha."

Chapter 17

A green smudge appeared on the horizon. The Torterat bared his teeth at Dram, indicating that she should walk faster. Kaldor was in sight. If they hurried he would be among his own by nightfall.

Dram licked her cracked lips. The desert crossing was torture, although it had been worse the first time. She flinched at the memory. Water had been essential, but she had given it no thought when she had led her supporters out of Kaldor after defecting from Tasha. *How stupid I was.* But Dram had learned from that experience and from the Torterat.

After the dunes, the waterbags of python skin had soon run dry. In the desert, Dram had been forced to become inventive. As she and the Torterat retraced the route taken by the Camarilla on their migration south, Dram had fossicked among the litter the clan had discarded. At night she had dug holes beside her sleeping place, lined them with pieces of python skin and using tiny leather funnels fashioned from the litter had collected dew. Dram's ingenuity had kept her and the Torterat alive.

In the distance the smudge had become a forest. Dram could see individual trees. She bent her head again and pulled her hood to better shade her face from the sun. In places on her face, the skin had peeled. She ran a hand across her ribs. They felt bony, protruding from her flesh. Dram smiled wryly at the desert sand. She was no longer the beautiful girl whom all admired.

The Torterat was almost running. Dram hurried to stay in front of him. They entered the forest. Patches of snow lay among the trees. Dram fell to lie in the snow, to feel it on her burnt face, to hold it cold in her mouth, to have it melt and run down her throat. Tears filled her eyes. She was in snow, experiencing again the world of white in which, until the exodus, she had spent her life. If only we had stayed in Homecave, she thought. If only... but the Torterats had forced the clan to leave the world of ice and she, a prisoner, was about to be taken before their leader.

Her captor nipped her leg and yipped. Dram rose from the snow and followed him deeper into the forest. Soon she was climbing over great trunks of long-fallen trees, the snow lying thicker on the ground. She would never have found her way, but the forest seemed familiar. When she saw the cathedral tree, Dram knew that she was at the entrance to the military bunker. She had been brought back to the place where she and Snotty had found Dumperty on the night he had run from the wraiths.

Dram followed the Torterat to stand within the thick sections of the trunk. He screeched at her. She knew what he wanted and climbed to stand on the lip of the concrete shaft. The moment she was there, the funky smell of Torterats hit her. Dram reeled and almost fell. The shaft with its metal ladder set into the concrete walls was like a chimney drawing the heat of the many Torterats in the underground complex. The heated air funnelled up the shaft, bringing with it the overpowering stink of furry bodies. Dram held a hand to cover her mouth and nose, shaking her head, saying to herself that there was no way she could go down the ladder. She shuddered at the thought that there would be no light. She would be blindly stumbling among hordes of stinking Trats.

"No, no," she shouted at her keeper and unable to bear the smell, Dram lowered herself to the ground.

The Torterat jumped on to the shaft uttering low pitched sounds, finally screeching. The reaction from below was immediate. From where Dram stood, Torterats seemed to pour from the shaft in excitement. They gathered around her showing their teeth, some darting forward to nip the air so close to her that she felt wet noses touch her skin. She backed away. Her movement triggered strong reaction from her tormentors. The sham nipping became real. The Torterats were no longer bluffing. Dram cried in pain and saw blood run from a wound on her leg.

She became hysterical, screaming at the animals. "There's no light down there, I won't be able to see." And mimed the actions of a blind girl. She continued the pantomime, playing the charade of making a torch. "I must have light."

The Torterat who had captured Dram by the river and who had lived with her for months of hardship, understood. He barked an order to the pack surrounding her. Dram could make her torch.

Once lit, she climbed again onto the shaft and with teeth snapping at her head descended the ladder. At its foot, another phalanx waited like drovers' dogs to keep her moving.

For the second time in her life, Dram stood in the control room. The uniformed mummies of the ancients sat at their consoles, staring sightless at dials. Despite occupation by the mutant rats, the war room seemed to be just as she remembered. Dram held the torch forward to shed more light and ran her eyes over shelves and desks and tables. The pistol that had frightened Dumperty lay where Snotty had left it. In holsters that hung on military belts around the waists of long dead soldiers, Dram could see other pistols. Every dried and darkened body was wearing one.

A Torterat snarled and screeched. Dram was to wait where she stood.

She kept staring at the holsters, seeing similarity with the quiver and bow and arrows she carried. *The dead warriors are wearing weapons.* No other possibility existed. Dram was convinced that she was right. Somehow Dumperty had set off the weapon. *It barks and it bites,* he had said. Wasn't that proof? She tried to make sense of the idea, but contrary thoughts whirled in her mind. Her bow was useless without arrows. When she hunted, it was the arrow which killed the hare-cousin or the raptor. Dram was thinking rapidly. The pistol, all the pistols, must be like her bow. *They must fire tiny arrows or something like an arrow.* The puzzle was, where was the ammunition kept? She looked at the pistol on the table, imagining how it might work. Dram, the clan's best archer, the girl who could put three arrows in the air within four seconds, realised that the pistol played the role of a bow, but a bow that held its arrows within itself.

For Dram, hunting had been a daily habit for years. She knew from long experience that the supply of arrows she could carry was limited. There had been times when her life had been endangered because she had emptied her quiver. She looked at the lifeless, uniformed figures, thinking that the ancient soldiers must have been confronted with the same problem. The pistol was small, too small to hold a good quantity of the missiles it fired. With Torterats guarding her, yet unaware of what she was thinking, Dram's eyes searched the control room. Boxes of ammunition – some broken open months before by Torterats searching for food – were on a shelf. She could see a jumble of bullets in the opened cases and scattered on the shelf. Dram knew immediately that this was ammunition for the pistols. The bullets even looked a little like tiny, metal arrows.

Grunting, as though she wished to be relieved of its weight, Dram shucked her pack from her back to leave it on the table close to her. She placed her bow beside the pack. Torterats snarled, but took no action. Dram walked to the shelf and as though checking what might be edible, handled a bullet, smelled it and tasted it. The Torterats watched the human express her disappointment. Had they been capable, they would have laughed. Dram placed a box of ammunition in her pack. The Torterats were unconcerned. She picked up the pistol and laid it with the ammunition. When I have time, she thought, I'll figure out how the weapon works.

A Torterat barked a command at Dram. She was to follow him. He led her through the connecting rooms of the bunker, other Torterats surrounding her, ensuring that she could cause no trouble. The flame of the torch flickered as she passed through the chamber that had been the schoolroom for children of the military families. The blond boy who had intrigued Dumperty remained at the desk where he had sat for the past four thousand years, his unseeing eyes fixed on the spot where the Swiss knife had been.

The Torterats hurried Dram on.

She was led into a large room. King Trat, as Snotty had named him, sat on a raised dais. Dram recognised the leader of the Torterats. He was much bigger and heavier than those he commanded. She had last seen him in the stomach of the mountain carved by ghosts. Dram shivered at the memory of that frightening night when the Torterats had attacked her, Tasha and Biscetti and the boys. Only luck had enabled the Foragers to escape.

King Trat also recognised Dram. He knew that it was she, who terrified, had tried to climb to safety in the dark and inadvertently turned on the solar current that had flooded the hollow mountain with light. On that occasion Dram's action had robbed the Torterats of the Foragers. Both knew that this time Dram would not get away. Escape from the bunker was impossible.

The Torterat leader had received the report from Dram's captor. The loss of a phalanx to Komodos was serious, but the death of so many Torterats would be avenged. First, the humans would be dealt with. King Trat looked at the girl standing before him. She would lead the Torterats to her people. If necessary, the king would then use the girl as bait to lure the Camarilla from their hiding place or whatever stronghold they occupied. The king and the whole Torterat nation had one ambition: annihilation of the last remaining members of the human race.

King Trat screeched an order. They would leave at once.

Tasha spoke again to the one Sleeper who had been wakened. The girl ignored her and walked to stand before the long mirror. For minutes she looked at her image full-face and then turned to examine her profile from each side.

Tasha stood next to the girl and spoke to the image in the mirror.

Tiny lines creased the space between the girl's brows.

"She doesn't understand you," Biscetti said.

"Guten Tag." The girl looked at Tasha and at Biscetti.

They stared at her, unable to give a response.

The girl persisted. "Bon jour, Buenas dias, Dobry den." She gave the greeting in French, Spanish and Russian; phrases she had been taught in preparation for the day she would be wakened. None made any sense to Tasha, Biscetti or to anyone among the crowd of onlookers.

The girl drank more water and her frown reappeared. The strange people who had woken her spoke in some unknown tongue. Worse, they did not understand English, or any word she had said.

The adults who had placed her in the capsule had warned her and all the Sleepers that those who woke them might not speak English and so the need for a few words in other languages. No one had taken into account that English would continue to change as living languages always do. Even if they had, changes are unpredictable. With each passing century the language altered a little more. After forty centuries, English bore no resemblance to what it had been in the Good Times. Tasha had greeted the girl in the English of the Camarilla. To the Sleeper, Tasha's words were incomprehensible.

Tasha touched one hand to her own chest and repeated her name.

A faint smile dimpled the girl's cheeks. She repeated the gesture Tasha had made. "Lianne. People call me Dolly."

"Dolly." Tasha returned her smile. "Dolly is a nice name."

Cloud had listened intently to the short exchange of words, concentrating, delving deep into her mind for the meaning of words hidden there.

"Lianne is her real name, Tasha. Dolly is her nickname."

"Do you think you can speak to her, Cloud?"

"I'll try."

Cloud introduced herself and with many pauses as she groped for a word – a word that she had never before used, yet had been

passed down to her in the genes of generations of ancestors –
explained to Dolly that she had been found by the Camarilla and
that Tasha was their Queen.

Dolly understood. She nodded to Tasha and pointed to the
rows of cylinders. "Open now." Speaking to Tasha as though she
were an infant and using her hands to demonstrate what should
be done.

"Okay, that's why we're here."

Tasha turned to the huddle around her. Every face was staring
at Dolly, intrigued by the girl, her voice and the strange words she
used, the suit of unusual material that, tight fitting, clothed her
from neck to ankle, the cut of her boots. For the clan, the recently
awakened Sleeper could have been an alien from another planet.

"Come on," Tasha said. "Let's get them up."

Ingamo and Jemma hung back, the rest of the clan dispersed
among the capsules, peering curiously through windows at the
faces of strangers. Each of the clan knew precisely what was
required. The vault filled with the soft sighs of escaping gas.

Tasha watched the lids of capsules folding back. No longer
coffins, the capsules had transformed the vault into a garden of
metal petals, opening as if in response to the changing season.
Tasha saw the Sleepers as the new born, leaving their protective
cocoons to step into a world they would not recognise. Doubt cast
its dark shadow over her. Had she been right to set the Sleepers
free?

She heard her name called. Kalich was agitated, beckoning
her to come quickly. "This one's eyes aren't opening."

The voices of Mangrove and Sola came loud from different
places in the room. They too had problems. More shouts followed
from Zita and Dumperty. Tasha ran from one to the other. Five
Sleepers had not responded. They remained with eyes closed
below the clear face piece of their cylinders. In each case the
valve had been opened and the exchange of gases had occurred.
Something was wrong.

Dolly saw the alarm on Tasha's face and the general
consternation within the room. She looked through each window

in turn, spending a moment to identify who it was that lay unmoving.

"They need oxygen immediately, perhaps adrenalin," she pleaded.

Tasha looked at Dolly blankly. "What did she say, Cloud?"

Cloud raised her hands empty of an answer. "She wants us to give them something, but I don't know what."

To Mangrove there was no logic to Dolly's request. "We followed the instructions of the drawings. What else can we do? We can't get inside these things to give anything to anyone."

"Maybe we can." Snotty left the vault, the light and shadow of his torch flickering down the corridor as he rushed away.

Within the vault a lot was happening. Most cylinders had opened and the clan was busy bringing food and drink to those they had helped from their resting places. Some of the Sleepers were at the mirror examining their reflections, but as they became oriented awareness grew that a few of their friends had not emerged.

Amid the movement and the hubbub created by the clan, with questions that flew from one to the other unanswered, Dolly pounded with her fists on the window of a capsule that grew wet with her tears.

Re-entering the commotion, Snotty gently moved Dolly away from the capsule. Raising his stone axe he brought it down hard on the Perspex. The sudden noise brought quiet. Snotty raised his axe again. With the entire room looking he smashed it down. The axe bounced from the rigid surface. The window remained unmarked. Again and again with all his strength he struck with the axe. Below the unbroken window, the Sleeper's eyes stayed shut.

Snotty dropped the axe. He took the Swiss knife from his pocket and flicked the file from its sheath. Leaning into it, using his weight and the force of shoulder and arm muscles, Snotty dragged the file back and forth on the surface of the window. The scratch he made deepened. Changing direction he scratched another groove to make a cross with the first.

Satisfied, Snotty closed the knife and tossed it to Mangrove. "Do the others."

"Right."

Snotty raised his axe again. His aim was good. Craze lines radiated from the centre point of the cross. With one final blow, the face piece shattered. Dolly reached into the capsule. It opened, the Sleeper, a boy, did not move.

Dolly tried to lift the boy. She managed to raise his head and shoulders. Snotty went to her assistance and together they laid him on the floor.

"Robby, Robby." On her knees, Dolly slapped his cheeks, begging him to open his eyes.

The boy's face had gone grey. Snotty knelt opposite Dolly. He bent low over the boy's face and felt no breath. Snotty put two fingers on the grey skin of the boy's neck. No pulse was beating.

Mangrove interrupted scratching at Perspex and shouted advice. "You saved *me* when I was like that. Do it for *him*, Snotty."

For the second time Snotty recalled the illustrations he had seen in the military bunker in Kaldor, the instructions for giving cardiac pulmonary resuscitation. He tilted the boy's head, blew twice into his mouth and then placed one hand over the other and pressed hard on the boy's chest. Snotty imagined the heart being squeezed by the pressure. He pressed and pressed again, repeating the cycle of forcing air into the boy's lungs and then compressing his chest.

"Come on, come on, breathe," he exhorted. But the boy did not breathe.

"I'm doing it right," Snotty muttered. "This is what I did for Manny. Why isn't it working now?"

In other parts of the vault Kalich and Situ were smashing at face pieces that Mangrove had weakened. Another four Sleepers were laid on the floor.

Dolly saw that Snotty was tiring. She took over, blowing and pressing, hoping for life to return.

Other Sleepers were standing before the mirror examining their images. Snotty screamed at them to give help to those needing it. "Stop looking at yourselves. Your friends are dying."

For a moment the mirror gazers focused on the image of Snotty, not understanding what he had said, merely looking to see from where the noise had come.

Snotty shouted again, this time at Dolly, demanding that she make the people at the mirror help. Dolly stared at him.

Disturbed by the yelling, Cloud squatted by Snotty. "They don't know what you're saying."

"It doesn't matter. They have eyes. They can see their friends are in trouble."

Dolly touched Cloud's arm and spoke to her.

"What did she say, Cloud?"

"That the Sleepers need to re-establish their identities, the mirror is there to let each boy and girl recall who they are. She says that it takes a little while for their brains to retrieve memory and begin thinking again."

"Hmm." Snotty was sceptical. But eventually the people at the mirror turned away from their reflections, knelt by the inert bodies and began resuscitation.

The attempts to give back life went on for a long time. Only when torches began to splutter, some dying completely, did the exhausted resuscitators sit back on their haunches. Their efforts had failed.

Hoping that some faint chance remained, Manny checked each of the five motionless Sleepers. He looked at Tasha and shook his head. "They've gone to Endless Night."

"That's so sad. They were asleep for such a long time and now..."

Yes, Manny thought, now what? We'll have funeral pyres, but after that... He did not even try to guess what the future would hold.

Chapter 18

The five piles of interlaced timber stood stark on the crown of the hill above Haven; turrets of a domed castle waiting to receive their final guests. Silhouetted against the dark volcanic cloud still pummelling the sky from the distant cone, the woven structures added gloom to an already dismal scene.

Tasha led the funeral procession. Behind her, lying on separate biers, the five Sleepers who could not be woken were carried by their friends. Walking in front of each bier, one of the clan held a bowl of smouldering embers.

The cortege wound its way up the hill in silence. Five bodies, the bodies of three boys and two girls, who had lived in a time long gone, were laid on their pyres. The bowl bearers knelt, emptied glowing coals and blew gently. Fire danced at kindling, took hold and flared. Flame spread, roaring, leaping into the air, consuming the wood and the corpses of those who had died so young.

Not since the cremation of Queen Avon had the clan given the final, fiery farewell to someone claimed by Endless Night. Most had memories of that morning on Home Mountain as they stood gazing at the flames and smoke. In the forefront of their minds was the irony of saying goodbye to people to whom they had never spoken and about whom they knew nothing.

Tasha looked at the faces of the assembled Sleepers, unable to read what they might be thinking. That five of them had gone to Endless Night had cast a cloud over the whole gathering from the beginning. The children of the ancients had preferred to keep their own company. Although invited to make their sleeping places on the platforms in the great chamber, they preferred to spend each night in the vault, continuing to use the capsules for sleeping. Tasha saw logic in this decision, but although the clan had been generous by giving furs to the strangers so that they might make their sleeping places more comfortable, this generosity seemed to have been taken as a right.

In the two days since their awakening, the Sleepers had sat down at mealtimes with the clan, shared the fish and hare-cousins that the clan had caught, eaten the fruit and drank milk. At Tasha's suggestion, her people had denied themselves the biscuits that Jemma had made and given them to their guests. Yes, she thought, they slept on our furs and sat with us and ate the food we readily gave them, but only Dolly and a few others have made any attempt to talk to us and to thank us.

A few of the Sleepers held her eyes as she examined a face. Tasha smiled. As with the food, there was no answering warmth. The attitude of the Sleepers troubled her. Did they not know common courtesy? Didn't the ancients teach their children manners? But it seemed to Tasha that some of the faces looked at her with contempt. In her mind, Ingamo's warning sounded again. *But I did the only thing possible. I couldn't let these people sleep on forever.* She grimaced. That may have been her intention, but it was apparent to Tasha that she had failed with the five now burning. *Do the other Sleepers blame me for that?*

Right or wrong, Tasha had made her decision and she realised that she would have to live with it, nevertheless the Sleepers worried her. She glanced at Mangrove, wondering if he had noticed anything and whether he had the same misgivings.

The flames lost intensity. Wood that had burned brightly dulled to glowing red and broke to pieces. The funeral pyres collapsed into mounds of hot embers and smoking ash. The ritual was complete, the farewells taken.

In silence the clan made its way down the hill. Tasha expected that the Sleepers would follow. They did not. She turned her head to see them standing, watching her and the others depart. It's a sad occasion, she thought. They must want to spend more time honouring their dead. Tasha looked around for Mangrove.

He listened to her concerns as they walked together by the creek. "Yes," he said. "Snotty and I have talked about the way the Sleepers treat us. We don't like it."

Mangrove looked up at the pyres smoking on the hill. The group had gathered more closely together and appeared to be listening to one who stood apart, facing the others.

"That's Jack." Mangrove indicated with a movement of his head. "I've seen him looking at us and laughing."

"Hmm." Tasha waved to Cloud and beckoned her to join them. "Have you ever overheard what the Sleepers are saying?"

"A lot of them mock us. The one they call Jack is the ringleader. They make fun of everything: the way we look, the way we speak, our clothing, the food we eat. The Sleepers think we are wild animals who know nothing. They have a name for us. They call us *ferals*."

"A lot of them, you said?"

Cloud nodded. "Dolly and some of her friends are nice. *They* don't talk like that."

"I see." But Tasha felt hurt that people she had brought back to life could speak that way. "After all we've done for them."

On the hill, more words were being spoken. Words that the Sleeper known as Jack hoped would stir his audience to action.

"We must take over or we'll become like them. Do you want to live like these uneducated, ignorant primitives?"

Murmurs of agreement drifted among the crowd. Jack let the idea float, seeking out faces, raising a finger in acknowledgement when he saw a nod.

"Do you want to eat raw meat, drink blood?" He saw support growing. "With all the knowledge we have, are we to use bows and arrows to survive?"

"What alternatives are you proposing, Jack?" Those around her stepped aside for Dolly to come to the front.

"I'm saying that we take over. We organise these savages. We give the orders. They do as they're told."

"Such as?"

"Such as bringing about a return to civilization."

"Look around you, Jack. What do you see?" Dolly scoffed. "Piles of hot ash, the cremated remains of Robby and the others, a volcano spewing stuff into the sky, a wilderness of hills and valleys. This isn't the world that existed when we were put to sleep. Everything has changed. We need these people. The clan and their ancestors have survived for generations in fierce environments. They're tough. They have to be. And don't ever forget that it was our people who destroyed civilization! Jack, Tasha and her people woke us. They feed us. They share their possessions with us. They are good, caring human beings. Don't dare to look down on them. Without Tasha, you, all of us, would still be lying in our time capsules."

"But we aren't! Come on, Dolly, we're superior. We have knowledge they couldn't dream of."

"And knowledge is power is it, Jack?"

"Yes."

Dolly shook her head in disbelief. "I won't be part of this."

"I will," a voice shouted.

Other voices rose in agreement, but not all. Dolly's views were shared by some of the Sleepers.

"Okay," said Jack. "If you're with me, stand by me. If you aren't, stand by her."

The group split. Jack counted. He had twenty-nine supporters and among them were Jason, Wayne and Peter. They were big strong boys. Jack smiled. Mary and Fiona had also joined him. He looked at the fourteen Dolly had attracted and wished that Tommy and David had chosen to be with him and not with her. They had skills Jack wanted. Jane and Emmy and Nicole were also standing by Dolly. Well, he thought, they might change their minds when they see what's coming.

Jack waved a dismissive arm at Dolly. "Go on. Go back to your new friends with their long hair and their dirty finger nails."

He turned to his own followers. "Can't you see Dolly with her bow and arrows and her stone axe? She'll be a real tribal girl."

Jack got the laugh he sought.

Dolly and the few who stood with her left the hill. There was sadness as they talked. The future in which they had woken was not the one they had hoped to find.

"Whatever," Dolly said. "This is the way it is and we can't change it. I'm going to tell Tasha that from here on we are with the Camarilla. She can treat us like one of them and we'll have to fit in."

Dolly got no objections.

"What do you think Jack will do?" Jane asked.

"I don't know, but I don't trust him. I didn't trust him way back and I don't trust him now."

In the great space of Haven, Cloud translated for Dolly and Tasha. "The Sleepers have split, Tasha. Dolly wants her group to become part of us. They'll live the way we do, do their share of the chores and so on."

Tasha smiled at Dolly and nodded. "Okay."

"They also want us to teach them how to hunt."

"Fine. Tell Dolly that she and her friends can make their sleeping places on the tiers with us. Everything else will fall into place as the days go by."

Tasha waited for Cloud to translate. "Now ask her what Jack is up to."

Dolly was non-committal, saying that Jack would learn that he could not get on without the help of the clan.

"Perhaps the best way is to be kind to Jack," Tasha said. "We'll treat him and those with him no differently from you."

"Yes." Dolly had her doubts, but what else could Tasha do?

Jack's clique did not move out of Haven. The cylinders were suitable places in which to sleep and the vault gave the privacy Jack sought. With his followers gathered around him, he laid out his plan.

"It will take time to achieve supremacy and until we are ready to act, we'll accept the ferals' hospitality."

Those around him grinned. Why not? It made life easy.

"We'll also need their help." Jack went on to explain that they needed to bring their knowledge of the countryside up to date. "Dolly's right in a way. A lot has changed. I think we should send out scouting parties. Some of the Foragers could act as guides. I'll ask Tasha about it."

"They talk about monsters, dragons that can eat horses," Mary said.

Jack laughed. "That's what I mean. They're primitives. Dragons, can you believe it?"

"Maybe dragons do exist."

Jack looked into faces lit by torches made by the Camarilla. "Dragons? Come on that's fairytale stuff. Anyway, we should take a close look at the volcano and do a bit of exploring generally."

Everyone agreed that it was a good idea.

"Okay," said Jack. "That's it. I'll talk to Tasha."

As the meeting broke up, Jack asked four of the Sleepers to stay for a few minutes. They were his closest allies. He had important things he wished to share with them that the others needn't know.

At the beginning of the journey to the volcano, Snotty kept Bucky close to the Sleepers. At Tasha's request he had agreed to accompany Jason and Fiona and do his best to see that no harm came their way. In Snotty's eyes, the Sleepers were like babies. They were unable to make fire, they had no weapons, and the packs on their backs were borrowed from Zita and Kalich.

The inability of the Sleepers to provide for themselves was evident on the first night. Although Snotty showed Jason how to use the wooden tools to generate heat that was turned into flame, Jason could not get the hang of it. It was Snotty who had to prepare the fire. Exasperated by the slowness of Jason and Fiona, Snotty cut the meat and did the cooking too.

In the morning, sitting on Bucky as they travelled further south, the thought kept recurring to Snotty that the age in which the Sleepers had lived, had taught them nothing. The Sleepers seemed to have no practical knowledge or skills. Snotty wondered how this could be.

Bucky ambled along. Snotty gazed around, taking stock of yet another valley. Movement caught his eye. He stopped the horse. In the distance he could make out dark shapes, so far off that they appeared ant sized. Snotty concentrated, trying to make out what the tiny shapes might be. Whatever they were they were grazing. It was further movement, the awkward gait that let Snotty know that he was looking at cattle. He made note of where they were. Another cow or two would be of great value to the clan.

By the third day Snotty's opinion of the Sleepers had softened a little. He was getting on quite well with both. Language was a problem, but the Sleepers had begun to pick up words and phrases from Snotty and he questioned them non-stop. Bit by bit he was becoming familiar with the English of the ancients.

They had come to within five hundred metres of the volcano. Since the first great eruption that had triggered the earthquake, the volcano had calmed a little. A mantle of snow clung to the peak of the cone, puzzling Snotty that cold and heat could exist together. The mountain rose very high and he had no understanding of air that became colder with altitude.

Explosions came intermittently, still hurling magma into the air, but Snotty and the Sleepers had become accustomed to the noise and the spectacle of pyroplastic debris hurtling high and then falling to earth. Only Bucky reacted to the unexpected bursts of sound, shying each time, his eyes wide.

Snotty turned his face from the volcano and pulled his hood closer. He was hot and would have taken off his jacket, but it offered some protection from the heat radiating from the magma. "Let's go home," he said.

Jason shook his head. "No. We must get closer."

Snotty argued that it was getting too hot, gesturing that they had seen enough. Jason refused. They should press on. He and Fiona were not afraid.

No one had ever suggested to Snotty that fear was stopping him. He stared at Jason wondering why the boy was daring him. What was the point of getting closer? What more was there to see?

Jason made the motion of cutting something. "Loan me your knife."

"Why?"

Jason explained that he wanted to collect stuff from the volcano. Snotty shrugged and reached for the flint in its scabbard.

Jason raised his hand. "Not that one. I want the steel knife, the one with all the blades."

He was not getting through to Snotty. Playing the role of weakening the plexiglass of the capsules he tried again. "You know, the Swiss Army knife. You used it to scratch the face panels."

Snotty understood, but shook his head. The metal knife belonged to the clan. It was a prized possession. If it was lost they would never have another.

Fiona smiled at Snotty, assuring him that she and Jason would take good care of the knife. Snotty would have it in sight all the time Jason had it. Reluctantly, Snotty handed the Swiss knife over.

The Sleepers moved off.

Snotty squeezed his heels against Bucky. The horse refused to move.

"C'mon, Bucky. We're as good as Sleepers."

Bucky hesitated and then began to walk in the tracks left in the ash by Jason and Fiona.

Noise was everywhere, a rough, oppressive blanket that wrapped tight around Snotty. Even mounted as he was, Snotty could feel the earth rumbling. A river of molten rock was flowing from the cone, dribbling like molasses, turgid and slow moving. Heat danced in the air.

As they got closer, the air thickened with the fumes of sulphur. The smell was terrible. Snotty watched the two ahead of him put their faces into the crook of their elbows.

"What are those two up to?" Snotty spoke softly to himself and was suddenly jerked forward. Bucky had stopped. He would go no further.

"Okay, boy. That's okay, we'll wait here."

The Sleepers were a little way up the slope of the cone. They had slowed. At different places around them, the pressure of smoke and steam had opened up the ground to form mounds of dirty yellow. Jason and Fiona were examining the smoking vents, moving from one to another. As Snotty watched, the two took clay bowls from their packs. Each knelt and using the knife, scraped yellow material into the bowls.

Bucky was restless, stamping his hooves into the ash, wanting to leave.

"Steady, boy."

The horse neighed. Sweat gleamed on his neck and flanks. Snotty leaned forward, patting Bucky, talking to the horse, but never taking his eyes from the Sleepers.

The explosion shattered the air, overcame every other sound with a blast of shock wave and earth and lava. Above the Sleepers part of the slope blew to smithereens, sending chunks of rock and magma flying, opening a great gap in the side of the cone. Lava spilled out, rolling down the slope in a wide, fiery ribbon.

"Get out of there." Snotty screamed.

His cry was lost in the tumult of sound as Bucky reared and Snotty fell from the horse, and as he fell saw the Sleepers drop and lie unmoving.

Snotty senses were overpowered. He could not hear. In eerie silence he saw Bucky bolt. In silence he saw earth erupting in gobbets of brown soil and glowing magma that began to fall all around him in deathly quiet. Hot ash fell on him, singeing his hood and sleeves, burning pin holes ringed with black and smoking. In those moments, when all was happening in a myriad of simultaneous events, he saw that the Sleepers had not risen.

Snotty searched for Bucky. The horse was no longer madly galloping. He had come to a stop hundreds of metres away. *I don't blame him. He's smarter than we are!* Snotty looked back to the Sleepers and the lava streaming down the slope. He cried out again and inside his skull felt a buzzing vibration, but heard no sound.

The Sleepers remained where they had fallen. Snotty began to run.

If they were to play the role of local guides, Mangrove and Dumperty had also decided that it was better to ride than walk. The party resembled explorers of ancient times on an expedition into unknown territory; the Foragers on their Palominos, three Sleepers on foot carrying backpacks loaned to them and Schmucky running about among horses and people.

The Sleepers had asked to see the land that lay between Haven and the mountains to the north. By doing so, with Snotty taking Jason and Fiona south, all the country between the volcano and the valley where the clan had first settled would be surveyed.

Dumperty watched Jack, Mary and Wayne climb yet another hill. Before they had set out, Jack had asked the Foragers whether they knew of any caves. Manny had assumed that Jack was keen to move from Haven and find a place for his group to live.

"Yeah, something like that," Jack had said.

After three days of searching valleys that the clan had crossed in torrential rain some months earlier, nothing had been found. The three Sleepers reached the top of the hill and sat down. Mangrove and Dumperty joined them. Star and Stripe, heads lowered, tugged at the grass. Schmucky, snuffled around, investigating things of interest.

"Perhaps there are no caves." Mary spoke slowly, mouthing each word carefully, looking at Mangrove to see if he understood.

"There's one that I know, but it's not suitable."

"Why not?" Jack sat forward.

"Well it's full of sparkling shapes that are beautiful, but the cave drips with water all the time. It's too wet."

Jack's interest had sharpened. He leaned closer to Mangrove. "What are these shapes like?"

Manny told of the stalagmites and stalactites, most of them white, but some that were tinted red or green and all glinting with crystals.

Jack glanced at Mary and winked; an unspoken message that she acknowledged with the barest of nods.

"Sounds interesting. I'd like to see that cave."

Mangrove shrugged. "If you want."

They crossed the floor of the next valley. Although Schmucky ran ahead and was at times out of sight, Mangrove guided Stripe on a course that zigzagged to avoid the woods and clumps of trees, insisting that the others stayed with him.

Jack grew tired of the constant change of direction. "Why are we wandering around like this?"

"We're in dragon country and dragons use trees for cover," Mangrove said. "On the open ground we get some warning if one attacks."

"You're kidding me."

"Take it as you like." Mangrove didn't bother to look at Jack. He was searching the area ahead and to left and right.

Dumperty was acting as rear guard. He whistled to Schmucky and changed station, riding Star to the front to be closer to Mangrove.

"Manny, this is where Dram and I found Schmucky. He was only a pup then, but he must recognise the place."

"I guess so." A wave of sadness washed over Mangrove. "We'll never know what happened to Dram."

Late in the afternoon the party climbed the far hill. The light had faded, not because of approaching nightfall, but because the sun, which had shone all day, had sunk behind the smoke streaming from the distant volcano.

Mangrove looked down at the river, dull in the smoke-screened light and pointed to the escarpment that ran the length of the tableland. "The cave has two entrances, one in the cliff, one where water empties from the cave to feed that creek."

The Sleepers smiled.

Dumperty could see the hare-cousin warren. On foot, with Schmucky for company, he went to shoot fresh meat for dinner. Mangrove made fire. The smell of salt was in the breeze coming from the sea. There was also another smell, not so pleasant.

"What's that?" Mary sniffed and sniffed again three of four times. She walked thirty or forty metres along the crown of the hill. "Hey, come and see this."

Jack and Wayne joined her. Mangrove looked up, but stayed by the fire. He knew what Mary had found.

The Sleepers returned. "That stinking mess, what is it?"

"A vomit ball. Dragons sick up the stuff they can't digest."

"You really are kidding me?" But Jack had seen the tangle of teeth and hair and bits of bone. Perhaps the feral was telling the truth.

Mangrove looked briefly at Jack and put more sticks on the fire. "Dragons are real, Jack. You'd better believe it."

His opinion of the Sleepers was no different from Snotty's. They could do nothing for themselves and they refused to see what was in front of their eyes.

Dumperty returned with three rabbits and laid them on the grass. The Sleepers watched as he skinned and gutted two.

"Here," he said and offered a steaming liver to Mary.

She backed away. Dumperty grinned and tossed the liver to Mangrove. Dark blood ran from Mangrove's mouth as he ate.

Dumperty gestured to Jack to pass him the third rabbit. Jack picked up the animal by the ears. Mangrove and Dumperty kept straight faces. Urine was dribbling onto Jack's leg. It took a moment for the warmth to register, to bring a look of horror to Jack's face. Only then did the Foragers laugh. The old trick worked every time. Mary and Wayne were laughing too. Jack wiped at his leg with grass, not amused. He looked hard at Dumperty. *You'll get yours one day, buddy. I'll make sure of it.*

The cloud of volcanic smoke brought dusk early. In the fading twilight, Dumperty and Mangrove sat with the Sleepers around the fire and ate roasted rabbit. Not much was said. The five human beings saw themselves as belonging to two groups of quite different people.

Only when morning sunlight hit the top of the hill, did the Sleepers stir. Not quite awake, they looked about. The Foragers had been up since dawn. Dumperty had been to the river with the horses, watered them and brought back water for the Sleepers. Mangrove had laid out fruit and some of the meat not eaten the previous night.

The sight of food prompted the Sleepers to rise. They dashed some of the water at their faces, washing sleep away before they ate. Mangrove watched them eating and when meat and fruit was gone, waited for the thanks he believed due. None was offered.

"Let's get going," Jack said.

"When I'm ready." Mangrove bent, plucked a few handfuls of dry grass and stuffed it in his pack. He straightened and waved his arm to take in the whole valley. "This is dragon country. We must take great care."

Jack looked at the river calm in the morning sun. A flock of cormorants skimmed the water, in flight to where they thought the fishing might be better. The tunes of songbirds confirmed the peacefulness of all that he could see.

"Yeah, right." Sarcasm in his tone.

At the river, Mangrove and Dumperty paused to check the far bank and what lay beyond. Carefree, as if on a picnic, the Sleepers jumped in and swam. The Foragers watched. The three Sleepers stroked powerfully, moving quickly through the water.

Satisfied that the way ahead was clear, Mangrove and Dumperty rode the Palominos across the shallows and into deeper water. The horses swam, their riders sitting on them, Schmucky swimming alongside.

Again Mangrove avoided the trees, keeping to open ground until they gained the slope of the mountainside. Half way up he stopped and dismounted. Dumperty would stay with the horses while Mangrove led the Sleepers to the cave.

Chatting as they went, they followed him in single file across the slope, Jack, Mary next, Wayne in the rear. On the rock shelf, edging their way with backs to the cliff face, the chatting ceased. Mangrove could hear the vibration in Jack's breathing. Mangrove looked back at him. Jack was sweating, his mouth open, staring at the treetops well below.

At the point where the strata of rock forming the ledge had come apart, Jack froze. Mangrove smiled and held out his hand. Jack forced himself against the cliff face, wanting to glue himself to the rock.

"Go on, Jack." Mary urged him.

Jack didn't move. He was looking down, seeing the ground between gaps in the leaves and branches. Solid earth was fifty metres below.

"Let him help you, Jack," Mary said. "I'll take your other hand. You'll be okay."

Stiff with fear, Jack took the step to stand beside Mangrove on the continuation of the ledge. Safe, he flicked Mangrove's hand away. Mangrove smiled again. He was getting to know more about Jack.

One after the other the Sleepers tossed their packs into the fissure and squeezed through to stand in the cave.

Mangrove was last to enter. He paused in the crevice and called to Jack. "Did you see these marks?" Mangrove slid his fingers along the deep, parallel scratches in the rock.

"So?"

"The claws of a dragon made them."

Jack looked, but made no comment.

With only the thin streak of light coming through the crevice, weakening as it dissipated into the depths of the cavern, the Sleepers were given a hint of the colours and shapes that existed.

Mary stepped among the stalactites and stalagmites, touching the shining crystals, entranced by the natural wonder. "This is so beautiful."

"I'll need more light." Jack's interest lay in the far parts of the cave.

"Be patient." Mangrove was gathering the torches that he and Tasha and Biscetti had left behind after the search for Cloud. He laid them down and took spindle and wood and grass from his pack. In turn the blackened torches were brought back to life to dance with shadows on the glistening limestone.

The Sleepers each took a torch and made their way deeper into the cavern. Mangrove watched them stepping around the whorls of white and pink and green that rose from the floor or hung from the roof as giant pendants. As the Sleepers moved further away, the aura of light around each torch shrank to a flicker and as the limestone formations hid the Sleepers Mangrove could see only a yellow glow in the darkness. He waited, amusing himself by looking at the eyeless fish that had attracted Cloud.

The Sleepers were busy. Jack had found what he hoped would be in the damp recesses of the cave. Crusts of white crystals had formed around cracks in the limestone wall. Jack broke some off and licked them. He tasted salt and grinned at Mary and Wayne. "This is what we came for."

Like ancient miners grubbing in some dark and dangerous mine, the three Sleepers chipped at the crystals, letting the freed material fall into their open packs. When one area was cleaned out, they sought another.

Over aeons the white crystals had formed around weeping hairline cracks in the limestone. Rain falling on the tableland above had percolated through vegetable matter, withdrawing minute traces of salts from fallen leaves and dead grass. The water had wound its way downward in the dark cracks and crevices of the limestone until, exposed to the air of the cavern, the salts had precipitated into white crystals, crystals that crowded together to resemble toadstools. The Sleepers harvested these toadstools from their mineral gardens and packed them away.

Chapter 19

Schmucky was the first to notice. He stiffened and growled, his eyes fixed on the trees growing below the entrance to the cavern. The horses stopped grazing, raised their heads and looked in the same direction. Dumperty scanned the trees and thought he saw movement. He squinted, but distance and the foliage made it difficult to distinguish whatever it was disturbing the animals.

"What is it, boy?" Dumperty got low and put his face next to Schmucky's.

The movement came again and Dumperty glimpsed red between the brown and grey of tree trunks. Another movement distracted him, not in the trees but much closer on the mountainside. Mangrove and the Sleepers were returning.

Dumperty looked again for the flash of red and saw the Komodo come from the cover of the forest. She was walking slowly, swinging one thick, bandy leg, planting it to look about while her yellow tongue licked the air, swinging the other leg to repeat the process.

"She's hunting." He whispered the words to Schmucky. The dog growled.

Mangrove waved. Dumperty signalled to him, holding a finger to his lips, pointing to the Komodo. The animal was a long way off, but sound could travel far.

The Sleepers, sweaty and breathing heavily, shucked their packs and sat down beside Dumperty.

"Look down there," he said. "That's a dragon."

The Komodo was in the open, head swinging from side to side, forked tongue darting and withdrawing.

Mangrove heard Mary's sharp intake of breath, the shock visible on her face.

"Jack, they do exist. That beast is huge."

"She's a female," Mangrove said. "We've seen her before, much closer."

Jack got to his feet. "Never mind, she won't bother us. We'll cross the valley well away from her."

Mangrove put it to Jack that crossing the valley was not a good idea. They should go to the mouth of the river and cross by the bar.

"No, our packs are heavy. We'll take the shortest way back."

Mangrove looked at the sky, wishing that in the great arc of blue he could find an answer to the troublesome Sleepers. Tasha had put their safety in his hands. The lives of the Sleepers were his responsibility, yet he couldn't force them to obey him. He checked the position of the sun; mid-morning. The breeze was light, coming from the west.

"Okay. We go now and we go fast."

"What's the rush?"

Dumperty saw Mangrove's annoyance and interrupted. "The wind will shift soon. If we get caught upwind of the dragon it won't be good."

"Whatever." Jack got to his feet.

Mangrove lifted Wayne's pack and put it by Mary's. She raised an arm to stop him.

"What are you doing?"

He linked the straps of the two packs together and laid them across Stripe. They hung like saddlebags.

"We'll travel faster this way."

Dumperty acknowledged Mangrove's good sense by slinging Jack's bag on his back and mounting Star. The Sleepers had been relieved of their burdens.

Mangrove took another fix on the sun. "We don't have long."

His heels prompted Stripe. They were on their way.

Half way across the open fields of the valley, still hundreds of metres from the river. Mangrove stopped. The lightest of breezes touched his cheeks. He sniffed the air and caught the faint tang of the sea. The onshore wind had begun to blow.

On Star, Dumperty was stretching high to get a view of the red Komodo. The big lizard was motionless, the split ribbon of her tongue flicking the air.

"Manny, she's picked up our scent." As he spoke, the Komodo was already moving toward them.

"Yeah, she can't see us yet, but she knows we're here."

The animal was ploughing her way through long grass. The Sleepers watched massive legs pound the ground, a flat track left to mark where the Komodo had been.

Jack slapped Mangrove's leg. "Well, don't hang around. Let's get to the river, swim across and get out of the thing's way."

"Dragons swim. They swim very well."

The news surprised Jack. The Komodo appeared to be too heavy, too ungainly to have any ability in water. He looked at her. Slime was dripping from her jaws.

"Manny, she'll soon see us." Anxiety was evident in Dumperty's voice, the picture of Torterats being torn to pieces flashing in his mind.

"Yeah." Manny was looking at Jack, watching fear replace nonchalance, taking enjoyment from seeing the Sleeper realise that he was in danger.

Schmucky began to bark, the hair on his back standing on end. Mangrove glanced at the Komodo. There was no doubt that the horses and the humans were visible to her. She was moving faster.

The Palominos were sidling, lifting their hooves in a nervous dance, wanting to get away. Jack had had enough. He was no longer cynical. Converted to the truth of Mangrove's warnings, he saw the threat looming large; too close, much too close. He tore Mangrove from Stripe, flinging him to the ground. Grabbing mane, Jack pulled himself onto the horse.

Mary held his leg. "Jack, don't leave me."

He reached for her arm and hauled. Mary straddled the horse behind him. Jack kicked at Stripe and slapped at his neck, shouting wildly, terrified that he might be caught by the Komodo.

Strangers on his back, the Komodo threatening, Stripe bolted.

As the ugly scene unfolded, Wayne's only thought was that he was being left behind. He grabbed Dumperty's tunic. Dumperty beat at the hand holding him, gripping Star with his legs so that Wayne would not pull him from the horse. Wayne did not let go, wrenching at Dumperty's clothing. Dumperty tried to tear the hand away, but being small, not strong enough, failed. Wayne, unable to unseat the little fellow, pulled himself onto the horse, took hold of the pack on Dumperty's back and kicked hard at Star's ribs. She whinnied in fear and took off after Stripe. Powerless to stop her, Dumperty looked back at Manny.

Mangrove lay stunned where he had been thrown. The Komodo, less than one hundred and fifty metres from Mangrove, was coming straight toward him.

Dumperty screamed into the wind that they must go back. "Manny will be eaten."

"No." Wayne kicked at Star. "No." There could be no going back.

"I can't leave Manny."

"Forget him."

On the galloping horse, careering down the valley, Dumperty knew that he had no time to argue. He slipped his arms from the straps of the pack. The unwanted tie with Wayne was severed.

Straddling the speeding, rising, falling, body of the galloping Palomino, Wayne clutched the pack. It no longer secured him to Dumperty, no longer gave him stability. He was bouncing wildly. Totally unbalanced, he fell from the horse, hitting hard, rolling along the ground, white crystals flying like snow to leave a trail.

Dumperty lay forward, stroking Star's neck, calling to her, settling her, wheeling her around to return to Manny.

Mangrove's eyes opened. His head ached. He realised that he was alone and that the dragon could not be far away. Fearful of rising and making himself an easier target, he parted stems of grass to check on where she might be. The Komodo was closing on him, near enough for him to see the outline of her scales. Her tongue was active, continually darting to taste the air.

She knows where I am.

He lay in the grass watching, turning ideas in his mind, trying to come up with some means of escape. How could he get away? He could run. Useless! If he could fly, take to the air and like a bird simply flap his wings and be gone. If... There was nothing he could do. Mangrove resigned himself to the fact that Endless Night was approaching.

He felt the earth vibrate under his body; a regular beat. He looked through the grass at the Komodo, watched the great, bowed legs swinging and felt the tremor as they pounded the ground. Mangrove held his breath, lying perfectly still. The earth was sending two different signals. He raised his head a little. The sound came echoing to him, the staccato of hooves, increasingly loud, coming closer.

Mangrove rolled to look. He saw Star, Dumperty stretched flat, urging her on. Mangrove rose from the grass and began to run toward the flying Palomino. From behind, he heard the bellow of the Komodo.

In the distance, Stripe's bolting had fizzled to nothing. With the Sleepers still upon his back, the horse stood with sides heaving.

"Look," Jack said.

He and Mary watched Star galloping toward Mangrove, Dumperty low on her neck, closing the distance.

"Dumperty won't make it." Jack grinned at Mary. "The dragon's moving too quickly. He'll have our friend Manny. You watch."

Dumperty was speaking constantly to Star, a stream of encouragement, telling the horse that Manny's life depended on her, that she must ignore her fear of the reptile and run like the wind. "You can do it, Star. Go girl, go."

The horse responded, the great muscles of her rump and shoulders driving her hooves hard at the turf, lengthening her stride so that she flew toward Manny.

Mangrove was sprinting, sucking air deep into his lungs, almost at the limit of his endurance, the oxygen levels of his blood falling, fatigue beginning to clog the cells that he needed to keep him running.

"Come on, come on." He called on his body to make the final effort.

With Star's mane thrashing at Dumperty's neck, he looked at the charging Komodo. It seemed impossible that the massive legs, thick as tree trunks, bowed as they were carrying the weight of the monster, could move so quickly. But he had to believe his eyes, and he wasn't sure that he would reach Manny before the Komodo.

"Manny, Manny." Screaming at him to swerve toward the river.

Mangrove understood. For him to meet Star head on would mean that they both had to stop. The dragon would have them all. If he swung to the right and Dumperty swung Star to the left they would meet still travelling fast, but moving in the same direction. Mangrove headed for the river.

On Star, Dumperty was gauging the distance to the point where he would come together with Manny. He glanced at the Komodo. The huge beast had altered course. All the players in the drama were racing for the river.

"Manny, I'll scoop you up." Dumperty was yelling, angling Star toward Mangrove.

The Komodo was level with him, both horse and reptile now closing in on Mangrove from the rear. Dumperty was so close he could see the bloodied saliva dripping from dragon teeth to be torn away by the wind. At the critical time, he would have to slow Star. Fear that he would not make it swept over Dumperty.

"No," he cried. "We can do it." And Dumperty yelled at Mangrove to be ready and holding mane in one hand he leaned low with elbow bent. Mangrove glanced back, turned, gripped the offered arm and swung himself on to Star.

The roar of the Komodo hammered the ears of the Foragers. She was so close that had Mangrove stretched out he could have touched the red scales. The animal swung her head at him, jaws widespread in one final lunge. The stink of her breath hit Mangrove, filled his nostrils and flowed hot on his skin. He was looking into a mouth of suppurating gums, at teeth that were about to sink into his flesh, drag him from Star and tear him apart.

But the Palomino had felt the blast of hot Komodo breath. With one wide, terrified eye she could see the huge reptile running at her side about to strike. Whether it was Mangrove or her own flank that felt the teeth of the Komodo didn't matter, Star's instinct was to get away. At full gallop the horse leapt as though clearing some unseen hurdle. The jaws of the Komodo snapped shut on empty air.

"How about that?" Dumperty half turned to grin at Mangrove.

"Yeah." It was all Mangrove could say. Another moment and by now chunks of his body would be disappearing down the dragon's throat.

Dumperty rode Star to finally stop by Stripe. Jack and Mary had dismounted and had been joined by Wayne. Spectators to the near death of Mangrove, they made no comment.

Mangrove slid from Star and stood with his face centimetres from Jack. "You took my horse. You hurt me and left me to die."

"Back off." Jack raised a hand ready to defend himself.

Mangrove had never hit another human being. He had never even thought that one person might intentionally hurt another. For countless centuries the custom of the Camarilla had been to help one another, never to harm. Mangrove was bound by these traditions, by his own good nature and by a sense that hitting another person was a barbaric thing to do. He held Jack's eyes, looking into the mind of the Sleeper. Mangrove did not like what he saw. Jack had lived in the time when the earth was in turmoil. He had seen mankind in the final throes of destroying all that was good, yet Jack had learned nothing. Mangrove looked at Mary and Wayne. They were no better. *We woke them, gave life back to them and this is how they treat us. What poor people they are.*

Mangrove walked away from Jack, went to Stripe and fussed over him.

Wayne waited for Dumperty to dismount and then accosted him, abusing him for the way Dumperty had caused him to fall so heavily from Star. Wayne was standing over Dumperty. The little fellow came only to Wayne's shoulder.

Wayne was threatening. "And you can pick up the crystals that were lost from the pack."

Dumperty didn't flinch. "What's so special about those crystals?"

"You wouldn't understand. Just pick 'em up."

The sound of a far away blast ended conversation and ended movement. Momentarily Foragers and Sleepers were figures in a tableau, all stilled by the ferocity of the noise. But the moment was brief. Every head turned to look south. Another pillar of smoke was rumbling and tumbling into the distant sky.

Snotty ran across ground that seemed to have gone mad. Steaming mud and glowing magma was falling all around. He saw the stuff fly high, spit-outs from the new born crater where the side of the mountain had blown away. As he ran, he watched the flung out, burning guts of the planet rain down and he ran a crazy, dodging path to avoid them. He knew that the air was crowded with noise, but he heard not a thing. Snotty was running in a silent world gone wild.

The Sleepers lay insensible, greying with the falling ash. From the vents in the earth near them, steam and smoke issued in irregular bursts; tiny geysers that rose in dirty, yellow puffs.

Snotty hurdled a vent and steam scalded his leg. He did not hear his own yelp of pain. He reached the slope. Running became more difficult. He was coughing, fumes of sulphur burning his lungs, hurting his eyes. When he got to the Sleepers he glanced upward at the lava crawling like some rosy, thickened snail and briefly wondered why it moved so slowly and how long it would take to reach him.

Covering his nose and mouth with his hand, Snotty looked down at Fiona and Jason, at the problem of how he might best take them out of danger. The Sleepers lay face down between fumaroles, the vents on whose rims grew the concentrates they had come to collect. Grubby yellow scrapings lay in the bowls by their outstretched arms.

Snotty looked again at the creeping lava. Radiated heat seared his face. The molten river was already closer. He placed the bowls in Fiona's pack and put the pack on his back. Taking her hands in his, he pulled her up until he could bend and, in the manner of a fireman from ancient times, flopped Fiona over his shoulder.

Snotty went down the hill with odd, jerking strides, the weight of his burden hampering him as he tried his best to run. One hundred metres clear of the slope he lowered Fiona to the ground and shucked the pack. In the clearer air, perhaps from the buffeting she had received as she bounced on Snotty's shoulder, Fiona regained consciousness.

"I'm going for Jason." Snotty was off again.

The stream of lava was perilously close. Snotty turned his head from it. The heat was intense. For the second time he used the fireman carry, finding the going tougher. Jason was heavier than Fiona, a deadweight that added to the time taken to get him to her and lay him by her side. Jason coughed a few times before opening his eyes.

"We have to get away from here," Snotty said. "Can you both walk?"

Jason opened the packs, checked that the bowls of yellow grit were there and nodded. "Yeah, we can go now."

Snotty pointed to his ears and gestured that he couldn't hear. "But you still have my knife." Holding out his hand for it.

Jason shook his head, miming that the knife must still be on the mountain.

"You left it there?" Hardly able to believe that the knife was gone.

"Hey, I passed out with the fumes. Anyway it's only a knife. Don't worry about it. Leave it."

Snotty looked back at the slope, at the fumaroles, at the advancing lava. "I have to get it."

The Sleepers watched him go.

"He's crazy," Jason said.

"Maybe he is, but that knife is the only metal the ferals own."

Jason shrugged. "Let's get out of here. This is no place to stay."

The two shouldered the packs with the yellow grit and began to walk. They did not look back to see how Snotty was faring.

Snotty was running with difficulty, often coughing, the fumes irritating his lungs. He had to keep going. The lava was metres from where the Sleepers had collapsed, metres from where the knife had to be. In minutes the river of molten rock would flow over the spot and all would be consumed in its fiery progress.

He stood where Jason had lain. The heat was unbearable. Snotty shielded his face as he searched the ground. Clods of mud and magma were still spewing from the gash in the mountainside, falling around him. He tried to make himself small, cringing from the hail of stuff coming down, suddenly realising that the knife could under his feet and he wouldn't know because mud had buried it. Snotty kicked at the ash and mud, knelt and felt blindly in the rubbish heaved from the core of the planet. Heat from the lava flow was burning through his clothing. His fingers sifted through the hot mud. *Where are you?* He couldn't stay. Without the knife, he couldn't go.

Snotty flung mud aside, used both hands in frantic effort, saw the glint of steel and grabbed. He held the Swiss knife and ran. Behind him molten rock crawled over the marks left by his knees in the mud.

Fiona and Jason were with Bucky. When Snotty reached them the horse neighed; a dual message of greeting and a warning that they should leave without delay.

Snotty mounted Bucky and firmly patted the horse's neck. "It's okay. You don't like it here, neither do I."

Jason held out the two packs to Snotty. "The horse can carry these."

As Mangrove had done, Snotty looped the packs together and laid them across Bucky's withers. He noticed that the scrapings from the fumaroles had left stains on the packs and could not understand why the Sleepers would risk their lives for yellow dirt.

Returning to Haven, sometimes riding, often walking beside Bucky, Snotty's hearing gradually recovered. In the twilight zone, shifting from deafness to the clarity of sound, he had time to think. He could see no value, none at all, in the scrapings the Sleepers had gone to such lengths to gather, but the yellow dirt sure had some attraction for them.

On more than one occasion he asked what that attraction was. Each time the Sleepers fobbed him off, laughing at the absurdity of the question or saying that the grit was just something they needed. Snotty did not react to the dismissive way in which he was treated, but came to the conclusion that the yellow dirt had been gathered for a purpose and the Sleepers were determined to keep that purpose hidden from him. But why?

Snotty looked across the horse at the boy and the girl. There was a lot about them he did not care for. They knew that the Swiss knife was a treasured possession, yet had shown no remorse at losing it. He had saved them from the black eternity of Endless Night, but neither one had expressed gratitude. *If I had been burned alive, they wouldn't care.*

It troubled Snotty that fellow human beings had no regard for him, that they placed more value on dumb dirt than they did on his life. The Sleepers talked to each other as they went along, but unless they wanted food or water, or had an urge to ask when they might arrive at Haven, they did not address him. He could have been a slave, whose only use was to serve his master and his mistress.

The packs swayed as Bucky plodded along. Snotty mulled over their contents and the way the Sleepers were treating him. Yeah, he thought, they're up to something and whatever that is will be of no benefit to the clan.

Chapter 20

Within hours of Snotty's return, Mangrove and Dumperty rode down the hillside above Haven. Tasha was waiting with Snotty and Biscetti. They waved to the riders and the answering wave came without a smile.

Tasha glanced at Snotty. He had already told her of his own experiences. "Something's not right."

"Are you surprised?"

The Foragers waited while the packs with the crystals were handed over. As she helped tether the horses, Tasha asked Manny what was wrong.

"Not yet." Mangrove gestured toward the Sleepers who had been with him. They were still close and might overhear.

Tasha watched them go through the doorway of Haven. "So, what happened?"

Mangrove's face puckered with concern. He shook his head. "These are not nice people." And with Biscetti and Snotty listening, he gave her an account of everything that had happened to him and to Dumperty.

"Understand this, Tasha," Snotty said. "The Sleepers didn't want to see the valleys north and south of here. The two with me, Jason and Fiona, were only interested in collecting the yellow stuff coming out of the ground. It was the same with Manny and Dumperty. Jack was keen to find caves because that's where the crystals grow."

"The Sleepers left you both to die? How could they do that?" Biscetti turned to Tasha. "We can't trust them."

Tasha was staring down the valley to where the ancient orchards had been planted. "Dolly and the ones with her aren't like that."

"How do you know?" Biscetti asked. "How can you be sure?"

"Well, that's what I think." But in her mind Tasha could see Cloud lying among the peach trees and hear the words she had spoken in her trance. *Past and present come and go, but past is future even so, future's past we'll come to know.* Tasha repeated the words aloud, searching the faces around her. "If only we knew what Cloud meant. What did she see?"

"Who knows," Snotty said. "But one thing's for sure, Jack and all those with him are already working to a plan. I don't know what that plan is, but we have to watch Jack, watch him like a raptor."

Biscetti was nodding vigorously. "Yeah."

"Hmm." Tasha turned to Manny. "What do you reckon?"

"Snotty's right about Jack and he may be part of Cloud's dream. The Sleepers have entered our lives. We're tangled up with them and they're from the past." Mangrove looked directly into Tasha's eyes. "Time will tell what part they play in our future."

"Yes." Tasha thought for a while. "It would be better if we were prepared. Whatever the Sleepers do, we should know. We must watch them... all the time."

"What about Dolly?" Biscetti would not let go.

"She's given us no reason to suspect her. She and her people live among us. They have their sleeping places by us. They do their share of the chores."

"Okay."

Tasha recalled the moments before the Sleepers had been woken, that brief period of time when the decision could have gone either way; to wake or leave to sleep undisturbed. Only Ingamo and Jemma had thought it best to leave the Sleepers be. What if Ingamo was right? Tasha looked at the smoke that hid part of the western sky. It hung like some dark, evil omen and she questioned what it might be that the Sleepers had taken from the volcano. And why was Jack happy to sacrifice Manny and Dumperty to get his hands on white crystals? What possible use could they have?

The presence of the Sleepers raised many questions to which Tasha had no answer. Nor were the Sleepers the only source of worry. Tasha thought of the Torterats. Manny was certain that the Trats would track them down. *They'll be back*, he had said. She knew that Manny was right. Tasha drew a deep breath. Manny had almost been taken by a dragon. Jack had abandoned Manny, uncaring whether he died or survived.

Thoughts whirled in Tasha's head. She pictured herself in falling snow, lying hungry in an ice coffin, waiting for dawn to continue the hunt for food. The new land had seemed so welcoming, so generous after the deprivation the clan had known in the north, yet the dangers the group now faced seemed far worse. The land of plenty was a chameleon that offered much, but in moments changed to threaten. It was a land the Camarilla could not trust.

Tasha heard her name called. Dolly was coming toward her.

"Jack wants some charcoal from the fire. Can he have it?"

"Yes, that's okay." Tasha hoped that showing kindness might yet bring Jack around.

Time will tell, Manny had said.

Epilogue

Time would tell! Tasha's life, the lives of all of the clan, were about to change. In visions that only Cloud could see, she had glimpsed the past and had been shown the future. In the strange way of dreams, past and future had fused so that Cloud had looked at a future repeating the past. What lay ahead was a terrible amalgam of danger far worse than any the Camarilla had ever known. Old enemies had debts to settle. These they would pursue while the earth shook and rivers flowed with fire. The clan could accept that animals would want to eliminate the clan. They could come to tolerate a seismic world. The Camarilla, however, could never imagine what would be the greatest threat of all.

www.ingramcontent.com/pod-product-compliance
Lightning Source LLC
Chambersburg PA
CBHW072208170626
46813CB00003B/843